A Dedalus Nobel Prize Winner

THE NOTEBOOK
or (SHOOT !)

Luigi Pirandello

Translated from the Italian by
C.K. Scott Moncrieff

The note books
SERAFINO *of* GUBBIO

or
(SHOOT!)

with a chronology
by Nicoletta Simborowski

Luigi Pirandello

DEDALUS

Published in the UK by Dedalus Ltd
Langford Lodge, St Judith's Lane, Sawtry, Cambs, PE17 5XE

ISBN 0 946626 58 8

First published in Italy in 1915
Dedalus edition 1990

Printed in England by Clays Ltd, St. Ives plc.

A C.I.P. listing for this title is available on request.

Dedalus would like to thank Juri Gabriel for originating this series
and David Bird and Tim Gray of Wide Eyed for designing it.

Chronology:

Life and works of Pirandello (1867 - 1936)

1867	Luigi Pirandello born on 28th June in Girgenti (Agrigento), Sicily.
1886	Starts studying law at Palermo University.
1887	Enrols at Rome University. Writes some plays, now lost.
1889/91	Publishes collection of poems, **Mal Giocondo.** Leaves Rome University and completes studies at Bonn University, where he writes more poetry.
1892	Returns to Rome and writes for various literary magazines.
1894	Marries Maria Antonietta Portulano (from whom has three children between 1895 and 1899). Publishes collection of short stories, **Amori senza Amore.**
1897	Starts teaching Italian literature.
1898	One-act play published in "Ariel", originally called L'Epilogo then retitled **La Morsa.**
1901	Publishes first novel, **L'Esclusa.**
1902	Publishes **Il Turno.**
1903	Father's sulphur mine destroyed in landslide and Pirandello loses all his own and his wife's money. Wife is ill, both mentally and physically. Pirandello thinks of suicide.
1904	Publishes **Il Fu Mattia Pascal** and it achieves immediate success in Italy and abroad. Increases literary activity, writes for press, including Il Corriere della Sera, becomes a well-known literary figure.
1910	Two one-act plays, **La Morsa** and **Lumié di Sicilia** performed in Rome. Short stories, **La Vita Nuda**, published.
1911 / 17	Increases literary activity still more: writes about fifty short stories, achieves success in theatre with Pensaci Giacomino! (1916)

	Publication of **The Young and The Old** and **The Notebooks of Serafino Gubbio.** Meanwhile wife's mental and physical health deteriorating.
1917	Writes **Cosi é (se vi pare), Il Berretto a Sonagli, La Giara** and **Il Piacere dell 'Onesta.** All are performed and can be described as the first truly characteristic 'Pirandellian' works.
1918 / 36	More highly successful literary activity: **Sei Personaggi in cerca d'Autore** produced in 1921 in Italy and then in 1922 in London and New York. **Enrico IV** produced in 1922. Now internationally established as playwright. Travels widely; plays produced all over world.
1934	Receives Nobel prize for literature.
1936	Dies on 10th December.

Book I

OF THE NOTES OF SERAFINO GUBBIO
CINEMATOGRAPH OPERATOR

SHOOT!

BOOK I

§ 1

I STUDY people in their most ordinary occupa-
tions, to see if I can succeed in discovering in
others what I feel that I myself lack in everything
that I do : the certainty that they understand what
they are doing.

At first sight it does indeed seem as though
many of them had this certainty, from the way
in which they look at and greet one another,
hurrying to and fro in pursuit of their business
or their pleasure. But afterwards, if I stop and
gaze for a moment in their eyes with my own
intent and silent eyes, at once they begin to take
offence. Some of them, in fact, are so disturbed
and perplexed that I have only to keep on gazing
at them for a little longer, for them to insult or
assault me.

No, go your ways in peace. This is enough for
me : to know, gentlemen, that there is nothing
clear or certain to you either, not even the little

that is determined for you from time to time by
the absolutely familiar conditions in which you
are living. There is a *something more* in everything. You do not wish or do not know how to
see it. But the moment this something more
gleams in the eyes of an idle person like myself,
who has set himself to observe you, why, you
become puzzled, disturbed or irritated.

I too am acquainted with the external, that is
to say the mechanical framework of the life which
keeps us clamorously and dizzily occupied and
gives us no rest. To-day, such-and-such; this and
that to be done hurrying to one place, watch in
hand, so as to be in time at another. "No, my
dear fellow, thank you: I can't!" "No, really?
Lucky fellow! I must be off. . . ." At eleven,
luncheon. The paper, the house, the office, school.
. . . "A fine day, worse luck! But business. . . ."
"What's this? Ah, a funeral." We lift our hats
as we pass to the man who has made his escape.
The shop, the works, the law courts. . . .

No one has the time or the capacity to stop for
a moment to consider whether what he sees other
people do, what he does himself, is really the right
thing, the thing that can give him that absolute
certainty, in which alone a man can find rest. The
rest that is given us after all the clamour and
dizziness is burdened with such a load of weariness, so stunned and deafened, that it is no longer
possible for us to snatch a moment for thought.

With one hand we hold our heads, the other we wave in a drunken sweep.

"Let us have a little amusement!"

Yes. More wearying and complicated than our work do we find the amusements that are offered us; since from our rest we derive nothing but an increase of weariness.

I look at the women in the street, note how they are dressed, how they walk, the hats they wear on their heads; at the men, and the airs they have or give themselves; I listen to their talk, their plans; and at times it seems to me so impossible to believe in the reality of all that I see and hear, that being incapable, on the other hand, of believing that they are all doing it as a joke, I ask myself whether really all this clamorous and dizzy machinery of life, which from day to day seems to become more complicated and to move with greater speed, has not reduced the human race to such a condition of insanity that presently we must break out in fury and overthrow and destroy everything. It would, perhaps, all things considered, be so much to the good. In one respect only, though: to make a clean sweep and start afresh.

Here in this country we have not yet reached the point of witnessing the spectacle, said to be quite common in America, of men who, while engaged in carrying on their business, amid the tumult of life, fall to the ground, paralysed. But perhaps, with the help of God, we shall soon reach it. I know that all sorts of things are in preparation. Ah, yes, the work goes on! And I, in my humble way, am one of those employed on this work *to provide amusement.*

I am an operator. But, as a matter of fact, being an operator, in the world in which I live and upon which I live, does not in the least mean operating. I operate nothing.

This is what I do. I set up my machine on its knock-kneed tripod. One or more stage hands, following my directions, mark out on the carpet or on the stage with a long wand and a blue pencil the limits within which the actors have to move to keep the picture in focus.

This is called *marking out the ground.*

The others mark it out, not I: I do nothing more than apply my eyes to the machine so that I can indicate how far it will manage to *take.*

When the stage is set, the producer arranges the actors on it, and outlines to them the action to be gone through.

I say to the producer:

"How many feet?"

The producer, according to the length of the scene, tells me approximately the number of feet of film that I shall need, then calls to the actors:

"Are you ready? Shoot!"

And I start turning the handle.

I might indulge myself in the illusion that, by turning the handle, I set these actors in motion, just as an organ-grinder creates the music by turning his handle. But I allow myself neither this nor any other illusion, and keep on turning until the scene is finished; then I look at the machine and inform the producer:

"Sixty feet," or "a hundred and twenty."

And that is all.

A gentleman, who had come out of curiosity, asked me once:

"Excuse me, but haven't they yet discovered a way of making the camera go by itself?"

I can still see that gentleman's face; delicate, pale, with thin, fair hair; keen, blue eyes; a pointed, yellowish beard, behind which there lurked a faint smile, that tried to appear timid and polite, but was really malicious. For by his question he meant to say to me:

"Is there any real necessity for *you?* What are you? *A hand that turns the handle.* Couldn't they do without this hand? Couldn't you be eliminated, replaced by some piece of machinery?"

I smiled as I answered:

"In time, Sir, perhaps. To tell you the truth, the chief quality that is required in a man of my profession is *impassivity* in face of the action that is going on in front of the camera. A piece of machinery, in that respect, would doubtless be better suited, and preferable to a man. But the most serious difficulty, at present, is this: where to find a machine that can regulate its movements according to the action that is going on in front of the camera. Because I, my dear Sir, do not always turn the handle at the same speed, but faster or slower as may be required. I have no doubt, however, that in time, Sir, they will succeed in eliminating me. The machine— this machine too, like all the other machines— will go by itself. But what mankind will do then, after all the machines have been taught to go by themselves, that, my dear Sir, still remains to be seen."

§ 2

I satisfy, by writing, a need to let off steam which is overpowering. I get rid of my professional impassivity, and avenge myself as well; and with myself avenge ever so many others, condemned like myself to be nothing more than *a hand that turns a handle.*

This was bound to happen, and it has happened at last!

Man who first of all, as a poet, deified his own feelings and worshipped them, now having flung aside every feeling, as an encumbrance not only useless but positively harmful, and having become clever and industrious, has set to work to fashion out of iron and steel his new deities, and has become a servant and a slave to them.

Long live the Machine that mechanises life!

Do you still retain, gentlemen, a little soul, a little heart and a little mind? Give them, give them over to the greedy machines, which are waiting for them! You shall see and hear the sort of product, the exquisite stupidities they will manage to extract from them.

To pacify their hunger, in the urgent haste to satiate them, what food can you extract from yourselves every day, every hour, every minute?

It is, perforce, the triumph of stupidity, after all the ingenuity and research that have been expended on the creation of these monsters, which ought to have remained instruments, and have instead become, perforce, our masters.

The machine is made to act, to move, it requires to swallow up our soul, to devour our life. And how do you expect them to be given back to us, our life and soul, in a contuplicated and continuous output, by the machines? Let me tell you: in bits and morsels, all of one pattern, stupid and precise, which would make, if placed one on top of another, a pyramid that might reach to the stars. Stars, gentlemen, no! Don't you believe it. Not even to the height of a telegraph pole. A breath stirs it and down it tumbles, and leaves such a litter, only not inside this time but outside us, that—Lord, look at all the

boxes, big, little, round, square—we no longer
know where to set our feet, how to move a step.
These are the products of our soul, the paste-
board boxes of our life.

What is to be done? I am here. I serve my
machine, in so far as I turn the handle so that
it may eat. But my soul does not serve me. My
hand serves me, that is to say serves the
machine. The human soul for food, life for food,
you must supply, gentlemen, to the machine
whose handle I turn. I shall be amused to see,
with your permission, the product that will come
out at the other end. 'A' fine product and a rare
entertainment, I can promise you.

Already my eyes and my ears too, from force
of habit, are beginning to see and hear everything in the guise of this rapid, quivering, ticking mechanical reproduction.

I don't deny it; the outward appearance is
light and vivid. We move, we fly. And the
breeze stirred by our flight produces an alert,
joyous, keen agitation, and sweeps away every
thought. On! On, that we may not have time
nor power to heed the burden of sorrow, the
degradation of shame which remain within us,
in our hearts. Outside, there is a continuous
glare, an incessant giddiness: everything flickers
and disappears.

"What was that?" Nothing, it has passed!

Perhaps it was something sad; but no matter, it has passed now.

There is one nuisance, however, that does not pass away. Do you hear it? A hornet that is always buzzing, forbidding, grim, surly, diffused, and never stops. What is it? The hum of the telegraph poles? The endless scream of the trolley along the overhead wire of the electric trams? The urgent throb of all those countless machines, near and far? That of the engine of the motor-car? Of the cinematograph?

The beating of the heart is not felt, nor do we feel the pulsing of our arteries. The worse for us if we did! But this buzzing, this perpetual ticking we do notice, and I say that all this furious haste is not natural, all this flickering and vanishing of images; but that there lies beneath it a machine which seems to pursue it, frantically screaming.

Will it break down?

Ah, we must not fix our attention upon it too closely. That would arouse in us an ever-increasing fury, an exasperation which finally we could endure no longer; would drive us mad.

On nothing, on nothing at all now, in this dizzy bustle which sweeps down upon us and overwhelms us, ought we to fix our attention. Take in, rather, moment by moment, this rapid passage of aspects and events, and so on, until we reach the point when for each of us the buzz shall cease.

§ 3

I cannot get out of my mind the man I met a year ago, on the night of my arrival in Rome.

It was in November, a bitterly cold night. I was wandering in search of a modest lodging, not so much for myself, accustomed to spend my nights in the open, on friendly terms with the bats and the stars, as for my portmanteau, which was my sole worldly possession, left behind in the railway cloakroom, when I happened to run into one of my friends from Sassari, of whom I had long lost sight: Simone Pau, a man of singular originality and freedom from prejudice. Hearing of my hapless plight, he proposed that I should come and sleep that night in his hotel. I accepted the invitation, and we set off on foot through the almost deserted streets. On our way, I told him of my many misadventures and of the frail hopes that had brought me to Rome. Every now and then Simone Pau raised his hatless head, on which the long, sleek, grey hair was parted down the middle in flowing locks, but zigzag, the parting being made with his fingers, for want of a comb. These locks, drawn back behind his ears on either side, gave him a curious, scanty, irregular mane. He expelled a large mouthful of smoke, and stood for a while listening to me, with his huge swollen lips held apart, like those of an ancient comic mask. His crafty, mouselike eyes, sharp as needles, seemed to dart to and fro, as though trapped in his big, rugged, massive face, the face of a savage and unsophisticated peasant. I supposed him to have adopted this attitude, with his mouth open, to laugh at me, at my misfortunes and hopes. But, at a certain point in my recital, I saw him stop in the middle of the street lugubriously lighted by its gas lamps, and heard him say aloud in the silence of the night:

"Excuse me, but what do I know about the mountain, the tree, the sea? The mountain is a mountain because I say: 'That is a mountain.' In other words: '*I am the mountain.*' What are we? We are whatever, at any given moment, occupies our attention. I am the mountain, I am the tree, I am the sea. I am also the star, which knows not its own existence!"

I remained speechless. But not for long. I too have, inextricably rooted in the very depths of my being, the same malady as my friend.

A malady which, to my mind, proves in the clearest manner that everything that happens happens probably because the earth was made not so much for mankind as for the animals. Because animals have in themselves by nature only so much as suffices them and is necessary for them to live in the conditions to which they

were, each after its own kind, ordained; whereas
men have in them a superfluity which constantly
and vainly torments them, never making them
satisfied with any conditions, and always leaving
them uncertain of their destiny. An inexplicable
superfluity, which, to afford itself an outlet,
creates in nature an artificial world, a world that
has a meaning and value for them alone, and
yet one with which they themselves cannot ever
be content, so that without pause they keep on
frantically arranging and rearranging it, like a
thing which, having been fashioned by themselves from a need to extend and relieve an
activity of which they can see neither the end
nor the reason, increases and complicates ever
more and more their torments, carrying them
farther from the simple conditions laid down by
nature for life on this earth, conditions to which
only dumb animals know how to remain faithful
and obedient.

My friend Simone Pau is convinced in good
faith that he is worth a great deal more than a
dumb animal, because the animal does not know
and is content always to repeat the same action.

I too am convinced that he is of far greater
value than an animal, but not for those reasons.
Of what benefit is it to a man not to be content
with always repeating the same action? Why,
those actions that are fundamental and indispensable to life, he too is obliged to perform and

to repeat, day after day, like the animals, if he does not wish to die. All the rest, arranged and rearranged continually and frantically, can hardly fail to reveal themselves sooner or later as illusions or vanities, being as they are the fruit of that superfluity, of which we do not see on this earth either the end or the reason. And where did my friend Simone Pau learn that the animal does not know? It knows what is necessary to itself, and does not bother about the rest, because the animal has not in its nature any superfluity. Man, who has a superfluity, and simply because he has it, torments himself with certain problems, destined on earth to remain insoluble. And this is where his superiority lies! Perhaps this torment is a sign and proof (not, let us hope, an earnest also) of another life beyond this earth; but, things being as they are upon earth, I feel that I am in the right when I say that it was made more for the animals than for men.

I do not wish to be misunderstood. What I mean is, that on this earth man is destined to fare ill, because he has in him more than is sufficient for him to fare well, that is to say in peace and contentment. And that it is indeed an excess, *for life on earth,* this element which man has within him (and which makes him a man and not a beast), is proved by the fact that it— this excess—never succeeds in finding rest in anything, nor in deriving contentment from anything here below, so that it seeks and demands elsewhere, beyond the life on earth, the reason and recompense for its torment. So much the worse, then, does man fare, the more he seeks to employ, upon the earth itself, in frantic constructions and complications, his own superfluity.

This I know, I who turn a handle.

As for my friend Simone Pau, the beauty of it is this: that he believes that he has set himself free from all superfluity, reducing all his wants to a minimum, depriving himself of every comfort and living the naked life of a snail. And he does not see that, on the contrary, he, by reducing himself thus, has immersed himself altogether in the superfluity and lives now by nothing else.

That evening, having just come to Rome, I was not yet aware of this. I knew him, I repeat, to be a man of singular originality and freedom from prejudice, but I could never have imagined that his originality and his freedom from prejudice would reach the point that I am about to relate.

§ 4

Coming to the end of the Corso Vittorio Emanuele, we crossed the bridge. I remember that I gazed almost with a religious awe at the dark rounded mass of Castel Sant' Angelo, high

and solemn under the twinkling of the stars.
The great works of human architecture, by night,
and the heavenly constellations seem to have a
mutual understanding. In the humid chill of
that immense nocturnal background, I felt this
awe start up, flicker as in a succession of spasms,
which were caused in me perhaps by the serpen-
tine reflexions of the lights on the other bridges
and on the banks, in the black mysterious water
of the river. But Simone Pau tore me from this
attitude of admiration, turning first in the direction of Saint Peter's, then dodging aside along
the Vicolo del Villano. Uncertain of the way,
uncertain of everything, in the empty horror of
the deserted streets, full of strange phantoms
quivering from the rusty reflectors of the infrequent lamps, at every breath of air, on the walls
of the old houses, I thought with terror and disgust of the people that were lying comfortably
asleep in those houses and had no idea how their
homes appeared from outside to such as wan-
dered homeless through the night, without there
being a single house anywhere which they might
enter. Now and again, Simone Pau shook his
head and tapped his chest with two fingers. Oh,
yes! The mountain was he, and the tree, and the
sea; but the hotel, where was it? There, in
Borgo Pio? Yes, close at hand, in the Vicolo del
Falco. I raised my eyes; I saw on the right hand
side of that alley a grim building, with a lantern

hung out above the door: a big lantern, in which the flame of the gas-jet yawned through the dirty glass. I stopped in front of this door which was standing ajar, and read over the arch:

Casual Shelter

"Do you sleep here?"

"Yes, and feed too. Lovely bowls of soup. In the best of company. Come in: this is my home."

Indeed the old porter and two other men of the night staff of the Shelter, huddled and crouching together round a copper brazier, welcomed him as a regular guest, greeting him with gestures and in words from their glass cage in the echoing corridor:

"Good evening, Signor Professore."

Simone Pau warned me, darkly, with great solemnity, that I must not be disappointed, for I should not be able to sleep in this hotel for more than six nights in succession. He explained to me that after every sixth night I should have to spend at least one outside, in the open, in order to start a fresh series.

I, sleep there?

In the presence of those three watchmen, I listened to his explanation with a melancholy smile, which, however, hovered gently over my lips, as though to preserve the buoyancy of my spirits and to keep them from sinking into the shame of this abyss.

Albeit in a wretched plight, with but a few lire in my pocket, I was well dressed, with gloves on my hands, spats on my ankles. I wanted to take the adventure, with this smile, as a whimsical caprice on the part of my strange friend. But Simone Pau was annoyed:

"You don't take me seriously?"

"No, my dear fellow, indeed I don't take you seriously."

"You are right," said Simone Pau, "serious, do you know who is really serious? The quack doctor with a black coat and no collar, with a big black beard and spectacles, who sends the medium to sleep in the market-place. I am not quite as serious as that yet. You may laugh, friend Serafino."

And he went on to explain to me that it was all free of charge there. In winter, on the hammocks, a pair of clean sheets, solid and fresh as the sails of a ship, and two thick woollen blankets; in summer, the sheets alone, and a counterpane for anyone who wanted it; also a wrapper and a pair of canvas slippers, washable.

"Remember that, washable!"

"And why?"

"Let me explain. With these slippers and wrapper they give you a ticket; you go into that dressing-room there—through that door on the right—undress, and hand in your clothes, including your shoes, to be disinfected, which is done in the ovens over there. Then, come over here, look. . . . Do you see this lovely pond?"

I lowered my eyes and looked.

A pond? It was a chasm, mouldy, narrow and deep, a sort of den to herd swine in, carved out of the living rock, to which one went down by five or six steps, and over which there hung a pungent odour of suds. A tin pipe, pierced with holes that were all yellow with rust, ran above it along the middle from end to end.

"Well?"

"You undress over there; hand in your clothes. . . . "

" . . . shoes included. . . . "

" . . . shoes included, to be disinfected, and step down here naked."

"Naked?"

"Naked, in company with six or seven other nudes. One of our dear friends in the cage there turns on the tap, and you, standing under the pipe, *zifff* . . . , you get, free for nothing, a most beautiful shower. Then you dry yourself sumptuously with your wrapper, put on your canvas slippers, and steal quietly out in procession with the other draped figures up the stairs; there they are; up there is the dormitory, and so goodnight."

"Is it compulsory?"

"What? The shower? Ah, because you are
wearing gloves and spats, friend Serafino? But
you can take them off without shame. Everyone here strips himself of his shame, and offers
himself naked to the baptism of this pond!
Haven't you the courage to descend to these
nudities?"

There was no need. The shower is obligatory
only for unclean mendicants. Simone Pau had
never taken it.

In this place he is, really, a schoolmaster.
Attached to the shelter there are a soup kitchen
and a refuge for homeless children of either sex,
beggars' children, prisoners' children, children
of every form of sin and shame. They are under
the care of certain Sisters of Charity, who have
managed to set up a little school for them as
well. Simone Pau, albeit by profession a bitter
enemy of humanity and of every form of teaching, gives lessons with the greatest pleasure to
these children, for two hours daily, in the early
morning, and the children are extremely grateful
to him. He is given, in return, his board and
lodging: that is to say a little room, all to himself, clean and neat, and a special service of
meals, shared with four other teachers, who are
a poor old pensioner of the Papal Government
and three spinster schoolmistresses, friends of
the Sisters and taken in here by them. But
Simone Pau dispenses with the special meals,

since at midday he is never in the Shelter, and
it is only in the evenings, when it suits his con-
venience, that he takes a bowlful or two of soup
from the common kitchen; he keeps the little
room, but he never uses it, because he goes and
sleeps in the dormitory of the Night Shelter, for
the sake of the company to be found there,
which he has grown to relish, of queer, vagrant
types. Apart from these two hours devoted to
teaching, he spends all his time in the libraries
and the *caffè;* every now and then, he publishes
in some philosophic review an essay which
amazes everyone by the bizarre novelty of the
views expressed in it, the strangeness of the
arguments and the abundance of learning displayed; and he flourishes again for a while.

At the time, I repeat, I was not aware of all
this. I supposed, and perhaps it was partly
true, that he had brought me there for the pleasure of bewildering me; and since there is no
better way of disconcerting a person who is seeking to bewilder one with extravagant paradoxes
or with the strangest, most fantastic suggestions
than to pretend to accept those paradoxes as
though they were the most obvious truisms, and
his suggestions as entirely natural and oppor-
tune; so I behaved that evening, to disconcert
my friend Simone Pau. He, realising my intention, looked me in the eyes and, seeing them to
be completely impassive, exclaimed with a smile:

"What an idiot you are!"

He offered me his room; I thought at first that he was joking; but when he assured me that he really had a room there to himself, I would not accept it and went with him to the dormitory of the Shelter. I am not sorry, since, for the discomfort and repulsion that I felt in that odious place, I had two compensations:

First; that of finding the post which I now hold, or rather the opportunity of going as an operator to the great cinematograph company, the Kosmograph;

Secondly; that of meeting the man who has remained for me ever since the symbol of the wretched fate to which continuous progress condemns the human race.

First of all, the man.

§ 5

Simone Pau pointed him out to me, the following morning, when we rose from our hammocks.

I shall not describe that barrack of a dormitory, foul with the breath of so many men, in the grey light of dawn, nor the exodus of the inmates, as they went downstairs, dishevelled and stupid with sleep, in their long white nightshirts, with their canvas slippers on their feet, and their tickets in their hands, to the dressing-room to recover their clothes.

There was one man among them who, amid
the folds of his white wrapper, gripped tightly
under his arm a violin, wrapped in a worn, dirty,
faded cover of green baize, and went on his way
frowning darkly, as though lost in contemplation of the hairs that overhung from his bushy,
knitted eyebrows.

"Friend, friend!" Simone Pau called to him.
The man came towards us, keeping his head
lowered, as though bowed down by the enormous
weight of his red, fleshy nose; and seemed to be
saying as he advanced:

"Make way! Make way! You see what life
can make of a man's nose?"

Simone Pau went up to him; lovingly with one
hand he lifted up the man's chin; with the other
he clapped him on the shoulder, to give him confidence, and repeated:

"My friend!"

Then, turning again to myself:

"Serafino," he said, "let me introduce to you
a great artist. They have labelled him with a
shocking nickname; but no matter; he is a great
artist. Gaze upon him: there he is, with his God
under his arm! It looks like a broom: it is a
violin."

I turned to observe the effect of Simone Pau's
words on the face of the stranger. Emotionless.
And Simone Pau went on:

"A violin, nothing else. And he never parts

from it. The attendants here even allow him to take it to bed with him, on the understanding that he does not play it at night and disturb the other inmates. But there is no danger of that. Out with it, my friend, and shew it to this gentleman, who can feel for you."

The man eyed me at first with misgivings; then, on a further request from Simone Pau, took from its case the old violin, a really priceless instrument, and shewed it to us, as a modest cripple might expose his stump.

Simone Pau went on, turning to me:

"You see? He lets you see it. A great concession, for which you ought to thank him! His father, many years ago, left him in possession of a printing press at Perugia, with all sorts of machines and type and a good connexion. Tell us, my friend, what you did with it, to consecrate yourself to the service of your God."

The man stood looking at Simone Pau, as though he had not understood the request.

Simone Pau made it clearer:

"What did you do with it, with your press?"

Thereupon the man waved his hand with a gesture of contemptuous indifference.

"He neglected it," Simone Pau explained this gesture. "He neglected it until he had brought himself to the verge of starvation. And then, with his violin under his arm, he came to Rome. He has not played for some time now, because he thinks that he cannot play any longer, after all that has happened to him. But until recently, he used to play in the wine-shops. In the wine-shops one drinks; and he would play first, and drink afterwards. He played divinely; the more divinely he played, the more he drank; so that often he was obliged to place his God, his violin, in pawn. And then he would call at some printing press to find work; gradually he would put together what he needed to redeem his violin, and back he would go to play in the wine-shops. But listen to what happened to him once, and has led, you understand, to a slight alteration of his . . . don't, for heaven's sake, let us say his reason, let us say his conception of life. Put it away, my friend, put your instrument away: I know it hurts you if I tell the story while you have your violin uncovered.''

The man nodded several times in the affirmative, gravely, with his towsled head, and wrapped up his violin.

''This is what happened to him,'' Simone Pau went on. ''He called at a big printing office where there is a foreman who, as a lad, used to work in his press at Perugia. 'There's no vacancy; I'm sorry,' he was told. And my friend was going away, crushed, when he heard himself called back. 'Wait,' said the foreman, 'if you can adapt yourself to it, we might have something for you. . . . It isn't the job for you; still,

if you are hard up. . . .' My friend shrugged
his shoulders and went with the foreman. He
was taken into a special room, all silent; and the
foreman shewed him a new machine: a pachyderm, flat, black, squat; a monstrous beast which
eats lead and voids books. It is a perfected
monotype, with none of the complications of rods
and wheels and bands, without the noisy jigging
of the fount. I tell you, a regular beast, a
pachyderm, quietly chewing away at its long
ribbon of perforated paper. 'It does everything
by itself,' the foreman said to my friend. 'You
have nothing to do but feed it now and then
with its cakes of lead, and keep an eye on it.'
My friend felt his breath fail and his arms sink.
To be brought down to such an office as that, a
man, an artist! Worse than being a stable-boy.
. . . To keep an eye on that black beast, which
did everything by itself, and required no other
service of him than to have put in its mouth,
from time to time, its food, those leaden cakes!
But this is nothing, Serafino! Crushed, mortified, bowed down with shame and poisoned with
spleen, my friend endured a week of this degrading slavery, and, as he handed the monster its
leaden cakes, dreamed of his deliverance, his
violin, his art; vowed and swore that he would
never go back to playing in the wine-shops, where
he is so strongly, so irresistibly tempted to drink,
and determined to find other places more befit-

ting the exercise of his art, the worship of his deity. Yes, my friends! No sooner had he redeemed the violin than he read in the advertisement columns of a newspaper, among the offers of employment, one from a cinematograph, addressed: such and such a street and number, which required a violin and clarinet for its orchestra. At once my friend hastened to the place; presented himself, joyful, exultant, with his violin under his arm. Well; he found himself face to face with another machine, an automatic pianoforte, what is called a piano player. They said to him: 'You with your violin have to accompany this instrument!' Do you understand? A violin, in the hands of a man, accompany a roll of perforated paper running through the belly of this other machine! The soul, which moves and guides the hands of the man, which now passes into the touch of the bow, now trembles in the fingers that press the strings, obliged to follow the register of this automatic instrument! My friend flew into such a towering passion that the police had to be called, and he was arrested and sentenced to a fortnight's imprisonment for assaulting the forces of law and order.

"He came out again, as you see him.

"He drinks now, and does not play any more."

§ 6

All the reflexions that I made at the beginning
with regard to my wretched plight, and that of
all the others who are condemned like myself to
be nothing more than a hand that turns a handle,
have as their starting point this man, whom I
met on the morning after my arrival in Rome.
Certainly I have been in a position to make them,
because I too have been reduced to this office of
being the servant of a machine; but that came
afterwards.

I say this, because this man presented to the
reader at this point, after the aforesaid reflexions, might appear to him to be a grotesque invention of my fancy. But let him remember that
I should perhaps never have thought of those
reflexions, had they not been, partly at least,
suggested to me by Simone Pau's introducing
the unfortunate creature to me; while, for that
matter, the whole of this first adventure of mine
is grotesque, and is so because Simone Pau himself is, and means to be, almost by profession,
grotesque, as he shewed on that first evening
when he chose to take me to a Casual Shelter.

I did not make any reflexion whatsoever at the
time; in the first place, because I could never,
even in my wildest dreams, have thought that I
should be reduced to this occupation; also,

because I should have been interrupted by a great hubbub on the stair leading to the dormitory, and by the tumultuous and joyful inrush of all the inmates who had already gone down to the dressing-room to recover their clothes.

What had happened?

They came upstairs again, still swathed in the white wrappers, and with the slippers on their feet.

Among them, together with the attendants and the Sisters of Charity attached to the Shelter and to the soup kitchen, were a number of gentlemen and some ladies, all well dressed and smiling, with an air of curiosity and novelty. Two of these gentlemen were carrying, one a machine, which now I know well, wrapped in a black cover, while the other had under his arm its knock-kneed tripod. They were actors and operators from a cinematograph company, and had come about a film to take a scene from real life in a Casual Shelter.

The cinematograph company which had sent these actors was the Kosmograph, in which I for the last eight months have held the post of operator; and the stage manager who was in charge of them was Nicola Polacco, or, as they all call him, Cocò Polacco, my playmate and schoolfellow at Naples in my early boyhood. I am indebted to him for my post, and to the fortunate coincidence of my happening to have

spent the night with Simone Pau in that Casual
Shelter.

But neither, I repeat, did it enter my mind,
that morning, that I should ever come down to
setting up a photographic camera on its tripod,
as I saw these two gentlemen doing, nor did it
occur to Cocò Polacco to suggest such an occupation to me. He, like the good fellow that he is,
made no bones about recognising me, whereas I,
having at once recognised him, was trying my
hardest not to catch his eye in that wretched
place, seeing him radiant with Parisian smart-
ness and with the air and in the setting of an
invincible leader of men, among all those actors
and actresses and all those recruits of poverty,
who were beside themselves with joy in their
white gowns at this unlooked-for source of profit.
He shewed surprise at finding me there, but only
because of the early hour, and asked me how I
had known that he and his company would be
coming that morning to the Shelter for a real
life interior. I left him under the illusion that
I had turned up there by chance, out of curiosity;
I introduced Simone Pau (the man with the violin,
in the confusion, had slipped away); and I remained to look on disgusted at the indecent contamination of this grim reality, the full horror
of which I had tasted overnight, by the stupid
fiction which Polacco had come there to stage.

My disgust, however, I perhaps feel only now.

That morning, I must have felt more than anything else curiosity at being present for the first time at the production of a film. This curiosity, though, was distracted at a certain point in the proceedings by one of the actresses, who, the moment I caught sight of her, aroused in me another curiosity far more keen.

Nestoroff? Was it possible? It seemed to be she and yet it seemed not to be. That hair of a strange tawny colour, almost coppery, that style of dress, sober, almost stiff, were not hers. But the motion of her slender, exquisite body, with a touch of the feline in the sway of her hips; the head raised high, inclined a little to one side, and that sweet smile on a pair of lips as fresh as a pair of rose-leaves, whenever anyone addressed her; those eyes, unnaturally wide, open, greenish, fixed and at the same time vacant, and cold in the shadow of their long lashes were hers, entirely hers, with that certainty all her own that everyone, whatever she might say or ask, would answer yes.

Varia Nestoroff? Was it possible? Acting for a cinematograph company?

There flashed through my mind Capri, the Russian colony, Naples, all those noisy gatherings of young artists, painters, sculptors, in strange eccentric haunts, full of sunshine and colour, and a house, a dear house in the country, near Sorrento, into which this woman had brought confusion and death.

When, after a second rehearsal of the scene for which the company had come to the Shelter, Cocò Polacco invited me to come and see him at the Kosmograph, I, still in doubt, asked him if this actress was really the Nestoroff.

"Yes, my dear fellow," he answered with a sigh. "You know her history, perhaps."

I nodded my head.

"Ah, but you can't know the rest of it!" Polacco went on. "Come, come and see me at the Kosmograph; I'll tell you the whole story. Gubbio, I don't know what I wouldn't pay to get that woman off my hands. But, I can tell you, it is easier . . . "

"Polacco! Polacco!" she called to him at that moment.

And from the haste with which Cocò Polacco obeyed her summons, I fully realised the power that she had with the firm, from which she held a contract as principal with one of the most lavish salaries.

A day or two later I went to the Kosmograph, for no reason except to learn the rest of this woman's story, of which I knew the beginning all too well.

Book II

OF THE NOTES OF SERAFINO GUBBIO
CINEMATOGRAPH OPERATOR

BOOK II

§ 1

DEAR house in the country, the *Grandparents'*, full of the indescribable fragrance of the oldest family memories, where all the old-fashioned chairs and tables, vitalised by these memories, were no longer inanimate objects but, so to speak, intimate parts of the people who lived in the house, since in them they came in contact with, became aware of the precious, tranquil, safe reality of their existence.

There really did linger in those rooms a peculiar aroma, which I seem to smell now as I write: an aroma of the life of long ago which seemed to have given a fragrance to all the things that were preserved there.

I see again the drawing-room, a trifle gloomy, it must be admitted, with its walls stuccoed in rectangular panels which strove to imitate ancient marbles: red and green alternately; and each panel was set in a handsome border of its own, of stucco likewise, in a pattern of foliage; except that in the course of time these imitation marbles had grown weary of their innocent make-believe, had bulged out a little here and there, and one

saw a few tiny cracks on the surface. All of
which said to me kindly:

"You are poor; the seams of your jacket are
rent; but you see that even in a gentleman's
house . . . "

Ah, yes! I had only to turn and look at those
curious brackets which seemed to shrink from
touching the floor with their gilded spidery legs.
The marble top of each was a trifle yellow, and
in the sloping mirror above were reflected exactly
in their immobility the pair of baskets that stood
upon the marble: baskets of fruit, also of marble,
coloured: figs, peaches, limes, corresponding
exactly, on either side, with their reflexions, as
though there were four baskets instead of two.

In that motionless, clear reflexion was embodied
all the limpid calm which reigned in that house.
It seemed as though nothing could ever happen
there. This was the message, also, of the little
bronze timepiece between the baskets, only the
back of which was to be seen in the mirror. It
represented a fountain, and had a spiral rod of
rock-crystal, which spun round and round with
the movement of the clockwork. How much
water had that fountain poured forth? And
yet the little basin beneath it was never full.

Next I see the room from which one goes down
to the garden. (From one room to the other
one passes between a pair of low doors, which
seem full of their own importance, and perfectly

aware of the treasures committed to their charge.) This room, leading down to the garden, is the favourite sitting-room at all times of the year. It has a floor of large, square tiles of terra-cotta, a trifle worn with use. The wall-paper, patterned with damask roses, is a trifle faded, as are the gauze curtains, also patterned with damask roses, screening the windows and the glass door beyond which one sees the landing of the little wooden outside stair, and the green railing and the pergola of the garden bathed in an enchantment of sunshine and stillness.

The light filters green and fervid between the slats of the little sun-blind outside the window, and does not pour into the room, which remains in a cool delicious shadow, embalmed with the scents from the garden.

What bliss, what a bath of purity for the soul, to sit at rest for a little upon that old sofa with its high back, its cylindrical cushions of green rep, likewise a trifle discoloured.

"Giorgio! Giorgio!"

Who is calling from the garden? It is Granny Rosa, who cannot succeed in reaching, even with the end of her cane, the flowers of the jasmine, now that the plant has grown so big and has climbed right up high upon the wall.

Granny Rosa does so love those jasmines! She has upstairs, in the cupboard in the wall of her

room, a box full of umbrella-shaped heads of
cummin, dried; she takes one out every morning,
before she goes down to the garden; and, when
she has gathered the blossoms with her cane, she
sits down in the shade of the pergola, puts on her
spectacles, and slips the jasmines one by one
into the spidery stems of that umbrella-shaped
head, until she has turned it into a lovely round
white rose, with an intense, delicious perfume,
which she goes and places religiously in a little
vase on the top of the chest of drawers in her
room, in front of the portrait of her only son,
who died long ago.

It is so intimate and sheltered, this little house,
so contented with the life that it encloses within
its walls, without any desire for the other life
that goes noisily on outside, far away. It
remains there, as though perched in a niche
behind the green hill, and has not wished for so
much as a glimpse of the sea and the marvellous
Bay. It has chosen to remain apart, unknown to
all the world, almost hidden away in that green,
deserted corner, outside and far away from all
the vicissitudes of life.

There was at one time on the gatepost a marble
tablet, which bore the name of the owner: *Carlo
Mirelli*. Grandfather Carlo decided to remove
it, when Death found his way, for the first time,
into that modest little house buried in the country, and carried off with him the son of the

house, barely thirty years old, already the father himself of two little children.

Did Grandfather Carlo think, perhaps, that when the tablet was removed from the gatepost, Death would not find his way back to the house again?

Grandfather Carlo was one of those old men who wore a velvet cap with a silken tassel, but could read Horace. He knew, therefore, that death, *aequo pede,* knocks at all doors alike, whether or not they have a name engraved on a tablet.

Were it not that each of us, blinded by what he considers the injustice of his own lot, feels an unreasoning need to vent the fury of his own grief upon somebody or something. Grandfather Carlo's fury, on that occasion, fell upon the innocent tablet on the gatepost.

If Death allowed us to catch hold of him, I would catch him by the arm and lead him in front of that mirror where with such limpid precision are reflected in their immobility the two baskets of fruit and the back of the bronze timepiece, and would say to him:

"You see? Now be off with you! Everything here must be allowed to remain as it is!"

But Death does not allow us to catch hold of him.

By taking down that tablet, perhaps Grandfather Carlo meant to imply that—once his son was dead—there was nobody left alive in the house.

A little later, Death came again.

There was one person left alive who called upon him desperately every night: the widowed daughter-in-law who, after her husband's death, felt as though she were divided from the family, a stranger in the house.

And so, the two little orphans: Lidia, the elder, who was nearly five, and Giorgetto who was three, remained in the sole charge of their grandparents, who were still not so very old.

To start life afresh when one is already beginning to grow feeble, and to rediscover in oneself all the first amazements of childhood; to create once again round a pair of rosy children the most innocent affection, the most pleasant dreams, and to drive away, as being importunate and tiresome, Experience, who from time to time thrusts in her head, the face of a withered old woman, to say, blinking behind her spectacles: "This will happen, that will happen," when as yet nothing has ever happened, and it is so delightful that nothing should have happened; and to act and think and speak as though really one knew nothing more than is already known to two little children who know nothing at all: to act as though things were seen not in retrospect but through the eyes of a person going forwards for the first time, and for the first time seeing and hearing: this miracle was performed by Grandfather Carlo and Granny Rosa; they did, that is to say, for the two little ones, far more than would have been done by the father and mother, who, if they had lived, young as they both were, might have wished to enjoy life a little longer themselves. Nor did their not having anything left to enjoy render the task more easy for the two old people, for we know that to the old everything is a heavy burden, when it no longer has any meaning or value for them.

The two grandparents accepted the meaning and value which their two grandchildren gradually, as they grew older, began to give to things, and all the world took on the bright colours of youth for them, and life recaptured the candour and freshness of innocence. But what could they know of a world so wide, of a life so different from their own, which was going on outside, far away, those two young creatures born and brought up in the house in the country? The old people had forgotten that life and that world, everything had become new again for them, the sky, the scenery, the song of the birds, the taste of food. Outside the gate, life existed no longer. Life began there, at the gate, and gilded afresh everything round about; nor did the old people imagine that anything could come to them from outside; and even Death, even Death they had almost forgotten, albeit he had already come there twice.

Have patience a little while, Death, to whom no house, however remote and hidden, can remain unknown! But how in the world, starting from thousands and thousands of miles away, thrust aside, or dragged, tossed hither and thither by the turmoil of ever so many mysterious changes of fortune, could there have found her way to that modest little house, perched in its niche there behind the green hill, a woman, to whom the peace and the affection that reigned there not only must have been incomprehensible, must have been not even conceivable?

I have no record, nor perhaps has anyone, of the path followed by this woman to bring her to the dear house in the country, near Sorrento.

There, at that very spot, before the gatepost, from which Grandfather Carlo, long ago, had had the tablet removed, she did not arrive of her own accord; that is certain; she did not raise her hand, uninvited, to ring the bell, to make them open the gate to her. But not far from there she stopped to wait for a young man, guarded until then with the life and soul of two old grand-parents, handsome, innocent, ardent, his soul borne on the wings of dreams, to come out of that gate and advance confidently towards life.

Oh, Granny Rosa, do you still call to him from

the garden, for him to pull down with your cane
your jasmine blossoms?

"Giorgio! Giorgio!"

There still rings in my ears, Granny Rosa, the
sound of your voice. And I feel a bitter delight,
which I cannot express in words, in imagining
you as still there, in your little house, which I
see again as though I were there at this moment,
and were at this moment breathing the atmosphere that lingers there of an old-fashioned existence; in imagining you as knowing nothing of
all that has happened, as you were at first, when
I, in the summer holidays, came out from Sorrento every morning to prepare for the October
examinations your grandson Giorgio, who refused
to learn a word of Latin or Greek, and instead
covered every scrap of paper that came into
his hands, the margins of his books, the top of
the schoolroom table, with sketches in pen and
pencil, with caricatures. There must even be
one of me, still, on the top of that table, covered
all over with scribblings.

"Ah, Signor Serafino," you sigh, Granny
Rosa, as you hand me in an old cup the familiar
coffee with essence of cinnamon, like the coffee
that our aunts in religion offer us in their con-
vents, "ah, Signor Serafino, Giorgio has bought
a box of paints; he wants to leave us; he wants
to become a painter . . . "

And over your shoulder opens her sweet, clear,

sky-blue eyes and blushes a deep red Lidiuccia,
your granddaughter; Duccella, as you call her.
Why?

Ah, because. . . . There has come now three
times from Naples a young gentleman, a fine
young gentleman all covered with scent, in a
velvet coat, with yellow chamois-leather gloves,
an eyeglass in his right eye and a baron's coronet
on his handkerchief and portfolio. He was sent
by his grandfather, Barone Nuti, a friend of
Grandfather Carlo, who was like a brother to
him before Grandfather Carlo, growing weary of
the world, retired from Naples, here, to the Sor-
rentine villa. You know this, Granny Rosa. But
you do not know that the young gentleman from
Naples is fervently encouraging Giorgio to devote himself to art and to go off to Naples with
him. Duccella knows, because young Aldo Nuti
(how very strange!), when speaking with such
fervour of art, never looks at Giorgio, but looks
at her, into her eyes, as though it were her that
he had to encourage, and not Giorgio; yes, yes,
her, to come to Naples to stay there for ever
with himself.

So that is why Duccella blushes a deep red,
over your shoulder, Granny Rosa, whenever she
hears you say that Giorgio wishes to become a
painter.

He too, the young gentleman from Naples, if
his grandfather would allow him . . . Not a

painter, no . . . He would like to go upon the
stage, to become an actor. How he would love
that! But his grandfather does not wish it. . . .

Dare we wager, Granny Rosa, that Duccella
does not wish it either?

§ 2

Of the sequel to this simple, innocent, idyllic
life, about four years later, I have a cursory
knowledge.

I acted as tutor to Giorgio Mirelli, but I was
myself a student also, a penniless student who
had grown old while waiting to complete his
studies, and whom the sacrifices borne by his
parents to keep him at school had automatically
inspired with the utmost zeal, the utmost diligence,
a shy, painful humility, a constraint which never
diminished, albeit this period of waiting had now
extended over many, many years.

Yet my time had perhaps not been wasted. I
studied by myself and meditated, in those years
of waiting, far more and with infinitely greater
profit than I had done in my years at school;
and I taught myself Latin and Greek, in an
attempt to pass from the technical side, in which
I had started, to the classical, in the hope that it
might be easier for me to enter the University
by that road.

Certainly this kind of study was far better

suited to my intelligence. I buried myself in it
with a passion so intense and vital that when,
at six-and-twenty, through an unexpected, tiny
legacy from an uncle in holy orders (who had
died in Apulia, and whose existence had long
been almost forgotten by my family), I was
finally able to enter the University, I remained
for long in doubt whether it would not be better
for me to leave behind in the drawer, where it
had slumbered undisturbed for all those years,
my qualifying diploma from the technical insti-
tute, and to procure another from the *liceo,* so
as to matriculate in the faculty of philosophy
and literature.

Family counsels prevailed, and I set off for
Liége, where, with this worm of philosophy
gnawing my brain, I acquired an intimate and
painful knowledge of all the machines invented
by man for his own happiness.

I have derived one great benefit from it, as
you can see. I have learned to draw back with
an instinctive shudder from reality, as others
see and handle it, without however managing
to arrest a reality of my own, since my distracted, wandering sentiments never succeed in
giving any value or meaning to this uncertain,
loveless life of mine. I look now at everything, myself included, as from a distance; and
from nothing does there ever come to me a loving signal, beckoning me to approach it with con-

fidence or with the hope of deriving some comfort from it. Pitying signals, yes, I seem to catch
in the eyes of many people, in the aspect of many
places which impel me not to receive comfort nor to
give it, since he that cannot receive it cannot give
it; but pity. Pity, ah yes . . . But I know that
pity is such a difficult thing either to give or to
receive.

For some years after my return to Naples I
found nothing to do; I led a dissolute life with
a group of young artists, until the last remains
of that modest legacy had gone. I owe to chance,
as I have said, and to the friendship of one of
my old school friends the post that I now occupy.
I fill it—yes, we may say so—honourably, and I
am well rewarded for my labour. Oh, they all
respect me, here, as a first rate operator: alert,
accurate, and *perfectly impassive*. If I ought
to be grateful to Polacco, Polacco ought in turn
to be grateful to me for the credit that he has
acquired with Commendator Borgalli, the Chair-
man and General Manager of the Kosmograph,
for the acquisition that the firm has made of an
operator like myself. Signor Gubbio is not,
properly speaking, attached to any of the four
companies among which the production is dis-
tributed, but is summoned here and there, from
one to another, to take the longest and most
difficult films. Signor Gubbio does far more
work than the firm's other five operators; but

for every film that proves a success he receives
a handsome commission and frequent bonuses.
I ought to be happy and contented. Instead of
which I think with longing of my lean years of
youthful folly at Naples among the young artists.

Immediately after my return from Liége, I
met Giorgio Mirelli, who had been at Naples
for two years. He had recently shown at an
exhibition two strange pictures, which had given
rise among the critics and the general public to
long and violent discussions. He still retained
the innocence and fervour of sixteen; he had no
eyes to see the neglected state of his clothes, his
towsled locks, the first few hairs that were sprout-
ing in long curls on his chin and hollow cheeks,
like the cheeks of a sick man: and sick he was
of a divine malady; a prey to a continual anxiety,
which made him neither observe nor feel what
was for others the reality of life; always on the
point of dashing off in response to some mysterious, distant summons, which he alone could
hear.

I asked after his people. He told me that
Grandfather Carlo had died a short time since.
I gazed at him surprised at the way in which he
gave me this news; he seemed not to have felt
any sorrow at his grandfather's death. But,
called back by the look in my eyes to his own
grief, he said: "Poor grandfather . . . " so
sadly and with such a smile that at once I

changed my mind and realised that he, in the
tumult of all the life that seethed round about
him, had neither the power nor the time to think
of his grief.

And Granny Rosa? Granny Rosa was keeping
well . . . yes, quite well, . . . as well as she
could, poor old soul, after such a bereavement.
Two heads of cummin, now, to be filled with
jasmine, every morning, one for the recently
dead, the other for him who had died long ago.

And Duccella, Duccella?

Ah, how her brother's eyes smiled at my
question!

"Rosy! Rosy!"

And he told me that for the last year she had
been engaged to the young Barone Aldo Nuti.
The wedding would soon be celebrated; it had
been postponed owing to the death of Grandfather Carlo.

But he shewed no sign of joy at this wedding;
indeed he told me that he did not regard Aldo
Nuti as a suitable match for Duccella; and, wav-
ing both his hands in the air with outstretched
fingers, he broke out in that exclamation of disgust which he was in the habit of using when I
endeavoured to make him understand the rules
and terminations of the second declension in
Greek:

"He's so complicated! He's so complicated!"

It was never possible to keep him still after

that exclamation. And as he used to escape then
from the schoolroom table, so now he escaped
from me again. I lost sight of him for more
than a year. I learned from his fellow-artists
that he had gone to Capri, to paint.

There he met Varia Nestoroff.

§ 3

I know this woman well now, as well, that is
to say, as it is possible to know her, and I can
now explain many things that long remained incomprehensible to me. Though there is still the
risk that the explanation I now offer myself of
them may perhaps appear incomprehensible to
others. But I offer it to myself and not to others;
and I have not the slightest intention of offering
it as an excuse for the Nestoroff.

To whom should I excuse her?

I keep away from people who are respectable
by profession, as from the plague.

It seems impossible that a person should not
enjoy his own wickedness when he practises it
with a cold-blooded calculation. But if such
unhappiness (and it must be tremendous) exists,
I mean that of not being able to enjoy one's own
wickedness, our contempt for such wicked
persons, as for all sorts of other unhappiness,
may perhaps be conquered, or at least modified,
by a certain pity. I speak, so as not to give
offence, as a moderately respectable person.

But we must, surely to goodness, admit this
fact: that we are all, more or less, wicked; but
that we do not enjoy our wickedness, and are unhappy.

Is it possible?

We all of us readily admit our own unhappiness; no one admits his own wickedness; and
the former we insist upon regarding as due to
no reason or fault of our own; whereas we labour
to find a hundred reasons, a hundred excuses and
justifications for every trifling act of wickedness
that we have committed, whether against other
people or against our own conscience.

Would you like me to shew you how we at
once rebel, and indignantly deny a wicked action,
even when it is undeniable, and when we have
undeniably enjoyed it?

The following two incidents have occurred.
(This is not a digression, for the Nestoroff has
been compared by someone to the beautiful tiger
purchased, a few days ago, by the Kosmograph.)
The following two incidents, I say, have occurred.

A flock of birds of passage—woodcock and
snipe—have alighted to rest for a little after
their long flight and to recuperate their strength
in the Roman Campagna. They have chosen a
bad spot. A snipe, more daring than the rest,
says to his comrades:

"You remain here, hidden in this brake. I

shall go and explore the country round, and, if I find a better place, I shall call you.''

An engineer friend of yours, of an adventurous spirit, a Fellow of the Geographical Society, has undertaken the mission of going to Africa, I do not exactly know (because you yourself do not know exactly) upon what scientific exploration. He is still a long way from his goal; you have had some news of him; his last letter has left you somewhat alarmed, because in it your friend explained to you the dangers which he was going to face, when he prepared to cross certain distant tracts, savage and deserted.

To-day is Sunday. You rise betimes to go out shooting. You have made all your preparations overnight, promising yourself a great enjoyment. You alight from the train, blithe and happy; off you go over the fresh, green Campagna, a trifle misty still, in search of a good place for the birds of passage. You wait there for half an hour, for an hour; you begin to feel bored and take from your pocket the newspaper you bought when you started, at the station. After a time, you hear what sounds like a flutter of wings in the dense foliage of the wood; you lay down the paper; you go creeping quietly up; you take aim; you fire. Oh, joy! A snipe!

Yes, indeed, a snipe. The very snipe, the explorer, that had left its comrades in the brake.

I know that you do not eat the birds you have

shot; you make presents of them to your friends:
for you everything consists in this, in the pleasure of killing what you call game.

The day does not promise well. But you, like
all sportsmen, are inclined to be superstitious:
you believe that reading the newspaper has
brought you luck, and you go back to read the
newspaper in the place where you left it. On the
second page you find the news that your friend
the engineer, who went to Africa on behalf of
the Geographical Society, while crossing those
savage and deserted tracts, has met a tragic
end: attacked, torn in pieces and devoured by a
wild beast.

As you read with a shudder the account in the
newspaper, it never enters your head even re-
motely to draw any comparison between the wild
beast that has killed your friend and yourself,
who have killed the snipe, an explorer like
him.

And yet such a comparison would be perfectly
logical, and, I fear, would give a certain advantage to the beast, since you have killed for pleasure, and without any risk of your being killed
yourself; whereas the beast has killed from
hunger, that is to say from necessity, and with
the risk of being killed by your friend, who must
certainly have been armed.

Rhetoric, you say? Ah, yes, my friend; do not
be too contemptuous; I admit as much, myself;

rhetoric, because we, by the grace of God, are men and not snipe.

The snipe, for his part, without any fear of being rhetorical, might draw the comparison and demand that at least men, who go out shooting for pleasure, should not call the beasts savage.

We, no. We cannot allow the comparison, because on one side we have a man who has killed a beast, and on the other a beast that has killed a man.

At the very utmost, my dear snipe, to make some concession to you, we can say that you were a poor innocent little creature. There! Does that satisfy you? But you are not to infer from this, that our wickedness is therefore the greater; and, above all, you are not to say that, by calling you an innocent little creature and killing you, we have forfeited the right to call the beast savage which, from hunger and not for pleasure, has killed a man.

But when a man, you say, makes himself lower than a beast?

Ah, yes; we must be prepared, certainly, for the consequences of our logic. Often we make a slip, and then heaven only knows where we shall land.

§ 4

The experience of seeing men sink lower than the beasts must frequently have occurred to Varia Nestoroff.

And yet she has not killed them. A huntress, as you are a hunter. The snipe, you have killed. She has never killed anyone. One only, for her sake, has killed himself, by his own hand: Giorgio Mirelli; but not for her sake alone.

The beast, moreover, which does harm from a necessity of its nature, is not, so far as we know, unhappy.

The Nestoroff, as we have abundant grounds for supposing, is most unhappy. She does not enjoy her own wickedness, for all that it is carried out with such cold-blooded calculation.

If I were to say openly what I think of her to my fellow-operators, to the actors and actresses of the firm, all of them would at once suspect that I too had fallen in love with the Nestoroff.

I ignore this suspicion.

The Nestoroff feels for me, like all her fellow-artists, an almost instinctive aversion. I do not reciprocate it in any way because I do not spend my time with her, except when I am in the service of my machine, and then, as I turn the handle, I am what I am supposed to be, that is to say perfectly *impassive*. I am unable either to hate or to love the Nestoroff, as I am unable either to hate or to love anyone. I am *a hand that turns the handle.* When, finally, I am restored to myself, that is to say when for me the torture of being *only a hand* is ended, and I can regain possession of the rest of my body, and marvel that I have still a head on my shoulders, and abandon myself once more to that wretched *superfluity* which exists in me nevertheless and of which for almost the whole day my profession condemns me to be deprived; then . . . ah, then the affections, the memories that come to life in me are certainly not such as can persuade me to love this woman. I was the friend of Giorgio Mirelli, and among the most cherished memories of my life is that of the dear house in the country by Sorrento, where Granny Rosa and poor Duccella still live and mourn.

I study. I go on studying, because that is perhaps my ruling passion: it nourished in times of poverty and sustained my dreams, and it is the sole comfort that I have left, now that they have ended so miserably.

I study this woman, then, without passion but intently, who, albeit she may seem to understand what she is doing and why she does it, yet has not in herself any of that quiet "systematisation" of concepts, affections, rights and duties, opinions and habits, which I abominate in other people.

She knows nothing for certain, except the harm that she can do to others, and she does it, I repeat, with cold-blooded calculation.

This, in the opinion of other people, of all the "systematised," debars her from any excuse. But I believe that she cannot offer any excuse, herself, for the harm which nevertheless she knows herself to have done.

She has something in her, this woman, which the others do not succeed in understanding, because even she herself does not clearly understand it. One guesses it, however, from the violent expressions which she assumes, involuntarily, unconsciously, in the parts that are assigned to her.

She alone takes them seriously, and all the more so the more illogical and extravagant they are, grotesquely heroic and contradictory. And there is no way of keeping her in check, of making her moderate the violence of those expressions. She alone ruins more films than all the other actors in the four companies put together. For one thing, she always moves out of the *picture;* when by any chance she does not move out, her action is so disordered, her face so strangely altered and disguised, that in the rehearsal theatre almost all the scenes in which she has taken part turn out useless and have to be done again.

Any other actress, who had not enjoyed and did not enjoy, as she does, the favour of the warm-hearted Commendator Borgalli, would long since have been given notice to leave.

Instead of which, "Dear, dear, dear . . ." exclaims the warm-hearted Commendatore, without the least annoyance, when he sees projected on the screen in the rehearsal theatre those demoniacal pictures, "dear, dear, dear . . . oh, come . . . no . . . is it possible? Oh, Lord, how horrible . . . cut it out, cut it out. . . ."

And he finds fault with Polacco, and with all the producers in general, who keep the *scenarios* to themselves, confining themselves to suggesting bit by bit to the actors the action to be performed in each separate scene, often disjointedly, because not all the scenes can be taken in order, one after another, in a studio. It often happens that the actors do not even know what part they are supposed to be taking in the play as a whole, and one hears some actor ask in the middle:

"I say, Polacco, am I the husband or the lover?"

In vain does Polacco protest that he has carefully explained the whole part to the Nestoroff. Commendator Borgalli knows that the fault does not lie with Polacco; so much so, that he has given him another leading lady, the Sgrelli, in order not to waste all the films that are allotted to his company. But the Nestoroff protests on her own account, if Polacco makes use of the Sgrelli alone, or of the Sgrelli more than of herself, the true leading lady of the company. Her ill-wishers say that she does this to ruin Polacco, and Polacco himself believes it and goes about saying so. It is untrue: the only thing ruined, here, is film; and the Nestoroff is genuinely in despair at what she has done; I repeat, involuntarily and unconsciously. She herself remains speechless and almost terror-stricken at her own image on the screen, so altered and disordered. She sees there some one who is herself but whom she does not know. She would like not to recognise herself in this person, but at least to know her.

Possibly for years and years, through all the mysterious adventures of her life, she has gone in quest of this demon which exists in her and always escapes her, to arrest it, to ask it what it wants, why it is suffering, what she ought to do to soothe it, to placate it, to give it peace.

No one, whose eyes are not clouded by a passionate antipathy, and who has seen her come out of the rehearsal theatre after the presentation of those pictures of herself, can retain any doubt as to that. She is really tragic: terrified and enthralled, with that sombre stupor in her eyes which we observe in the eyes of the dying, and can barely restrain the convulsive tremor of her entire person.

I know the answer I should receive, were I to point this out to anyone:

"But it is rage! She is quivering with rage!"

It is rage, yes; but not the sort of rage that they all suppose, namely at a film that has gone wrong. A cold rage, colder than a blade of steel, is indeed this woman's weapon against all her enemies. Now Cocò Polacco is not an enemy in her eyes. If he were, she would not tremble like that: with the utmost coldness she would avenge herself on him.

Enemies, to her, all the men become to whom she attaches herself, in order that they may help her to arrest the secret thing in her that escapes her: she herself, yes, but a thing that lives and suffers, so to speak, *outside herself.*

Well, no one has ever taken any notice of this thing, which to her is more pressing than anything else; everyone, rather, remains dazzled by her exquisite form, and does not wish to possess or to know anything else of her. And then she punishes them with a cold rage, just where their desires prick them; and first of all she exasperates those desires with the most perfidious art, that her revenge may be all the greater. She avenges herself by flinging her body, suddenly and coldly, at those whom they least expected to see thus favoured: like that, so as to shew them in what contempt she holds the thing that they prize most of all in her.

I do not believe that there can be any other explanation of certain sudden changes in her

amorous relations, which appear to everyone, at
first sight, inexplicable, because no one can deny
that she has done harm to herself by them.

Except that the others, thinking it over and
considering, on the one hand the nature of the
men with whom she had consorted previously,
and on the other that of the men at whom she
has suddenly flung herself, say that this is due
to the fact that with the former sort she could
not remain, *could not breathe;* whereas to the
latter she felt herself attracted by a "gutter"
affinity; and this sudden and unexpected flinging
of herself they explain as the sudden spring of
a person who, after a long suffocation, seeks to
obtain at last, *wherever he can,* a mouthful of
air.

And if it should be just the opposite? If *in
order to breathe,* to secure that help of which I
have already spoken, she had attached herself
to the former sort, and instead of having the
breathing-space, the help for which she hoped,
had found no breathing-space and no help from
them, but rather an anger and disgust all the
stronger because increased and embittered by
disappointment, and also by a certain contempt
which a person feels for the needs of another's
soul who sees and cares for nothing but his
own SOUL, like that, in capital letters? No one
knows; but of these "gutter" refinements those
men may well be capable who mostly highly

esteem themselves, and are deemed *superior* by
their fellows. And then . . . then, better the
gutter which offers itself as such, which, if it
makes you sad, does not delude you; and which
may have, as often it does have, a good side to
it, and, now and then, certain traces of innocence,
which cheer and refresh you all the more, the
less you expected to find them there.

The fact remains that, for more than a year,
the Nestoroff has been living with the Sicilian
actor Carlo Ferro, who also is engaged by the
Kosmograph: she is dominated by him and
passionately in love with him. She knows what
she may expect from such a man, and asks for
nothing more. But it seems that she obtains far
more from him than the others are capable of
imagining.

This explains why, for some time back, I have
set myself to study, with keen interest, Carlo
Ferro also.

§ 5

A problem which I find it far more difficult to
solve is this: how in the world Giorgio Mirelli,
who would fly with such impatience from every
complication, can have lost himself to this woman,
to the point of laying down his life on her
account.

Almost all the details are lacking that would
enable me to solve this problem, and I have said

already that I have no more than a summary
report of the drama.

I know from various sources that the Nestoroff, at Capri, when Giorgio Mirelli saw her
for the first time, was in distinctly bad odour,
and was treated with great diffidence by the little
Russian colony, which for some years past has
been settled upon that island.

Some even suspected her of being a spy, perhaps because she, not very prudently, had introduced herself as the widow of an old conspirator,
who had died some years before her coming to
Capri, a refugee in Berlin. It appears that some
one wrote for information, both to Berlin and
to Petersburg, with regard to her and to this unknown conspirator, and that it came to light that
a certain Nikolai Nestoroff had indeed been for
some years in exile in Berlin, and had died there,
but without ever having given anyone to understand that he was exiled for political reasons. It
appears to have become known also that this
Nikolai Nestoroff had taken her, as a little girl,
from the streets, in one of the poorest and most
disreputable quarters of Petersburg, and, after
having her educated, had married her; and then,
reduced by his vices to the verge of starvation,
had lived upon her, sending her out to sing in music-
halls of the lowest order, until, with the police
on his track, he had made his escape, alone, into
Germany. But the Nestoroff, to my knowledge,

indignantly denies all these stories. That she may have complained privately to some one of the ill-treatment, not to say the cruelty she received from her girlhood at the hands of this old man is quite possible; but she does not say that he lived upon her; she says rather that, of her own accord, obeying the call of her passion, and also, perhaps, to supply the necessities of life, having overcome his opposition, she took to acting in the provinces, a-c-t-i-n-g, mind, on the legitimate stage; and that then, her husband having fled from Russia for political reasons and settled in Berlin, she, knowing him to be in frail health and in need of attention, taking pity on him, had joined him there and remained with him till his death. What she did then, in Berlin, as a widow, and afterwards in Paris and Vienna, cities to which she often refers, shewing a thorough knowledge of their life and customs, she neither says herself nor certainly does anyone ever venture to ask her.

For certain people, for innumerable people, I should say, who are incapable of seeing anything but themselves, love of humanity often, if not always, means nothing more than being pleased with themselves.

Thoroughly pleased with himself, with his art, with his studies of landscape, must Giorgio Mirelli, unquestionably, have been in those days at Capri.

Indeed—and I seem to have said this before—
his habitual state of mind was one of rapture
and amazement. Given such a state of mind, it
is easy to imagine that this woman did not
appear to him as she really was, with the needs
that she felt, wounded, scourged, poisoned by the
distrust and evil gossip that surrounded her; but
in the fantastic transfiguration that he at once
made of her, and illuminated by the light in
which he beheld her. For him feelings must take
the form of colours, and, perhaps, entirely en-
grossed in his art, he had no other feeling left
save for colour. All the impressions that he
formed of her were derived exclusively, perhaps,
from the light which he shed upon her; impressions, therefore, that were felt by him alone. She
need not, perhaps could not participate in them.
Now, nothing irritates us more than to be shut
out from an enjoyment, vividly present before
our eyes, round about us, the reason of which
we can neither discover nor guess. But even if
Giorgio Mirelli had told her of his enjoyment,
he could not have conveyed it to her mind. It
was a joy felt by him alone, and proved that he
too, in his heart, prayed and wished for nothing
else of her than her body; not, it is true, like
other men, with base intent; but even this, in
the long run—if you think it over carefully—
could not but increase the woman's irritation.
Because, if the failure to derive any assistance,

in the maddening uncertainties of her spirit,
from the many who saw and desired nothing in
her save her body, to satisfy on it the brutal
appetite of the senses, filled her with anger and
disgust; her anger with the one man, who also desired her body and nothing more; her body, but
only to extract from it an ideal and absolutely
self-sufficient pleasure, must have been all the
stronger, in so far as every provocative of disgust was entirely lacking, and must have rendered more difficult, if not absolutely futile, the
vengeance which she was in the habit of wreak-
ing upon other people. An angel, to a woman,
is always more irritating than a beast.

I know from all Giorgio Mirelli's artist friends
in Naples that he was spotlessly chaste, not because he did not know how to make an impression
upon women, but because he instinctively avoided
every vulgar distraction.

To account for his suicide, which beyond question was largely due to the Nestoroff, we ought
to assume that she, not cared for, not helped, and
irritated to madness, in order to be avenged,
must with the finest and subtlest art have con-
trived that her body should gradually come to
life before his eyes, not for the delight of his
eyes alone; and that, when she saw him, like all
the rest, conquered and enslaved, she forbade
him, the better to taste her revenge, to take any
other pleasure from her than that with which,

until then, he had been content, as the only one
desired, because the only one worthy of him.

We ought, I say, to assume this, but only if we
wish to be ill-natured. The Nestoroff might say,
and perhaps does say, that she did nothing to
alter that relation of pure friendship which had
grown up between herself and Mirelli; so much
so that when he, no longer contented with that
pure friendship, more impetuous than ever owing to the severe repulse with which she met his
advances, yet, to obtain his purpose, offered to
marry her, she struggled for a long time—and
this is true; I learned it on good authority—to
dissuade him, and proposed to leave Capri, to
disappear; and in the end remained there only
because of his acute despair.

But it is true that, if we wish to be ill-natured,
we may also be of opinion that both the early
repulse and the later struggle and threat and
attempt to leave the island, to disappear, were
perhaps so many artifices carefully planned and
put into practice to reduce this young man to
despair after having seduced him, and to obtain
from him all sorts of things which otherwise he
would never, perhaps, have conceded to her.
Foremost among them, that she should be introduced as his future bride at the Villa by Sorrento
to that dear Granny, to that sweet little sister,
of whom he had spoken to her, and to the sister's
betrothed.

It seems that he, Aldo Nuti, more than the two women, resolutely opposed this claim. Authority and power to oppose and to prevent this marriage he did not possess, for Giorgio was now his own master, free to act as he chose, and considered that he need no longer give an account of himself to anyone; but that he should bring this woman to the house and place her in contact with his sister, and expect the latter to welcome her and to treat her as a sister, this, by Jove, he could and must oppose, and oppose it he did with all his strength. But were they, Granny Rosa and Duccella, aware what sort of woman this was that Giorgio proposed to bring to the house and to marry? A Russian adventuress, an actress, if not something worse! How could he allow such a thing, how not oppose it with all his strength?

Again "with all his strength" . . . Ah, yes, who knows how hard Granny Rosa and Duccella had to fight in order to overcome, little by little, by their sweet and gentle persuasion, all the strength of Aldo Nuti. How could they have imagined what was to become of that strength at the sight of Varia Nestoroff, as soon as she set foot, timid, ethereal and smiling, in the dear villa by Sorrento!

Perhaps Giorgio, to account for the delay which Granny Rosa and Duccella shewed in answering, may have said to the Nestoroff that this

delay was due to the opposition "with all his
strength" of his sister's future husband; so that
the Nestoroff felt the temptation to measure her
own strength against this other, at once, as soon
as she set foot in the villa. I know nothing! I
know that Aldo Nuti was drawn in as though
into a whirlpool and at once carried away like a
wisp of straw by passion for this woman.

I do not know him. I saw him as a boy, once
only, when I was acting as Giorgio's tutor, and
he struck me as a fool. This impression of mine
does not agree with what Mirelli said to me about
him, on my return from Liége, namely that he
was *complicated*. Nor does what I have heard
from other people, with regard to him correspond in the least with this first impression,
which however has irresistibly led me to speak
of him according to the idea that I had formed
of him from it. I must, really, have been mistaken. Duccella found it possible to love him!
And this, to my mind, does more than anything
else to prove me in the wrong. But we cannot
control our impressions. He may be, as people
tell me, a serious young man, albeit of a most
ardent temperament; for me, until I see him
again, he will remain that fool of a boy, with
the baron's coronet on his handkerchiefs and
portfolios, the young gentleman who *would so
love to become an actor.*

He became one, and not by way of make-

believe, with the Nestoroff, at Giorgio Mirelli's
expense. The drama was unfolded at Naples,
shortly after the Nestoroff's introduction and
brief visit to the house at Sorrento. It seems
that Nuti returned to Naples with the engaged
couple, after that brief visit, to help the inex-
perienced Giorgio and her who was not yet
familiar with the town, to set their house in order
before the wedding.

Perhaps the drama would not have happened,
or would have had a different ending, had it not
been for the complication of Duccella's engagement to, or rather her love for Nuti. For this
reason Giorgio Mirelli was obliged to concentrate
on himself the violence of the unendurable horror
that overcame him at the sudden discovery of
his betrayal.

Aldo Nuti rushed from Naples like a madman
before there arrived from Sorrento at the news
of Giorgio's suicide Granny Rosa and Duccella.

Poor Duccella, poor Granny Rosa! The woman
who from thousands and thousands of miles away
came to bring confusion and death into your
little house where with the jasmines bloomed
the most innocent of idylls, I have her here, now,
in front of my machine, every day; and, if the
news I have heard from Polacco be true, I shall
presently have him here as well, Aldo Nuti, who
appears to have heard that the Nestoroff is leading lady with the Kosmograph.

I do not know why, my heart tells me that, as I turn the handle of this photographic machine, I am destined to carry out both your revenge and your poor Giorgio's, dear Duccella, dear Granny Rosa!

OF THE NOTES OF SERAFINO GUBBIO
CINEMATOGRAPH OPERATOR

BOOK III

§ 1

A SLIGHT swerve. There is a one-horse carriage in front. *"Peu, pepeeeu, peeeu."*

What? The horn of the motor-car is pulling it back? Why, yes! It does really seem to be making it run backwards, with the most comic effect.

The three ladies in the motor-car laugh, turn round, wave their arms in greeting with great vivacity, amid a gay, confused flutter of many-coloured veils; and the poor little carriage, hidden in an arid, sickening cloud of smoke and dust, however hard the cadaverous little horse may try to pull it along with his weary trot, continues to fall behind, far behind, with the houses, the trees, the occasional pedestrians, until it vanishes down the long straight vista of the suburban avenue. Vanishes? Not at all! The motor-car has vanished. The carriage, meanwhile, is still here, still slowly advancing, at the weary, level trot of its cadaverous horse. And the whole of the avenue seems to come forward again, slowly, with it.

You have invented machines, have you? And

77

now you enjoy these and similar sensations of
stylish pace.

The three ladies in the motor-car are three
actresses from the Kosmograph, and have
greeted with such vivacity the carriage flung into
the background by their mechanical progress not
because there is anyone in the carriage particularly dear to them; but because the motor-car,
the machinery intoxicates them and excites this
uncontrollable vivacity in them. They have it
at their disposal; free of charge; the Kosmograph pays. In the carriage there is myself.
They have seen me disappear in an instant, drop-
ping ludicrously behind, down the receding vista
of the avenue; they have laughed at me; by this
time they have already arrived. But here am I
creeping forward again, my dear ladies. Ever
so slowly, yes; but what have you seen? A carriage drop behind, as though pulled by a string,
and the whole avenue rush past you in a long,
confused, violent, dizzy streak. I, on the other
hand, am still here; I can console myself for my
slow progress by admiring one by one, at my
leisure, these great green plane trees by the roadside, not uprooted by the hurricane of your passage, but firmly planted in the ground, which turn
towards me at every breath of wind in the gold
of the sunlight between their dark boughs a cool
patch of violet shadow: giants of the road,
halted in file, ever so many of them, they open

and uplift on muscular arms their huge palpi-
tating wreaths of foliage to the sky.

Drive on, yes, but not too fast, my coachman!
He is so tired, your old cadaverous horse. Everything passes him by: motor-cars, bicycles, electric trams; and the frenzy of all that motion
along the road urges him on as well, unconsciously and involuntarily, gives an irresistible
impetus to his poor stiff legs, weary with conveying, from end to end of the great city, so many
people afflicted, oppressed, excited, by necessities, hardships, engagements, aspirations which
he is incapable of understanding! And perhaps
none of them makes him so tired as the few who
get into the carriage with the object of amusing
themselves, and do not know where or how. Poor
little horse, his head droops gradually lower, and he
never raises it again, not even if you flay him
with your whip, coachman!

"Here, on the right . . . turn to the right!"
The Kosmograph is here, on this remote side
road, outside the city gate.

§ 2

Freshly dug, dusty, barely traced in outline, it
has the air and the ungraciousness of a person
who, expecting to be left in peace, finds that,
on the contrary, he is continually being disturbed.

But if the right to a few fresh tufts of grass,

to all those fine, wandering threads of sound,
with which the silence weaves a cloak of peace
in solitary places, to the croak of an occasional
frog when it rains and the pools of rain-water
mirror back the stars when the sky is clear
again; in short, to all the delights of nature in
the open and unpeopled country: if this right
be not enjoyed by a country road some miles outside the gate of the city, then indeed I do not
know who does enjoy it.

Instead of this: motor-cars, carriages, carts,
bicycles, and all day long an uninterrupted coming and going of actors, operators, mechanics,
labourers, messengers, and a din of hammers,
saws, planes, and clouds of dust and the stench
of petrol.

The buildings, high and low, of the great
cinematograph company rise at the far end of
the road, on either side; a few more stand up
farther off, scattered in confusion, within the vast
enclosure, which extends far over the Campagna:
one of them, higher than all the rest, is capped
with a sort of glazed tower, with opaque windows, which glitter in the sunlight; and on the
wall that is visible from both avenue and side road,
on the dazzling whitewashed surface, in black
letters a foot high, is painted:

THE KOSMOGRAPH

The entrance is to the left, through a little
door by the side of the gate, which is rarely
opened. Opposite is a wayside tavern, pom-
pously surnamed *Trattoria della Kosmograph,*
with a fine trellised pergola which encloses the
whole of the so-called garden and creates a patch
of green within. Five or six rustic tables, inside, none too steady on their legs, and chairs
and benches. A number of actors, made up and
dressed in strange costumes, are seated there and
engaged in an animated discussion; one of them
shouts louder than the rest, bringing his hand
down furiously upon his thigh:

"I tell you, you've got to hit her here, here,
here!"

And the bang of his hand on his leather
breeches sounds like so many rifle shots.

They are speaking, of course, of the tigress,
bought a short time ago by the Kosmograph;
of the way in which she is to be killed; of the
exact spot in which the bullet must hit her. It
has become an obsession with them. To hear
them talk, you would think that they were all
professional hunters of wild beasts.

Crowding round the entrance, stand listening
to them with grinning faces the chauffeurs of the
dusty, dilapidated motor-cars; the drivers of the
carriages that stand waiting, there in the background, where the side road is barred by a fence
of stakes and iron spikes; and ever so many

other people, the most wretched that I know, albeit they are dressed with a certain gentility. They are (I apologise, but everything here has a French or an English name) the casual *cachets*, that is to say the people who come to offer their services, should the need arise, as *supers*. Their petulance is insufferable, worse than that of beggars, because they come here to display a penury which asks not for the charity of a copper, but for five lire, in reward for dressing themselves up, often grotesquely. You ought to see the rush, on some days, to the dressing-room to snatch and put on at once a heap of gaudy rags, and the airs with which they strut up and down on the stage and in the open, knowing full well that, if they succeed in *dressing,* even if they do not *come on,* they draw half-salary.

Two or three actors come out of the tavern, making their way through the crowd. They are dressed in saffron-coloured vests, their faces and arms plastered a dirty yellow, and with a sort of crest of coloured feathers on their heads. Indians. They greet me:

"Hallo, Gubbio."

"Hallo, *Shoot!* . . . "

Shoot, you understand, is my nickname.

The difficulties of life!

You have lost an eye in it, and your case has been serious. But we are all of us more or less

marked, and we never notice it. Life marks us;
and fastens a beauty-spot on one, a grimace on
another.

No? But excuse me, you, yes, you who said no
just now . . . there now, *absolutely* . . . do you
not continually load all your conversation with
that adverb in *-ly?*

"I went absolutely to the place they told me:
I saw him, and said to him absolutely: What,
you, absolutely . . . "

Have patience! Nobody yet calls you *Mr.
Absolutely* . . . Serafino Gubbio (*Shoot!*) has
been less fortunate. Without my noticing it, I
may have happened once or twice, or several
times in succession, to repeat, after the producer,
the sacramental word: *"Shoot!"* I must have
repeated it with my face composed in that expression which is proper to me, of professional
impassivity, and this was enough to make everyone here, at Fantappiè's suggestion, address me
now as *Shoot.*

Every town in Italy knows Fantappiè, the
comedian of the Kosmograph, who has special-
ised in travesties of military life: *Fantappiè, C.
B.* and *Fantappiè on the range; Fantappiè on
manœuvres* and *Fantappiè steers the airship;
Fantappiè on guard* and *Fantappiè in the Colonies.*

---

[1] *Fantappiè,* or *fante a piede,* is equivalent to the English
footslogger. C. K. S. M.

He stuck it on himself, this nickname; a nickname that goes well with his special form of
art.   In private life he is called Roberto
Chismicò.

"You aren't angry with me, laddie, for calling
you *Shoot?*" he asked me, some time ago.

"No, my dear fellow," I answered him with a
smile.   "You have stamped me."

"I've stamped myself too, if it comes to that!"

All of us stamped, yes.   And most of all, those
of us who are least aware of it, my dear
Fantappiè.

§ 3

I go in through the entrance hall on the left,
and come out upon the gravelled path from the
gate, shut in by the buildings of the second department, the *Photographic* or *Positive.*

In my capacity as operator I have the privilege
of keeping one foot in this, and the other in the
Art, or *Negative Department.*   And all the mar-
vels of the industrial and so-called artistic maze
are familiar to me.

Here the work of the machines is mysteriously
completed.

All the life that the machines have devoured
with the voracity of animals gnawed by a tape-
worm, is turned out here, in the large under-
ground rooms, their darkness barely broken by
dim red lamps, which strike a sinister blood-red

gleam from the enormous dishes prepared for the developing bath.

The life swallowed by the machines is there, in those tapeworms, I mean in the films, now coiled on their reels.

We have to fix this life, which has ceased to be life, so that another machine may restore to it the movement here suspended in a series of instantaneous sections.

We are as it were in a womb, in which is developing and taking shape a monstrous mechanical birth.

And how many hands are at work there in the dark! There is a whole army of men and women employed here: operators, technicians, watchmen, men employed on the dynamos and on the other machinery, drying, soaking, winding, colouring, perforating the films and joining up the pieces.

I have only to enter here, in this darkness foul with the breath of the machines, with the exhalations of chemical substances, for all my *superfluity* to evaporate.

Hands, I see nothing but hands, in these dark rooms; hands busily hovering over the dishes; hands to which the murky light of the red lamps gives a spectral appearance. I reflect that these hands belong to men who are men no longer; who are condemned here to be hands only: these hands, instruments. Have they a heart? Of what use is it? It is of no use here. Only as an instrument, it too, of a machine, to serve, to move these hands. And so with the head: only to think of what these hands may need. And gradually I am filled with all the horror of the necessity that impels me to become a hand myself also, and nothing more.

I go to the store-keeper to provide myself with a stock of fresh film, and I prepare my machine for its meal.

I at once assume, with it in my hand, my mask of impassivity. Or rather I cease to exist. *It* walks, now, upon my legs. From head to foot, I belong to it: I form part of its equipment. My head is here, inside the machine, and I carry it in my hand.

Outside, in the daylight, throughout the vast enclosure, is the gay animation of an undertaking that prospers and pays punctually and hand, somely for every service rendered, that easy run of work in the confidence that there will be no complications, and that every difficulty, with the abundance of means at our disposal, will be neatly overcome; indeed a feverish desire to introduce, as though by way of challenge, the strangest and most unusual difficulties, without a thought of the cost, with the certainty that the money, spent now without reckoning, will before long return multiplied an hundredfold.

Scenario writers, stage hands, scene painters,

carpenters, builders and plasterers, electricians, tailors and dressmakers, milliners, florists, countless other workers employed as shoemakers, hatters, armourers, in the store-rooms of antique and modern furniture, in the wardrobe, are all kept busy, but are not seriously busy, nor are they playing a game.

Only children have the divine gift of taking their play seriously. The wonder is in themselves; they impart it to the things with which they are playing, and let themselves be deceived by them. It is no longer a game; it is a wonderful reality.

Here it is just the opposite.

We do not play at our work, for no one has any desire to play. But how are we to take seriously a work that has no other object than to deceive, not ourselves, but other people? And to deceive them by putting together the most idiotic fictions, to which the machine is responsible for giving a wonderful reality?

There results from this, of necessity, and with no possibility of deception, a hybrid game. Hybrid, because in it the stupidity of the fiction is all the more revealed and obvious inasmuch as one sees it to be placed on record by the method that least lends itself to deception: namely, photography. It ought to be understood that the fantastic cannot acquire reality except by means of art, and that the reality which a machine is capable of giving it kills it, for the very reason that it is given it by a machine, that is to say by a method which discovers and exposes the fiction, simply by giving it and presenting it as real. If it is mechanical, how can it be life, how can it be art? It is almost like entering one of those galleries of living statuary, waxworks, clothed and tinted. We feel nothing but surprise (which may even amount to disgust) at their movements, in which there is no possible illusion of a material reality.

And no one seriously believes that he can create this illusion. At the most, he tries to provide *something to take* for the machine, here in the workshops, there in the four studios or on the stage. The public, like the machine, takes it all. They make stacks of money, and can cheerfully spend thousands and thousands of lire on the construction of a scene which on the screen will not last for more than a couple of minutes.

Scene painters, stage hands, actors all give themselves the air of deceiving the machine, which will give an appearance of reality to all their fictions.

What am I to them, I who with the utmost seriousness stand by impassive, turning the handle, at that stupid game of theirs?

§ 4

Excuse me for a moment. I am going to pay a visit to the tiger. I shall talk, I shall go on talking, I shall pick up the thread of my discourse later on, never fear. At present, I must go and see the tiger.

Ever since they bought her, I have gone every day to pay her a visit, before starting my work. On two days only have I not been able to go, because they did not give me time.

We have had other animals here that were wild, although greatly subdued by melancholy: a couple of polar bears which used to spend the whole day standing on their hind legs beating their breasts, like Trinitarians doing penance: three shivering lion cubs, always huddled in a corner of the cage, one on top of another; other animals as well, that were not exactly wild: a poor ostrich, terrified at every sound, like a chicken, and always uncertain where to set its feet: a number of mischievous monkeys. The Kosmograph is provided with everything, including a menagerie, albeit its inmates remain there but a short time.

No animal has ever *talked to me* like this tiger.

When we first secured her, she had but recently arrived, a gift from some illustrious foreign personage, at the Zoological Gardens in Rome.

At the Zoological Gardens they were unable to keep her, because she was absolutely incapable of learning, I do not say to blow her nose with a handkerchief, but even to respect the most elementary rules of social intercourse. Three or four times she threatened to jump the ditch, or rather attempted to jump it, to hurl herself upon the visitors to the gardens who stood quietly gazing at her from a distance.

But what other thought could arise more spontaneously in the mind of a tiger (if you object to the word *mind,* let us say the paws) than that the ditch in question was put there on purpose so that she might try to jump it, and that those ladies and gentlemen stopped there in front of her in order that she might devour them if she succeeded in jumping it?

It is certainly an advantage to be able to stand a joke; but we know that not everyone possesses this advantage. Many people cannot even endure the thought that some one else thinks he is at liberty to joke at their expense. I speak of men, who, nevertheless, in the abstract, are all capable of realising that at times a joke is permissible.

The tiger, you say, is not placed on show in a zoological garden for a joke. I agree. But does it not seem a joke to you to think that she can suppose that you keep her there on show to give the public a "living idea" of natural history?

Here we are back at our starting-point. This,

inasmuch as we are not tigers, but men, is rhetoric.

We may feel compassion for a man who is unable to stand a joke; we ought not to feel any for a beast; especially if the joke for which we have placed it on show, I mean the "living idea," may have fatal consequences: that is to say, for the visitors to the Zoological Gardens, a too practical illustration of its ferocity.

This tiger was, therefore, wisely condemned to death. The Kosmograph Company managed to hear of it in time, and bought her. Now she is here, in a cage in our menagerie. Since she has been here, her behaviour has been exemplary. How are we to explain this? Our treatment, no doubt, seems to her far more logical. Here she is not at liberty to attempt to jump any ditch, has no illusion of *local colour*, as in the Zoological Gardens. Here she has in front of her the bars of her cage, which say to her continually: "You cannot escape; you are a prisoner"; and she lies on the ground there almost all day long, resigned to her fate, gazing out through the bars, quietly, wonderingly waiting.

Alas, poor beast, she does not know that here there is something far more serious in store for her, than that joke of the "living idea"!

The scenario is already completed, an Indian subject, in which she is destined to represent one of the principal parts. A spectacular scenario, upon which several hundred thousand lire will be spent; but the stupidest and most vulgar that could be imagined. I need only give the title: *The Lady and the Tiger*. The usual lady, more tigerish than the tiger. I seem to have heard that she is to be an English *Miss* travelling in the Indies with a train of admirers.

India will be a sham, the jungle will be a sham, the travels will be a sham, with a sham *Miss* and sham admirers: only the death of this poor beast will not be a sham. Do you follow me? And does it not make you writhe in anger?

To kill her in self-defence, or to save the life of another person, well and good. ι Albeit not of her own accord, for her own pleasure, has the beast come here to place herself on show among a lot of men, but men themselves, for their pleasure, have gone out to hunt her, to drag her from her savage lair. But to kill her like this, in a sham forest, in a sham hunt, for a stupid make-believe, is a real iniquity and is going too far. One of the admirers, at a certain stage, will fire point-blank at a rival. You will see this rival fall to the ground, dead. Yes, my friends. But when the scene is finished, there he is getting up again, brushing the dust of the stage off his clothes. But this poor beast will never get up again, after they have shot her. The scene shifters will carry off the sham forest, and at the same time clear the stage of her carcase. In the midst of a universal sham, her death alone will be genuine.

And if it were only a sham that could by its beauty and nobility compensate in a measure for the sacrifice of this beast. But no. It is utterly stupid. The actor who is to kill her will not even know, perhaps, why he has killed her. The scene will last for a minute or two at most, when projected upon the screen, and will pass without leaving any permanent impression in the minds of the spectators, who will come away from the theatre yawning:

"Oh Lord, what rubbish!"

This, you beautiful wild creature, is what awaits you. You do not know it, and gaze through the bars of your cage with those terror-stricken eyes in which the slit pupils contract and dilate by turns. I see your wild nature as it were steaming from your whole body, like the vapour of a blazing coal; I see marked on the black stripes of your coat the elastic force of your irrepressible spring. Whoever studies you closely is glad of the cage that imprisons you and checks in him also the savage instinct which the sight of you stirs irresistibly in his blood.

You cannot remain here on any other terms. Either you must be imprisoned like this, or you must be killed; because your ferocity—we quite understand—is innocent; nature has implanted it in you, and you, in employing it, are obeying

nature and cannot feel any remorse. We cannot
endure that you, after a gory feast, should be
able to sleep calmly. Your very innocence makes
us innocent of your death, when we inflict it in
self-defence. We can kill you, and then, like you,
sleep calmly. But out there, in the savage lands,
where you do not allow any stranger to pass;
not here, not here, where you have not come of
your own accord, for your own pleasure. The
beautiful, ingenuous innocence of your ferocity
makes the iniquity of ours seem disgusting here.
We seek to defend ourselves against you, after
bringing you here, for our pleasure, and we keep
you in prison: this is no longer your kind of
ferocity; it is a treacherous ferocity! But we
know, you may be sure, we know how to go
even farther, to do better still: we shall kill you
for amusement, stupidly. A sham hunter, in a
sham forest, among sham trees. . . . We shall be
worthy in every respect, truly, of the concocted
plot. Tigers, more tigerish than a tiger. And to
think that the sentiment which this film, now in
preparation, is intended to arouse in the spectators is contempt for human ferocity! It will be
part of our day's work, this ferocity practised
for amusement, and we count moreover upon
making a handsome profit out of it, should the
film prove successful.

You stare. At what do you stare, you beautiful, innocent creature? That is just how things

stand. You are here for no other purpose. And I, who love and admire you, when they kill you, shall be *impassively* turning the handle of this pretty machine here, do you see? They have invented it. It has to act; it has to eat. It eats everything, whatever stupidity they may set before it. It will eat you too; it eats everything, I tell you! And I am its servant. I shall come and plant it closer to you, when you, mortally wounded, are writhing in your last agony. Ah, do not fear, it will extract the utmost penny of profit from your death! It does not have the luck to taste such a dinner every day. You can have that consolation. And, if you like, another as well.

There comes every day, like myself, in front of your cage here, a lady intent on studying how you move, how you turn your head, how you look out of your eyes. The Nestoroff. Is that nothing to you? She has chosen you to be her teacher. Luck such as this does not come the way of every tiger.

As usual, she is taking her part seriously. But I have heard it said that the part of the *Miss,* "more tigerish than the tiger," will not be assigned to her. Perhaps she does not yet know this; she thinks that the part is hers; and she comes here to study.

People have told me this, and laughed at it. But I myself, the other day, took her by surprise,

on one of her visits here, and remained talking to
her for some time.

§ 5

It is no mere waste of time, you will understand, to spend half an hour in watching and considering a tiger, seeing in it a manifestation of
Earth, guileless, beyond good and evil, incom-
parably beautiful and innocent in its savage
power. Before we can come down from this
"aboriginality" and reach the stage of being
able to see before us a man or woman of our
own time, and to recognise and consider him or
her as an inhabitant of the same earth, we require—I do, at least; I cannot answer for you—
a wide stretch of imagination.

And so I remained for a while looking at Signora Nestoroff before I was able to understand
what she was saying to me.

But the fault, as a matter of fact, was not only
mine and the tiger's. The fact of her addressing
me at all was unusual; and it is quite natural,
when anyone addresses us suddenly with whom
we have not been on speaking terms, that we
should find it hard at first to take in the meaning, sometimes even the sound of the most ordinary words, and should ask:

"Excuse me, what was it you said?"

In a little more than eight months, since I

came here, between her and myself, apart from formal greetings, barely a score of words have passed.

Then she—yes, this happened too—coming up to me, began to speak to me with great volubility, as we do when we wish to distract the attention of some one who has caught us in some action or thought which we are anxious to keep secret. (The Nestoroff speaks our language with marvellous ease and with a perfect accent, as though she had lived for many years in Italy: but she at once breaks into French whenever, if only for a moment, she changes her tone or grows excited.) She wished to find out from me whether I believed that the actor's profession was such that any animal whatsoever (not necessarily in a metaphorical sense) could regard itself as qualified, without preliminary training, to practise it.

"Where?" I asked her.

She did not understand my question.

"Well," I explained to her; "if you mean, practise it here, where there is no need of speech, perhaps even an animal—why not?—may be capable of succeeding."

I saw her face cloud over.

"That will be it," she said mysteriously.

I seemed at first to divine that she (like all the professional actors who are employed here) was speaking out of contempt for certain others who, without actually needing, but at the same time not despising an easy source of revenue, either from vanity or from predilection, or for some other reason, had managed to have their services accepted by the firm and to take their place among the actors, with no great difficulty, that supreme difficulty being eliminated which it would have been most arduous for them and perhaps impossible to overcome without a long training and a genuine aptitude, I mean the difficulty of speaking in public. We have a number of them at the Kosmograph who are real gentlemen, young fellows between twenty and thirty, either friends of some big shareholder on the Board, or shareholders themselves, who make a hobby of playing some part or other that has taken their fancy in a film, solely for their own amusement; and play their parts in the most gentlemanly fashion, some of them even with a grace that a real actor might envy.

But, reflecting afterwards on the mysterious tone in which she, her face suddenly clouding over, had uttered the words: "That will be it," the suspicion occurred to me that perhaps she had heard the news that Aldo Nuti, I do not yet know from what part of the horizon, was trying to find an opening here.

This suspicion disturbed me not a little.

Why did she come to ask me, of all people, with Aldo Nuti in her mind, whether I believed

that the actor's profession was such that any
animal might consider itself qualified, without
preliminary training, to practise it? Did she
then know of my friendship with Giorgio Mirelli?

I had not then, nor have I now any reason to
think so. At least the questions with which I
have adroitly plied her in the hope of enlighten-
ment have brought me no certainty.

I do not know why, but I should dislike intensely her knowing that I was a friend of
Giorgio Mirelli, in his boyhood, and a familiar
inmate of the villa by Sorrento into which she
brought confusion and death.

"I do not know why," I have said: but it is
not true; I do know why, and I have already
given a hint of the reason. I feel no love, I
repeat again, nor could I feel any, for this
woman; hatred, if anything. Everyone hates her
here; and that by itself would be an overwhelm-
ing reason for me not to hate her. Always, in
judging other people, I have endeavoured to
break the circle of my own affections, to gather
from the clamour of life, composed more of tears
than of laughter, as many notes as I could outside the chord of my own feelings. I knew
Giorgio Mirelli; but how, in what capacity? Such
as he was in his relations with me. He was the
sort of person that I liked. But who, and what
was he in his relations with this woman? The
sort that she could like? I do not know. Cer-

tainly he was not, he could not be one and the same person to her and to myself. And how then am I to judge this woman by him? We have all of us a false conception of an individual whole. Every whole consists in the mutual relations of its constituent elements; which means that, by altering those relations however slightly, we are bound to alter the whole. This explains how some one who is reasonably loved by me can reasonably be hated by a third person. I who love and the other who hates are two: not only that, but the one whom I love, and the one whom the third person hates, are by no means identical; they are one and one: therefore they are two also. And we ourselves can never know what reality is accorded to us by other people; who we are to this person and to that.

Now, if the Nesteroff came to hear that I had been a great friend of Giorgio Mirelli, she would perhaps suspect me of a hatred for herself which I do not feel: and this suspicion would be enough to make her at once become another person to me, I myself remaining meanwhile in the same attitude towards her; she would assume in my eyes an aspect that would hide all the rest; and I should no longer be able to study her, as I am now studying her, as a whole.

I spoke to her of the tiger, of the feelings which its presence in this place and the fate in store for it aroused in me; but I at once became aware that she was not in a position to understand me, not perhaps because she was incapable of doing so, but because the relations that have grown up between her and the animal do not allow her to feel either pity for it or anger at the deed that is to be done.

Her answer was shrewd:

"A sham, yes; stupid too, if you like; but when the door of the cage is opened and the animal is driven into the other, bigger cage representing a glade in a forest, with the bars hidden by branches, the hunter, even if he is a sham like the forest, will still be entitled to defend himself against it, simply because it, as you say, is not a sham animal but a real one."

"But that is just where the harm lies," I exclaimed: "in using a real animal where everything else is a sham."

"Where do you get that?" she promptly rejoined. "The part of the hunter will be a sham; but when he is face to face with this real animal he will be a *real* man! And I can assure you that if he does not kill it with his first shot, or does not wound it so as to bring it down, it will not stop to think that the hunter is a sham and the hunt a sham, but will spring upon him and *really* tear a *real* man to pieces."

I smiled at the acuteness of her logic and said:

"But who will have wished such a thing. Look at her as she lies there. She knows nothing, the beautiful creature, she is not to blame for her ferocity."

There was a strange look in her eyes, as though she suspected that I was trying to make fun of her; then she smiled as well, shrugged her shoulders slightly and went on:

"Do you feel is to deeply? Tame her! Make her a stage tiger, trained to sham death at a sham bullet from a sham hunter, and then all will be right."

We should never have come to an understanding; because if my sympathies were with the tiger, hers were with the hunter.

In fact, the hunter appointed to kill the animal is Carlo Ferro. The Nestoroff must be greatly upset by this; and perhaps she comes here not, as her enemies assert, to study her part, but to estimate the risk which her lover will be running.

He too, for all that he shews a scornful indifference, must, in his heart of hearts, feel apprehensive. I know that, in conversation with the General Manager, Commendator Borgalli, and also upstairs in the office, he has put forward a number of claims: the insurance of his life for at least one hundred thousand lire, to be paid to his parents in Sicily, in the event of his death, which heaven forbid; another insurance, for a more modest sum, in the event of his being incapacitated for work by any serious injury, which heaven forbid also; a handsome bonus, if every-

thing, as is to be hoped, turns out well, and lastly
—a curious claim, and one that was certainly not
suggested, like the rest, by a lawyer—the skin
of the dead tiger.

The tigerskin is presumably for the Nestoroff;
for her little feet; a costly rug. Oh, she must
certainly have warned her lover, with prayers
and entreaties, against undertaking so dangerous
a part; but then, seeing him determined and
bound by contract, she must, she and no one else,
have suggested to Ferro that he should claim
at least the skin of the tiger. "At least?" you
say. Why, yes! That she used the words "at
least" seems to me beyond question. *At least,*
that is to say in compensation for the tense
anxiety that she must feel for the risk to which
he will be exposing himself. It is not possible
that the idea can have originated with him, Carlo
Ferro, of having the skin of the dead animal to
spread under the little feet of his mistress.
Carlo Ferro is incapable of such an idea. You
have only to look at him to be convinced of it;
look at that great black hairy arrogant goat's
head on his shoulders.

He appeared, the other day, and interrupted
my conversation with the Nestoroff in front of
the cage. He did not even trouble to inquire
what we were discussing, as though a conversation with myself could not be of the slightest importance to him. He barely glanced at me, barely

raised his bamboo cane to the brim of his hat in sign of greeting, looked with his usual contemptuous indifference at the tiger in the cage, saying to his mistress:

"Come along: Polacco is ready; he is waiting for us."

And he turned his back, confident of being followed by the Nestoroff, as a tyrant by his slave.

No one feels or shews so much as he that instinctive antipathy, which as I have said is shared by almost all the actors for myself, and which is to be explained, or so at least I explain it, as an effect, which they themselves do not see clearly, of my profession.

Carlo Ferro feels it more strongly than any of them, because, among all his other advantages, he has that of seriously believing himself to be a great actor.

§ 6

It is not so much for me, Gubbio, this antipathy, as for my machine. It recoils upon me, because I am the man who turns the handle.

They do not realise it clearly, but I, with the handle in my hand, am to them in reality a sort of executioner.

Each of them—I refer, of course, to the real actors, to those, that is to say, who really love their art, whatever their merits may be—is here against his will, is here because he is better paid, and for work which, even if it requires some exertion, does not call for any intellectual effort. Often, as I have said before, they do not even know what part they are playing.

The machine, with the enormous profits that it produces, if it engages them, can reward them far better than any manager or proprietor of a dramatic company. Not only that; but it, with its mechanical reproduction, being able to offer at a low price to the general public a spectacle that is always new, fills the cinematograph halls and empties the theatres, so that all, or nearly all the dramatic companies are now doing wretched business; and the actors, if they are not to starve, see themselves compelled to knock at the doors of the cinematograph companies. But they do not hate the machine merely for the degradation of the stupid and silent work to which it condemns them; they hate it, first and foremost, because they see themselves withdrawn, feel themselves torn from that direct communion with the public from which in the past they derived their richest reward, their greatest satisfaction: that of seeing, of hearing from the stage, in a theatre, an eager, anxious multitude follow their *live* action, stirred with emotion, tremble, laugh, become excited, break out in applause.

Here they feel as though they were in exile.

In exile, not only from the stage, but also in a sense from themselves. Because their action, the *live* action of their *live* bodies, there, on the screen of the cinematograph, no longer exists: it is *their image* alone, caught in a moment, in a gesture, an expression, that flickers and disappears. They are confusedly aware, with a maddening, indefinable sense of emptiness, that their bodies are so to speak subtracted, suppressed, deprived of their reality, of breath, of voice, of the sound that they make in moving about, to become only a dumb image which quivers for a moment on the screen and disappears, in silence, in an instant, like an unsubstantial phantom, the play of illusion upon a dingy sheet of cloth.

They feel that they too are slaves to this strident machine, which suggests on its knock-kneed tripod a huge spider watching for its prey, a spider that sucks in and absorbs their live reality to render it up an evanescent, momentary appearance, the play of a mechanical illusion in the eyes of the public. And the man who strips them of their reality and offers it as food to the machine; who reduces their bodies to phantoms, who is he? It is I, Gubbio.

They remain here, as on a daylight stage, when they rehearse. The first night, for them, never arrives. The public they never see again. The machine is responsible for the performance before the public, with their phantoms; and they have

to be content with performing only before it.
When they have performed their parts, their
performance is film.

Can they feel any affection for me?

A certain comfort they have for their degradation in seeing not themselves only subjugated to
the service of this machine, which moves, stirs,
attracts ever so many people round it. Eminent
authors, dramatists, poets, novelists, come here,
all of them regularly and solemnly proposing the
"artistic regeneration" of the industry. And
to all of them Commendator Borgalli speaks in
one tone, and Cocò Polacco in another: the former, with the gloved hands of a General Manager; the other, openly, as a stage manager. He
listens patiently, does Cocò Polacco, to all their
suggestions of plots; but at a certain stage in
the discussion he raises his hand, saying:

"Oh no, that is a trifle crude. We must always
keep an eye on the English, my dear Sir!"

A most brilliant discovery, this of the English.
Indeed the majority of the films produced by
the Kosmograph go to England. We must therefore, in selecting our plots, adapt ourselves to
English taste. And is there any limit to the
things that the English will not have in a film,
according to Cocò Polacco?

"English prudery, you understand! They have
only to say 'shocking,' and there's an end of the
matter!"

If the films went straight before the judgment
of the public, then, perhaps, many things might
pass; but no: for the importation of films into
England there are the agents, there is the reef,
the pitfall of the agents. They decide, the agents,
and there is no appeal. And for every film that
will not *go,* there are hundreds of thousands of
lire wasted or not forthcoming.

Or else Cocò Polacco exclaims:

"Excellent! But that, my dear fellow, is a
play, a perfect play! A certain success! Do you
want to make a film of it? I won't hear of it!
As a film it won't go: I tell you, my dear fellow,
it's too subtle, too subtle. That is not the sort
of thing we want here! You are too clever, and
you know it."

In short, Cocò Polacco, if he refuses their
plots, pays them a compliment: he tells them
that they are not stupid enough to write for the
cinematograph. From one point of view, therefore, they would like to understand, would resign
themselves to understanding; but, from another,
they would like also to have their plots accepted.
A hundred, two hundred and fifty, three hundred
lire, at certain moments. . . . The suspicion that
this praise of their intelligence and depreciation
of the cinematograph as a form of art have been
advanced as a polite way of refusing their plots
flashes across the minds of some of them; but

their dignity is saved and they can go away with their heads erect. As they pass, the actors salute them as companions in misfortune.

"Everyone has to pass through here!" they think to themselves with malicious joy. "Even crowned heads! All of them in here, printed for a moment on a sheet!"

A few days ago, I was with Fantappiè in the courtyard on which the rehearsal theatre and the office of the Art Department open, when we noticed an old man with long hair, in a tall hat, with a huge nose and eyes that peered through his gold-rimmed spectacles, and a straggling beard, who seemed to be shrinking into himself with fear at the big coloured posters pasted on the wall, red, yellow, blue, glaring, terrible, of the films that have brought most honour to the firm.

"Illustrious Senator," Fantappiè exclaimed with a bound, springing towards him and then bringing himself to attention, his hand comically raised in the military salute. "Have you come for the rehearsal?"

"Why . . . yes . . . they told me ten o'clock," replied the illustrious Senator, endeavouring to make out whom he was addressing.

"Ten o'clock? Who told you that? The Pole?"

"I don't understand . . . "

"The Pole, the producer?"

"No, an Italian . . . one they call the engineer. . . ."

"Ah! Now I know: Bertini! He told you ten o'clock? That's all right. It is half past ten now. He's sure to be here by eleven."

It was the venerable Professor Zeme, the eminent astronomer, head of the Observatory and a Member of the Senate, an Academician of the Lincei, covered with ever so many Italian and foreign decorations, invited to all the Court banquets.

"Excuse me, though, Senator," went on that buffoon Fantappiè. "May I ask one favour: couldn't you make me go to the Moon?"

"I? To the Moon?"

"Yes, I mean cinematographically, you know . . . *Fantappiè in the Moon:* it would be lovely! Scouting, with a patrol of eight men. Think it over, Senator. I would arrange the business. . . . No? You say no?"

Senator Zeme said no, with a wave of the hand, if not contemptuously, certainly with great austerity. A scientist of his standing could not allow himself to place his science at the service of a clown. He has allowed himself, it is true, to be taken in every conceivable attitude in his Observatory; he has even asked to have projected on the screen a page containing the signatures of the most illustrious visitors to the

Observatory, so that the public may read there
the signatures of T.M. the King and Queen and
of T. R. H. the Crown Prince and the Princesses
and of H. M. the King of Spain and of other
Kings and Cabinet Ministers and Ambassadors;
but all this to the greater glory of his science and
to give the public some sort of idea of the *Mar-
vels of the Heavens* (the title of the film) and of
the formidable greatness in the midst of which
he, Senator Zeme, insignificant little creature as
he is, lives and labours.

"Martuf!" muttered Fantappiè, like a good
Piedmontese, with one of his characteristic
grimaces, as he strolled away with me.

But we turned back, a moment later, at the
sound of a great clamour of voices which had
arisen in the courtyard.

Actors, actresses, operators, producers, stage
hands had come pouring out from the dressing-
rooms and rehearsal theatre and were gathered
round Senator Zeme at loggerheads with Simone
Pau, who is in the habit of coming to see me now
and again at the Kosmograph.

"Educating the people, indeed!" shouted
Simone Pau. "Do me a favour! Send Fantappiè to the Moon! Make him play skittles with
the stars! Or perhaps you think that they belong to you, the stars? Hand them over here
to the divine Folly of man, which has every right
to appropriate them and to play skittles with

them! Besides . . . excuse me, but what do you
do? What do you suppose you are? You see
nothing but the object! You have no consciousness of anything but the object! And so, a
religion. And your God is your telescope! You
imagine that it is your instrument? Not a bit of
it! It is your God, and you worship it! You
are like Gubbio here, with his machine! The servant. . . . I don't wish to hurt your feelings, let
me say the priest, the supreme pontiff (does
that satisfy you?) of this God of yours, and you
swear by the dogma of its infallibility. Where
is Gubbio? Three cheers for Gubbio! Wait,
don't go away, Senator! I came here this morning, to comfort an unhappy man. I made an ap-
pointment with him here: he ought to be here
by now. An unhappy man, my fellow-lodger in
the Falcon Hostelry. . . . There is no better
way of comforting an unhappy man, than by
proving to him by actual contact that he is not
alone. So I have invited him here, among these
good artist friends. He is an artist too! Here
he comes!"

And the man with the violin, long and lanky,
bowed and sombre, whom I first saw more than
a year ago in the Casual Shelter, came forward,
apparently absorbed as before in gazing at the
hairs that drooped from his bushy, frowning
brows.

The crowd made way for him. In the silence

that had fallen, a titter of merriment sounded here and there. But stupefaction and a certain sense of revulsion held most of us spellbound as we watched this man come towards us with bent head, his eyes fastened like that on the hairs of his eyebrows, as though he refused to look at his red, fleshy nose, the enormous burden and punishment of his intemperance. More than ever, now, as he advanced, he seemed to be saying:

"Silence! Make way! You see what life can bring a man's nose to?"

Simone Pau introduced him to Senator Zeme, who made off, indignant; everyone laughed, but Simone Pau, quite serious, went on introducing him to the actresses, the actors, the producers, relating to one and another of them in snatches the story of his friend's life, and how and why, after that last famous rebuff, he had never played again. Finally, thoroughly aroused, he shouted:

"But he will play to-day, ladies and gentlemen! He will play! He will break the evil spell! He has promised me that he will play! But not to you, ladies and gentlemen! You will keep in the background. He has promised me that he will play to the tiger. Yes, yes, to the tiger! To the tiger! We must respect his wishes. He is certain to have excellent reasons for them! Come along, come along now all of

you. . . . We must keep in the background. . . .
He shall go in, by himself, in front of the cage,
and play!"

Amid shouts, laughter, applause, impelled, all
of us, by the keenest curiosity as to this strange
adventure, we followed Simone Pau, who had
taken his man by the arm and was urging him
on, following the instructions shouted at him
from behind, telling him the way to the menagerie. On coming in sight of the cages he stopped
us all, bidding us be silent, and sent on ahead,
by himself, the man with the violin.

At the sound of our coming, from shops and
stores, workmen, stage hands, scene painters
came running out in full force to watch the scene
over our shoulders: there was quite a crowd.

The animal had withdrawn with a bound to the
back of its cage; and crouched there with arched
back, lowered head, snarling teeth, bared claws,
ready to spring: terrible!

The man stood gazing at it, speechless; then
turned in bewilderment and let his eyes range
over us in search of Simone Pau.

"Play!" Simone shouted at him. "Don't be
afraid! Play! She will understand you!"

Whereupon the man, as though freeing himself
by a tremendous effort from an obsession, at
length raised his head, shook it, flung his shape-
less hat on the ground, passed a hand over his
long, unkempt locks, took the violin from its old

green baize cover, and threw the cover down also, on top of his hat.

A catcall or two came from the workmen who had crowded in behind us, followed by laughter and comments, while he tuned his violin; but a great silence fell as soon as he began to play, at first a little uncertainly, hesitating, as though he felt hurt by the sound of his instrument which he had not heard for so long; then, all of a sudden, overcoming his uncertainty, and perhaps his painful tremors with a few vigorous strokes. These strokes were followed by a sort of groan of anguish, that grew steadily louder, more insistent, strange notes, harsh and toneless, a tight coil, from which every now and then a single note emerged to prolong itself, like a person trying to breathe a sigh amid sobs. Finally this note spread, developed, let itself go, freed from its suffocation, in a phrase melodious, limpid, honey-sweet, intense, throbbing with infinite pain: and then a profound emotion swept over us all, which in Simone Pau took the form of tears. Raising his arms he signalled to us to keep quiet, not to betray our admiration in any way, so that in the silence this queer, marvellous wastrel might listen to the voice of his soul.

It did not last long. He let his hands fall, as though exhausted, with the violin and bow, and turned to us with a face transfigured, bathed in tears, saying:

"There . . ."

The applause was deafening. He was seized, carried off in triumph. Then, taken to the neighbouring tavern, notwithstanding the prayers and threats of Simone Pau, he drank and lost his senses.

Polacco was kicking himself with rage, at not having thought of sending me off at once to fetch my machine to place on record this scene of sere‧nading the tiger.

How perfectly he understands everything, always, Cocò Polacco! I was not able to answer him because I was thinking of the eyes of Signora Nestoroff, who had looked on at the scene, as though in an ecstasy instinct with terror.

Book IV

OF THE NOTES OF SERAFINO GUBBIO
CINEMATOGRAPH OPERATOR

BOOK IV

§ 1

I HAVE no longer the slightest doubt about it:
she is aware of my friendship with Giorgio
Mirelli, and knows that Aldo Nuti is coming here
shortly.

Both these pieces of information have come
to her, obviously, through Carlo Ferro.

But how is it that nobody here takes the
trouble to remember what has happened between
the two, and why have they not at once cancelled
their arrangement with Nuti? To help on this
arrangement a great deal of work has been done,
behind the scenes, by Cocò Polacco, a friend of
Nuti, on whom Nuti has been relying from the
first. It appears that Polacco has obtained from
one of the young men who parade here as
"amateurs," one Fleccia, the sale at a high
premium of the ten shares which this young man
held in the company. For some days, indeed,
Fleccia has gone about saying that he is bored
with life in Rome and is going to Paris.

We know that the majority of these young
men hang about here, more than for any other
reason, because of the friendly relations they

have formed, or hope to form, with some young
actress; and that many of them leave when they
have not succeeded in forming such relations, or
have grown tired of them. Friendly relations,
we say: fortunately, words cannot blush.

This is what happens: a young actress,
dressed as a *divette* or a *ballerina,* goes running
about stripped to the waist, on the stage or
lawn; she stops here and there to talk, with her
bosom offered to every eye; very well, the young
man who is her friend follows after her with a
powder-box and puff in his hand, and every now
and then powders her shoulders, her arms, her
neck, her throat, proud that such a duty should
fall to his lot. How many times, since I joined
the Kosmograph, have I seen Gigetto Fleccia run
like this after the little Sgrelli? But now he, for
about a month, has been out of favour with her.
He has served his apprenticeship: he is going
to Paris.

It cannot, therefore, come as a surprise to
anyone that Nuti, a rich gentleman also, and an
amateur actor, should be coming to take his
place. It is perhaps not sufficiently known, or
else people have already forgotten the drama of
his former adventure with the Nestoroff.

But I am often such an innocent creature!
Who remembers anything a year after it has
happened? Have we time now to consider, in a
town, among all the turmoil of life, that any-

thing—a man, a work, an event—deserves to be
remembered for a year? You, in the solitude of
the country, Duccella and Granny Rosa, you can
remember! Here, even if anyone does remember, well, was there a drama? There are ever so
many, and for none of them does this turmoil
of life pause for a moment. It does not appear
to be a matter in which other people, from outside, ought to interfere, to prevent the consequences of a renewal. What consequences? A
meeting with Carlo Ferro? But he is so hated
by everyone, that fellow, not only for his ill
manners, but precisely because he is the Nestoroff's lover! Should this meeting come about,
and give rise to any disturbance, it will be for the
outsiders one spectacle the more to enjoy: and as
for those whose duty it is to see that no disorder
does arise, they hope perhaps to find in it an excuse
for getting rid of both Carlo Ferro and the Nestoroff, who, if she is loyally protected by Commendator Burgalli, is a perfect nuisance to everyone else. Or, is it perhaps hoped that the Nestoroff herself, to escape from Nuti, will resign
of her own accord?

Certainly Polacco has toiled with such energy
to make Nuti come here for this reason alone;
and from the very first, secretly, has intended
that Nuti should be strengthened, against any influence that Commendator Borgalli might bring
to bear, by the acquisition, at a high price, of the

shares held by Gigetto Fleccia, with the right to take his place, as well, in the parts assigned to him.

What reason, then, have all these people to be so alarmed about the spirit in which Nuti will arrive? They anticipate, if anything, only the shock of meeting with Carlo Ferro, because Carlo Ferro is here, before their eyes; they see him, they can touch him; and they do not imagine that there can be any other connecting link between the Nestoroff and Nuti.

"You?" they would ask me, were I to begin to speak to them of such matters.

I, my friends? Ah, you will have your joke. One whom you do not see; one whom you cannot touch; a spectre, as in the story-books.

As soon as one of them tries to approach the other, this spectre is bound to rise up between them. Immediately after the suicide, it rose; and made them fly from one another with horror. A splendid cinematographic effect, to you! But not to Aldo Nuti. How in the world can he, now, propose and attempt to approach this woman again? It is not possible that he, of all people, can have forgotten the spectre. But he must have heard that the Nestoroff is here with another man. And this other man gives him of course, now, the courage to approach her again. Perhaps he hopes that this man, with the solidity of his body, will hide that spectre, will prevent

him from seeing it, engaging him in a *tangible*
struggle, in a struggle, that is, not with a spectre,
but of man with man. And perhaps also he will
pretend to think that he is coming to engage in
this struggle for *his* sake, to avenge *him*. For
obviously the Nestoroff, in calling this other man
to her side, has shewn that she has forgotten the
"poor victim."

It is not so. The Nestoroff has not forgotten
him. This I have seen clearly written in her
eyes, in the way in which she has looked at me
for the last two days, that is since Carlo Ferro,
acting upon information received, must have let
her know that I was a friend of Giorgio Mirelli.

Irritation, or rather contempt, an unmistakable
aversion: that is what I have observed for the
last two days in the eyes of the Nestoroff, whenever, for a moment or two, they have rested upon
myself. And I am glad of it. Because I am now
certain that everything that I have imagined and
assumed with regard to her, in studying her, is
correct, and corresponds to the reality, as though
she herself, in a sincere effusion of all her most
secret feelings, had opened to me her wounded
and tortured soul.

For the last two days she has displayed in my
presence a devoted and submissive affection for
Ferro; she clings to him, hangs on him, albeit she
lets it be seen by anyone who observes her closely
that she, like everyone else, more than anyone

else, knows and sees the mental limitations, the
coarse manners, in short the bestial nature of
the man. She knows and sees it. But do not the
rest of us—intelligent and well-mannered—despise and avoid him? Well, she values him and
attaches herself to him for that very reason;
precisely because he is neither intelligent nor
well-mannered.

A better proof of this I could not have. And
yet, apart from this arrogant disdain, something else must be stirring at this moment in her
heart! Certainly, she is planning something.
Certainly, Carlo Ferro is nothing more to her
than a strong, bitter medicine to which, setting
her teeth, making an enormous effort to control
herself, she has submitted in order to cure a desperate malady in herself. And now, more than
ever, she is holding fast to this medicine, seeing in a flash the peril, with Nuti's coming, of
a relapse into her malady. Not, I think, because
Aldo Nuti has any great power over her. Im-
pulsively, like a doll, that other time, she took
him up, broke him, flung him from her. But
his coming, now, has no other object, surely, than
to take her, to tear her from her medicine, setting before her once again the spectre of Giorgio
Mirelli, in which she perhaps sees her malady
embodied: the maddening torment of her strange
spirit, which none of the men to whom she has

attached herself has understood, or has cared to
take any interest in it.

She does not wish to suffer any more from her
malady; she wishes to be cured of it at all costs.
She knows that, if Carlo Ferro clasps her in his
arms, there is a risk of her being crushed. And
this fear pleases her.

"But what good will it do you"—I would like
to shout at her—"what good will it do you if
Aldo Nuti does not come to bring it back before
you, your malady, when you have it still inside
you, stifled by an effort but not conquered? You
do not wish to see your own soul? Is that possible? It follows you, it follows you always, it
pursues you like a mad thing! To escape from
it, you cling for refuge, take shelter in the arms
of a man whom you know to be without a soul
and capable of killing you, if your own soul, by
any chance, to-day or to-morrow, takes command
of you afresh, to renew the old torment within
you! Ah, is it better to be killed? Is it better
to be killed than to fall back into that torment,
to feel a soul within you, a soul that suffers and
does not know why?"

Well, this morning, as I turned the handle of
my machine, I suddenly conceived the terrible
suspicion that she—playing her part, as usual,
like a mad creature—wished to kill herself: yes,
really to kill herself, before my eyes. I do not

know how I managed to preserve my impassivity; to say to myself:

"You are a hand; go on turning! She is looking at you, looking at you fixedly, looking only at you, to make you understand something; but you know nothing, you are not to understand anything; keep on turning!"

They have begun to stage the film of the tiger, which is to be immensely long, and in which all four companies will take part. I shall not make the slightest effort to find the clue to that tangled skein of vulgar, idiotic scenes. I know that the Nestoroff will not be taking part in it, having failed to secure the principal part for herself. Only this morning, as a special concession to Bertini, she posed for a brief scene of local colour, in a subordinate but by no means easy part, as a young Indian woman, savage and fanatical, who kills herself in the course of the "dagger dance."

The ground having been marked out on the lawn, Bertini arranged a score of supers in a semicircle, disguised as Indian savages. The Nestoroff came forward almost completely naked, with nothing but a striped loincloth, yellow, green, red and blue. But the marvellous nudity of her firm, slender, shapely body was so to speak draped in the contemptuous indifference to its charms with which she presented herself in the midst of all those men, her head held high, her arms lowered with a pair of razor-keen daggers, one in each hand.

Bertini explained the action briefly:

"She dances. It is a sort of rite. All the rest stand round watching reverently. Suddenly, at a shout from me, in the middle of the dance, she plunges both daggers into her breast and falls to the ground. The crowd run up and stand over her, registering terror and dismay. Pay attention, there, all of you! You there, do you follow me? First of all you stand and look serious, watching her; as soon as the lady falls, you all run up. Pay attention now, keep in the picture!"

The Nestoroff, advancing to the chord of the semicircle brandishing the pair of daggers, began to gaze at me with so keen and hard a stare that I, behind my big black spider crouching on its tripod, felt my eyes waver and my sight grow dim. For a wonder I managed to obey Bertini's order:

"Shoot!"

And I set to work, like an automaton, to turn my handle.

Through the painful contortions of that strange, morbid dance, behind the sinister gleam of the daggers, she did not take her eyes for a minute from mine, which followed her movements, fascinated. I saw the sweat on her heaving bosom make furrows in the ochreous paint with which

she was daubed all over. Without giving a
thought to her nudity, she dashed about the
ground as in a frenzy, panted for breath, and
softly, in a gasping whisper, still with her eyes
fixed on mine, asked now and again:

"Bien comme ça? Bien comme ça?"

As though she wished to be told by me; and
her eyes were the eyes of a madwoman. Certainly, they could read in mine, apart from wonder, a dismay that hovered on the verge of
terror in the tension of waiting for Bertini to
shout. When the shout came, and she pointed
both daggers at her bosom and fell to the ground,
I really had for a moment the impression that
she had stabbed herself, and was for running to
the rescue myself, leaving my handle, when
Bertini in a fury called up the supers:

"You there, good God! Get round her! Take
your cue! Like that . . . that will do . . .
Stop!"

I was utterly exhausted; my hand had become
a lump of lead, which went on, of its own accord, mechanically, turning the handle.

I saw Carlo Ferro run forward scowling, full
of rage and tenderness, with a long purple cloak,
help the woman to rise, wrap her in the cloak
and lead her off, almost carrying her, to her
dressing-room.

I looked at the machine, and found in my

throat a curious somnolent voice in which to
announce to Bertini:

"Seventy-two feet."

§ 2

We were waiting to-day, beneath the pergola
of the tavern, for the arrival of a certain "young
lady of good family," recommended by Bertini,
who was to take a small part in a film which has
been left for some months unfinished and which
they now wish to complete.

More than an hour had passed since a boy
had been sent on a bicycle to this young lady's
house, and still there was no sign of anyone, not
even of the boy returning.

Polacco was sitting with me at one table, the
Nestoroff and Carlo Ferro were at another. All
four of us, with the young lady we were expecting, were to go in a motor-car for a "nature
scene" in the Bosco Flavio.

The sultry afternoon heat, the nuisance of the
myriad flies of the tavern, the enforced silence
among us four, obliged to remain together notwithstanding the openly declared and for that
matter obvious aversion felt by the other two for
Polacco and also for myself, increased the strain
of waiting until it became quite intolerable.

The Nestoroff was obstinately restraining herself from turning her eyes in our direction. But she was certainly aware that I was looking at her, covertly, while apparently paying her no attention; and more than once she had shewn signs of annoyance. Carlo Ferro had noticed this and had knitted his brows, keeping a close watch on her; and then she had pretended for his benefit to be annoyed, not indeed by myself who was looking at her, but by the sun which, through the vine leaves of the pergola, was beating upon her face. It was true; and a wonderful sight was the play, on that face, of the purple shadows, straying and shot with threads of golden sunlight, which lighted up now one of her nostrils, and part of her upper lip, now the lobe of her ear and a patch of her throat.

I find myself assailed, at times, with such violence by the external aspects of things that the clear, outstanding sharpness of my perceptions almost terrifies me. It becomes so much a part of myself, what I see with so sharp a perception, that I am powerless to conceive how in the world a given object—thing or person—can be other than what I would have it be. The Nestoroff's aversion, in that moment of such intensely lucid perception, was intolerable to me. How in the world did she not understand that I was not her enemy?

Suddenly, after peering out for a little through the trellis, she rose, and we saw her stroll out, towards a hired carriage, which also had been standing there for an hour outside the entrance to the Kosmograph, waiting under the blazing sun. I too had noticed the carriage; but the foliage of the vine prevented me from seeing who was waiting in it. It had been waiting there for so long that I could not believe that there was anybody in it. Polacco rose; I rose also, and we looked out.

A young girl, dressed in a sky-blue frock, of Swiss material, very light, with a straw hat, trimmed with black velvet ribbons, sat waiting in the carriage. Holding in her lap an aged dog with a shaggy coat, black and white, she was timidly and anxiously watching the taximeter of the carriage, which every now and then gave a click, and must already be indicating a considerable sum. The Nestoroff went up to her with great civility and invited her to come inside, to escape from the rays of the sun. Would it not be better to wait beneath the pergola of the tavern?

"Plenty of flies, of course. But at any rate one can sit in the shade."

The shaggy dog had begun to growl at the Nestoroff, baring its teeth in defence of its young mistress. She, turning suddenly crimson, perhaps at the unexpected pleasure of seeing this beautiful lady shew an interest in her with such courtesy; perhaps also from the annoyance that her stupid old pet was causing her, which received the other's cordial invitation in so unfriendly a spirit, thanked her, accepted the invitation with some confusion, and stepped down from the carriage with the dog under her arm. I had the impression that she left the carriage chiefly to make amends for the old dog's hostile reception of the lady. And indeed she slapped it hard on the muzzle with her hand, calling out:

"Be quiet, Piccinì!"

And then, turning to the Nestoroff:

"I apologise for her, she doesn't understand. . . ."

And they came in together beneath the pergola. I studied the old dog which was angrily looking its young mistress up and down, with the eyes of a human being. It seemed to be saying to her: "And what do *you* understand?"

Polacco, in the mean time, had advanced towards her and was asking politely:

"Signorina Luisetta?"

She turned a deep crimson, as though lost in a painful surprise, at being recognised by some one whom she did not know; smiled; nodded her head in the affirmative, and all the black ribbons on her straw hat nodded with her.

Polacco went on to ask her:

"Is Papa here?"

Yes, once more, with her head, as though amid her blushes and confusion she could not find

words with which to answer. At length, with an
effort, she found a timid utterance:

"He went inside some time ago: he said that
he would have finished his business at once, and
now . . ."

She raised her eyes to look at the Nestoroff
and smiled at her, as though she were sorry that
this gentleman with his questions had distracted
her attention from the lady, who had been so
kind to her without even knowing who she was.
Polacco thereupon introduced them:

"Signorina Luisetta Cavalena; Signora Nestoroff."

He then turned and beckoned to Carlo Ferro,
who at once sprang to his feet and bowed
awkwardly.

"Carlo Ferro, the actor."

Last of all, he introduced me:

"Gubbio."

It seemed to me that, among the lot of us, I
was the one who frightened her least.

I knew by repute Cavalena, her father, notori-
ous at the Kosmograph by the nickname of
Suicide. It seems that the poor man is terribly
oppressed by a jealous wife. Owing to his wife's
jealousy he has been obliged to renounce first of
all a commission in the Militia, as Surgeon
Lieutenant, and one good practice after another;
then, his independent work, as well, and journal-
ism, in which he had found an opening,

and finally teaching also, to which he had
turned in desperation, in the technical schools,
as a lecturer on physics and natural history.
Now, not being able (still on account of his wife)
to devote himself to the drama, for which he has
for some time past believed himself to have a
distinct talent, he has turned to the composition
of scenarios for the cinematograph, with great
loathing, *obtorto collo,* in order to supply the
wants of his family, since they are unable to live
exclusively upon his wife's fortune, and what
little they make by letting a pair of furnished
rooms.   Unfortunately, in the hell of his home
life, having now grown accustomed to viewing
the world as a prison, it seems that, however hard
he may try, he can never succeed in composing a
plot for a film without dragging in, somewhere
or other, a suicide.   Which accounts for Polacco's
having steadily, up to the present, rejected all
his scenarios, in view of the fact that the English
decline, absolutely, to hear of a suicide in their
films.

"Has he come to see me?" Polacco asked Signorina Luisetta.

Signorina Luisetta stammered in confusion:

"No," she said . . . "I don't think so; Bertini, I think it was."

"Ah, the rascal!   He has gone to Bertini, has
he?   But tell me, Signorina, did he go in
alone?"

Fresh, and still more vivid blushes on the part of Signorina Luisetta.

"With Mamma."

Polacco threw up his hands and waved them in the air, pulling a long face and winking.

"Let us hope that nothing dreadful is going to happen!"

Signorina Luisetta made an effort to smile; and echoed:

"Let us hope so . . . "

And it hurt me so to see her smile like that, with her little face aflame! I would have liked to shout at Polacco:

"Stop tormenting her with these questions! Can't you see that you are making her utterly miserable?"

But Polacco, all of a sudden, had an idea; he clapped his hands:

"Why shouldn't we take Signorina Luisetta? By Jove, yes; we have been waiting here for the last hour! Why yes, of course. My dear young lady, you will be helping us out of a difficulty, and you will see that we shall give you plenty of fun. It will all be over in half an hour. I shall tell the porter, as soon as your father and mother come out, to let them know that you have gone for half an hour with me and this lady and gentleman. I am such a friend of your father that I can venture to take the liberty. I shall give you a little part to play, you will like that?"

Signorina Luisetta had evidently a great fear
of appearing timid, embarrassed, foolish; and, as
for coming with us, said: "Why not?" But,
when it came to acting, she could not, she did
not know how . . . and in those clothes, too—
really? . . . she had never tried . . . she felt
ashamed . . . besides . . .

Polacco explained to her that nothing serious
was required: she would not have to open her
mouth, nor to mount a stage, nor to appear
before the public. Nothing at all. It would be
in the country. Among the trees. Without a
word spoken.

"You will be sitting on a bench, beside this
gentleman," he pointed to Ferro. "This gentleman will pretend to be making love to you. You,
naturally, do not believe him, and laugh at him.
. . . Like that. . . . Splendid! You laugh and
shake your head, plucking the petals off a flower.
All of a sudden, a motor-car dashes up. This
gentleman starts to his feet, frowns, looks round
him, scenting danger in the air. You stop plucking at the flower and adopt an attitude of doubt,
dismay. Suddenly this lady," here he pointed to
the Nestoroff, "jumps down from the car, takes
a revolver from her muff and fires at you . . ."

Signorina Luisetta opened her eyes wide and
stared at the Nestoroff, in terror.

"In make-believe! Don't be frightened!"
Polacco went on with a smile. "The gentleman

runs forward, disarms the lady; meanwhile you
have sunk down, first of all, on the bench, mortally wounded; from the bench you fall to the
ground—without hurting yourself, please! and
it is all over. . . . Come, come, don't let us waste
any more time! We can rehearse the scene on
the spot; you will see, it will go off splendidly
. . . and what a fine present you will get afterwards from the Kosmograph!''

"But if Papa . . . "

"We shall leave a message for him!"

"And Piccinì?"

"We can take her with us; I shall carry her
myself. . . . You will see, the Kosmograph will
give Piccinì a fine present too. . . . Come along,
let us be off!"

As we got into the motor-car (again, I am certain, so as not to appear timid and foolish), she,
who had not given me a second thought, looked
at me doubtfully.

Why was I coming too? What part was I to
play?

No one had uttered a word to me; I had been
barely introduced, named as a dog might be;
I had not opened my mouth; I remained
silent. . . .

I noticed that my silent presence, the necessity
for which she failed to see, but which impressed
her, nevertheless, as being mysteriously necessary, was beginning to disturb her. No one

thought of offering her any explanation; I could
not offer her one myself. I had seemed to her
a person like the rest; or rather, at first sight,
a person *more akin to herself* than the rest. Now
she was beginning to be aware that for these
other people and also for herself (in a vague
way) I was not, properly speaking, a person.
She began to feel that my person was not necessary; but that my presence there had the necessity of a *thing,* which she as yet did not understand; and that I remained silent for that reason.
They might speak, yes, they, all four of them—
because they were people, each of them represented a person, his or her own; but I, no: I was
a thing: why, perhaps the thing that was resting
on my knees, wrapped in a black cloth.

And yet I too had a mouth to speak with,
eyes to see with, and the said eyes, look, were
shining as they rested on her; and certainly
within myself I felt . . .

Oh, Signorina Luisetta, if you only knew the
joy that his own feelings were affording the person—*not necessary* as such, but as a thing—who
sat opposite to you! Did it occur to you that I
—albeit seated in front of you like that, like a
thing—was capable of feeling within myself?
Perhaps. But what I was feeling, behind my
mask of impassivity, that you certainly could not
imagine.

Feelings that were *not necessary,* Signorina

Luisetta! You do not know what they are, nor
do you know the intoxicating joy that they can
give! This machine here, for instance: does
it seem to you that there can be any necessity
for it to feel? There cannot be! If it could feel,
what feelings would it have? Not necessary
feelings, surely. Something that was a luxury
for it. Fantastic things. . . .

Well, among the four of you, to-day, I—a pair
of legs, a lap, and on it a machine—I felt *fan-
tastically.*

You, Signorina Luisetta, were, with everything
round about you, contained in my feelings, which
rejoiced in your innocence, in the pleasure that
you derived from the breeze in your face, the
view of the open country, the proximity of the
beautiful lady. Does it seem strange to you that
you entered like that, with everything round
about you, into my feelings? But may not a
beggar by the roadside perhaps see the road
and all the people who go past, comprised in
that feeling of pity which he seeks to arouse?
You, being more sensitive than the rest, as you
pass, notice that you enter into his feeling, and
stop and give him the charity of a copper. Many
others do not enter in, and it does not occur to
the beggar that they are outside his feeling, inside another of their own, in which he too is
included as a shadowy nuisance; the beggar
thinks that they are hard-hearted. What was I

to you in your feelings, Signorina Luisetta? A mysterious man? Yes, you are quite right. Mysterious. If you knew how I feel, at certain moments, my *inanimate silence!* And I revel in the mystery that is exhaled by this silence for such as are capable of remarking it. I should like never to speak at all; to receive everyone and everything in this silence of mine, every tear, every smile; not to provide, myself, an echo to the smile; I could not; not to wipe away, myself, the tear; I should not know how; but so that all might find in me, not only for their griefs, but also and even more for their joys, a tender pity that would make us brothers if only for a moment.

I am so grateful for the good that you have done with the freshness of your timid, smiling innocence, to the lady who was sitting by your side! So at times, when the rain does not come, parched plants find refreshment in a breath of air. And this breath of air you yourself were, for a moment, in the burning desert of the feelings of that woman who sat beside you; a burning desert that does not know the refreshing coolness of tears.

At one point she, looking at you almost with a frightened admiration, took your hand in her own and stroked it. Who knows what bitter envy of you was torturing her heart at that moment?

Did you see how, immediately afterwards, her face darkened?

A cloud had passed. . . . What cloud?

§ 3

A parenthesis. Yes, another. The things that I am obliged to do all day long, I do not speak of them; the beastlinesses that I have to serve up all day long as food for this black spider on its tripod, which eats and is never filled, I do not speak of them; beastlinesses incarnate in these actors and actresses, in all the people who are driven by necessity to feed this machine upon their own modesty, their own dignity, I do not speak of them; I must, all the same, have a little breathing-space, now and again, absolutely, draw a mouthful of air for my *superfluity;* or die. I am interested in the history of this woman, the Nestoroff I mean; I have filled with it many pages of these notes; but I do not, for all that, intend to be carried away by her history; I intend her, the lady, to remain in front of my machine, or rather I intend myself to remain in front of her what I am to her, an operator, and nothing more.

When my friend Simone Pau has failed for some days in succession to pay me a visit at the Kosmograph, I go myself in the evening to visit him in Borgo Pio, at his Falcon Hostelry.

The reason why, for some days, he has not

come to see me, is the saddest imaginable. The man with the violin is dying.

I found keeping watch in the room set apart for Pau in the Shelter, Paù himself, his aged colleague, the pensioner of the Papal Government, and the three old spinster schoolmistresses, friends of the Sisters of Charity. On Simone Pau's bed, with an ice-pack on his head, lay the man with the violin, struck down three evenings ago by an apoplectic stroke.

"He is freeing himself," Simone Pau said to me, with a wave of his hand, by way of comfort. "Sit down here, Serafino. Science has placed on his head that cap of ice, which is completely useless. We are helping him to pass away amid serene philosophic discussions, in return for the precious gift which he leaves as an heirloom to us: his violin. Sit down, man, sit here. They have washed him thoroughly, all over; they have put him in order with the sacraments; they have anointed him. Now we are waiting for the end, which cannot be far distant. You remember when he played before the tiger? It made him ill. But perhaps it is better so: he is gaining his freedom!"

How genially the old man smiled at these words, sitting there so clean and neat, with his cap on his head and the bone snuff-box in his hand with the portrait of the Holy Father on the lid!

"Continue," Simone Pau went on, turning to the old man, "continue, Signor Cesarino, your panegyric of the three-wicked oil-lamps, please."

"Panegyric indeed!" exclaimed Signor Cesarino. "You insist that I am making a panegyric of them! I tell you that they belong to that generation, that is all."

"And is not that a panegyric?"

"Why, no; I say that it all comes to the same thing in the end: it is an idea of mine: so many things I used to see in the dark with those lamps, which you are perhaps unable to see by electric light; but then, on the other hand, you see other things with these lights here which I fail to see; because four generations of lights, four, my dear Professor, oil, paraffin, gas and electricity, in the course of sixty years, eh . . . eh . . . eh . . . it's too much, you know? and it's bad for our eyesight, and for our heads too; yes, it's bad for the head too, it is."

The three old maids, who were sitting, all three of them, with their hands, in thread mittens, quietly folded in their laps, shewed their approval by nodding silently with their heads: yes, yes, yes.

"Light, a fine light, I don't say it isn't! Eh, but I know it is," sighed the old man, "I can remember when you went about with a lantern in your hand, so as not to break your neck. But light for outside, that's what it is. . . . Does it help us to see better indoors? No."

The three quiet old maids, still keeping their hands, in their thread mittens, folded in their laps, agreed in silence, with their heads: no, no, no.

The old man rose and offered those pure and peaceful hands the reward of a pinch of snuff. Simone Pau held out two fingers.

"You too?" the old man asked him.

"I too, I too," answered Simone Pau, slightly irritated by the question. "And you too, Serafino. Take it, I tell you! Don't you see that it is a rite?"

The little old man, with the pinch between his fingers, shut one eye wickedly:

"Contraband tobacco," he said softly. "It comes from over there. . . . "

And with the thumb of his other hand he made a furtive sign, as though to say: "Saint Peter's, Vatican."

"You understand?" Simone Pau turned to me, thrusting his pinch out before my eyes. "It sets you free from Italy! Does that seem to you nothing? You snuff it, and you no longer smell the stench of the Kingdom!"

"Come, come, do not say that . . ." the little old man pleaded in distress, for he wished to enjoy in peace the benefits of toleration, by tolerating others.

"It is I who say it, not you," replied Simone Pau. "I say it, who have a right to say it. If you said it, I should ask you not to say it in my presence, is that all right? But you are a wise man, Signor Cesarino! Go on, go on, please, describing to us, with your courtly, old-fashioned grace, the good old oil-lamps, with three wicks, of days gone by . . . I saw one, do you know, in Beethoven's house, at Bonn on the Rhine, when I was travelling in Germany. There, this evening we must recall the memory of all the good old things, round this poor violin, shattered by an automatic piano. I confess that I am not over pleased to see my friend in the room here, at such a moment. Yes, you, Serafino. My friend, ladies and gentlemen—let me introduce him to you: Serafino Gubbio—is an operator: poor fellow, he turns the handle of a cinematograph machine."

"Ah," said the little old man, with a note of pleasure.

And the three old maids gazed at me in admiration.

"You see?" Simone Pau said to me. "You spoil everything with your presence here. I wager that you now, Signor Cesarino, and you too, ladies, have a burning desire to learn from my friend how the machine works, and how a film is made. But for pity's sake!"

And he pointed to the dying man, who was

breathing heavily in a profound coma under the ice-pack.

"You know that I . . ." I attempted to put in, quietly.

"I know!" he interrupted me. "You do not enter into your profession, but that does not mean, my dear fellow, that your profession does not enter into you! Try to disabuse these colleagues of mine of the idea that I am a professor. I am the Professor, for them: a trifle eccentric, but still a professor! We may easily fail to recognise ourselves in what we do, but what we do, my dear fellow, remains done: an action which circumscribes you, my dear fellow, gives you a form of sorts, and imprisons you in it. Do you seek to rebel? You cannot. In the first place, we are not free to do as we wish: the age we live in, the habits of other people, our means, the conditions of our existence, ever so many other reasons, outside and inside us, compel us often to do what we do not wish; and then, the spirit is not detached from the flesh; and the flesh, however closely you guard it, has a will of its own. And what is our intelligence worth, if it does not feel compassion for the beast that is within us? I do not say excuse it. The intelligence that excuses the beast, bestialises itself as well. But to feel pity for it is another matter! Christ preached it; am I not right, Signor Cesarino? So you are the prisoner of what

you have done, of the form that your actions
have given you. Duties, responsibilities, a chain
of consequences, coils, tentacles which are wound
about you, and do not leave you room to breathe.
You must do nothing more, or as little as possible, like me, so as to remain as free as possible?
Ah, yes! Life itself is an action! When your
father brought you into the world, my dear fellow, the deed was done. You can never free yourself again until you end by dying. And not even
after your death, Signor Cesarino here will tell
you, eh? He never frees himself again, eh?
Not even after death. Keep calm, my dear fellow. You will go on turning the handle of your
machine even beyond the grave! But yes, yes,
because it is not for your being, for which you are
not to blame, but for your actions and the consequences of your actions that you have to answer,
am I not right, Signor Cesarino?"

"Quite right, yes; but it is not a sin, Professor, to turn the handle of a cinematograph
machine," Signor Cesarino observed.

"Not a sin? You ask him!" said Pau.

The little old man and the three old maids
gazed at me stupefied and dismayed to see me
assent with a nod of my head, smiling, to Simone
Pau's verdict.

I smiled because I was picturing myself in the
presence of the Creator, in the presence of the
Angels and of the blessed souls in Paradise

standing behind my great black spider on its
knock-kneed tripod, condemned to turn the handle, in the next world also, after my death.

"Why, of course," sighed the little old man,
"when the cinematograph represents certain in-
decencies, certain stupid scenes. . . ."

The three old maids, with lowered eyes, made
a sign of outraged modesty with their hands.

"But this gentleman would not be responsible
for it," Signor Cesarino hastened to add, courteous and still friendly.

There came from the staircase a sound of
sweeping garments and of the heavy beads of
a rosary with a dangling crucifix. There appeared, under the broad white wings of her coif,
a Sister of Charity. Who had sent for her?
The fact remains that, as soon as she appeared
on the threshold, the dying man ceased to
breathe. And she was quite ready to perform
the last duties. She lifted the ice-pack from his
head; turned to look at us, in silence, with a
simple, rapid movement of her eyes towards the
ceiling; then stooped to arrange the deathbed and
fell on her knees. The three old maids and Signor Cesarino followed her example. Simone Pau
summoned me from the room.

"Count," he bade me, as we began to go downstairs, pointing to the steps. "One, two, three,
four, five, six, seven, eight, nine. The steps of a
stair; of this stair, which ends in this dark pas-

sage. . . . The hands that hewed them, and placed them here, one upon another. . . . Dead. The hands that erected this building. . . . Dead. Like other hands, which erected all the other houses in this quarter. . . . Rome; what do you think of it? A great city. . . . Think of this little earth in the firmament. . . . Do you see? What is it? . . . A man has died. . . . Myself, yourself . . . no matter: a man. . . . And five people, in there, have gone on their knees round him to pray to some one, to something, which they believe to be outside and over everything and everyone, and not in themselves, a sentiment of theirs which rises independent of their judgment and invokes that same pity which they hope to receive themselves, and it brings them comfort and peace. Well, people must act like that. You and I, who cannot act thus, are a pair of fools. Because, in saying these stupid things that I am now saying, we are doing the same thing, on our feet, uncomfortably, with only this result for our trouble, that we derive from it neither comfort nor peace. And fools like us are all those who seek God within themselves and despise Him without, who fail, that is to say, to see the value of the actions, of all the actions, even the most worthless, which man has performed since the world began, always the same, however different they may appear. Different, forsooth? Different because we credit them with another value, which, in any event, is arbitrary. We know nothing for certain. And there is nothing to be known beyond that which, in one way or another, is represented outwardly, in actions. Within is torment and weariness. Go, go and turn your handle, Serafino! Be assured that yours is a profession to be envied! And do not regard as more stupid than any others the actions that are arranged before your eyes, to be taken by your machine. They are all stupid in the same way, always: life is all a mass of stupidity, always, because it never comes to an end and can never come to an end. Go, my dear fellow, go and turn your handle, and leave me to go and sleep with the wisdom which, by always sleeping, dogs shew us. Good night."

I came away from the Shelter, comforted. Philosophy is like religion: it is always comforting, even when it is a philosophy of despair, because it is born of the need to overcome a torment, and even when it does not overcome it, the action of setting that torment before our eyes is already a relief, inasmuch as, for a while at least, we no longer feel it within us. The comfort I derived from Simone Pau's words had come to me, however, principally from what he had said with regard to my profession.

Enviable, yes, perhaps; but if it were applied to the recording, without any stupid invention or imaginary construction of scenes and actions, of life, life as it comes, without selection and without any plan; the actions of life as they are performed without a thought, when people are alive and do not know that a machine is lurking in concealment to surprise them. Who knows how ridiculous they would appear to us! Most of all, ourselves. We should not recognise ourselves, at first; we should exclaim, shocked, mortified, indignant: "What? I, like that? I, that person? Do I walk like that? Do I laugh like that? Is that my action? My face?" Ah, no, my friend, not you: your haste, your wish to do this or that, your impatience, your frenzy, your anger, your joy, your grief. . . . How can you know, you who have them within you, in what manner all these things are represented outwardly? A man who is alive, when he is alive, does not see himself: he lives. . . . To see how one lived would indeed be a ridiculous spectacle!

Ah, if my profession were destined to this end only! If it had the sole object of presenting to men the ridiculous spectacle of their heedless actions, an immediate view of their passions, of their life as it is. Of this life without rest, which never comes to an end.

"Signor Gubbio, please: I have something to say to you."

Night had fallen: I was hurrying along beneath the big planes of the avenue. I knew that he—Carlo Ferro—was following me, in breathless haste, so as to pass me and then perhaps to turn round, pretending to have remembered all of a sudden that he had something to say to me. I wished to deprive him of this pleasure, and kept increasing my pace, expecting at every moment that he—growing tired at length—would admit himself beaten and call out to me. As indeed he did. . . . I turned, as though in surprise. He overtook me and with ill-concealed annoyance asked:

"Do you mind?"

"Go on."

"Are you going home?"

"Yes."

"Do you live far off?"

"Some way."

"I have something to say to you," he repeated, and stood still, looking at me with an evil glint in his eye. "You probably know that, thank God, I can spit on the contract I have with the Kosmograph. I can secure another, just as good and better, at any moment, whenever I

choose, anywhere, for myself and my lady friend.
Do you know that or don't you?"

I smiled, shrugging my shoulders:

"I can believe it, if it gives you any pleasure."

"You can believe it, because it is the truth!"
he shouted back at me, in a provocative, chal-
lenging tone.

I continued to smile; and said:

"It may be; but I do not see why you come
and tell me about it, and in that tone."

"This is why," he went on. "I intend to
remain, my dear Sir, with the Kosmograph."

"Remain? Why; I never even knew that you
had any idea of leaving."

"Some one else had the idea," Carlo Ferro
retorted, laying stress on the words *some one
else*. "But I tell you that I intend to remain:
do you understand?"

"I understand."

"And I remain, not because I care about the
contract, which doesn't matter a damn to me;
but because I have never yet run away from
anyone!"

So saying, he took the lapel of my coat between his fingers, and gave it a tug.

"Do you mind?" it was now my turn to ask,
calmly, as I removed his hand; and I felt in
my pocket for a box of matches; I struck one of
them to light the cigarette which I had already

taken from my case and held between my lips;
I drew in a mouthful or two of smoke; stood
for a while with the burning match in my fingers
to let him see that his words, his threatening
tone, his aggressive manner, were not causing
me the slightest uneasiness; then I went on,
quietly: "I may possibly understand to what
you wish to allude; but, I repeat, I do not understand why you come and say these things to
me."

"It is not true," Carlo Ferro shouted. "You
are pretending not to understand."

Placidly, but in a firm voice, I replied:

"I do not see why. If you, my dear Sir, wish
to provoke me, you are making a mistake; not
only because you have no reason, but also because, precisely like yourself, I am not in the
habit of running away from anyone."

Whereupon, "What do you mean?" he sneered.
"I have had to run pretty fast to catch you!"

I gave a hearty laugh:

"Oh, so that's it! You really thought that I
was running away from you? You are mistaken,
my dear Sir, and I can prove it to you straight
away. You suspect, perhaps, that I have something to do with the arrival here, shortly, of a
certain person who annoys you?"

"He doesn't annoy me in the least!"

"All the better. On the strength of this sus-

picion, you were capable of believing that I was
running away from you?"

"I know that you were a friend of a certain
painter, who committed suicide at Naples."

"Yes. Well?"

"Well, you who have mixed yourself up in this
business. . . . "

"I? Nothing of the sort! Who told you so?
I know as much about it as you; perhaps not so
much as you."

"But you must know this Signor Nuti!"

"Nothing of the sort! I saw him, some years
ago, as a young man on one or two occasions,
not more. I have never spoken to him."

"Which means . . . "

"Which means, my dear Sir, that not knowing
this Signor Nuti, and feeling annoyed at seeing
myself looked at askance for the last few days
by you, from the suspicion that I had mixed
myself up, or wished to mix myself up in this
business, I did not wish you, just now, to over-
take me, and so increased my pace. That is the
explanation of my *running away*. Are you
satisfied?"

With a sudden change of expression Carlo
Ferro held out his hand, saying with emotion:

"May I have the honour and pleasure of becoming your friend?"

I took his hand and answered:

"You know very well that I am so unimportant a person compared with yourself, that the honour will be mine."

Carlo Ferro shook himself like a bear.

"Don't say that! You are a man who knows his own business, more than any of the others; you know, you see, and you don't speak. . . . What a world, Signor Gubbio, what a wicked world we live in! How revolting! Everyone seems . . . what shall I say? But why must it be like this? Disguised, disguised, always disguised! Can you tell me? Why, as soon as we come together, face to face, do we become like a lot of puppets? Yes, I too; I include myself; all of us! Disguised! One putting on this air, another that. . . . And inside we are different! We have a heart, inside us, like . . . like a child hiding in a corner, whose feelings are hurt, crying and ashamed! Yes, I assure you: the heart is ashamed! I am longing, Signor Gubbio, I am longing for a little sincerity . . . to be with other people as I so often am with myself, inside myself; a child, I swear to you, a new-born infant that whimpers because its precious mother, scolding it, has told it that she does not love it any more! I myself, always, when I feel the blood rush to my eyes, think of that old mother of mine, away in Sicily, don't you know? But look out for trouble if I begin to cry! The tears in my eyes, if anyone doesn't understand me and thinks that I am crying from fear, may at any moment turn to blood on my hands; I know it, and that is why I am always afraid when I feel the tears start to my eyes! My fingers, look, become like this!"

In the darkness of the wide, empty avenue, I saw him thrust out beneath my eyes a pair of muscular fists, savagely clenched and clawed.

Concealing with a great effort the disturbance which this unexpected outburst of sincerity aroused in me, so as not to exacerbate the secret grief that was doubtless preying upon him and had found in this outburst, unintentionally I was certain on his part, a relief which he already regretted; I modulated my voice until I felt that I could speak in such a way that he, while appreciating my sympathy for his sincerity, might be led to think rather than to feel; and said:

"You are right; that is just how it is, Signor Ferro! But inevitably, don't you see, we put constructions upon ourselves, living as we do in a social environment. . . . Why, society by its very nature is no longer the natural world. It is a constructed world, even in the material sense! Nature knows no home but the den or the cave."

"Are you alluding to me?"

"To you? No."

"Am I of the den or of the cave?"

"Why, of course not! I was trying to explain to you why, as I look at it, people invariably lie. And I say that while nature knows no other house than the den or cave, society *constructs* houses; and man, when he comes from a *constructed* house, where as it is he no longer leads a natural life, entering into relations with his fellows, *constructs* himself also, that is all; presents himself, not as he is, but as he thinks he ought to be or is capable of being, that is to say in a construction adapted to the relations which each of us thinks that he can form with his neighbour. And so in the heart of things, that is to say inside these constructions of ours set face to face in this way, there remain carefully hidden, behind the blinds and shutters, our most intimate thoughts, our most secret feelings. But every now and then we feel that we are stifling; we are overcome by an irresistible need to tear down blinds and shutters, and shout out into the street, in everyone's face, our thoughts, our feelings that we have so long kept hidden and secret.''

''Quite so . . . quite so . . . '' Carlo Ferro repeated his endorsement several times, his face again darkening. ''But there is a person who takes up his post behind those constructions of which you speak, like a dirty cutthroat at a street corner, to spring on you behind your back, in a treacherous assault! I know such a man, here with the Kosmograph, and you know him too.''

He was alluding of course to Polacco. I at once realised that he at that moment could not be made to think. He was feeling too keenly.

"Signor Gubbio," he went on resolutely, "I see that you are a man, and I feel that to you I can speak openly. You might give this *constructed* gentleman, whom we both know, a hint of what we have been saying. I cannot talk to him; I know my own violent nature; if I once start talking to him, I may know how I shall begin, I cannot tell where I may end. Because covert thoughts, and people who act covertly, who *construct* themselves, to use your expression, I simply cannot stand. To me they are like serpents, and I want to crush their heads, like that . . . look, like that. . . . "

He stamped twice on the ground with his heel, furiously. Then he went on:

"What harm have I done him? What harm has my lady friend done him, that he should plot against us so desperately in secret? Don't refuse, please . . . please don't . . . you must be straight with me, for God's sake! You won't do it?"

"Why, yes . . . "

"You can see that I am speaking to you frankly? So please! Listen; it was he, knowing that I as a matter of honour would never try to back out, it was he that suggested my name to Commendator Borgalli for killing the tiger. . . .

He went as far as that, do you understand? To
the length of catching me on a point of honour
and getting rid of me! You don't agree? But
that is the idea; the intention is that and nothing else: I tell you it is, and you've got to believe
me! Because it doesn't require any courage, as
you know, to shoot a tiger in a cage: it requires
calm, coolness is what it requires, a firm hand,
a keen eye. Very well, he nominates me! He
puts me down for the part, because he knows
that I can, at a pinch, be a wild beast when I'm
face to face with a man, but that as a man face
to face with a wild beast I am worth nothing! I
have dash, calm is just what I lack! When I see
a wild beast in front of me, my instinct tells me
to rush at it; I have not the coolness to stand
still where I am and take aim at it carefully so
as to hit it in the right place. I have never shot;
I don't know how to hold a gun; I am capable of
flinging it away, of feeling it a burden on my
hands, do you understand? And he knows this!
He knows it perfectly! And so he has deliberately wished to expose me to the risk of being
torn in pieces by that animal. And with what
object? But just look, just look to what a pitch
that man's perfidy has reached! He makes Nuti
come here; he acts as his agent; he clears the
way for him, by getting rid of me! 'Yes, my dear
fellow, come,' will be what he has written to him,
'I shall look after you, I shall get him out of

your way! Don't worry, but come!' You don't agree?"

So aggressive and peremptory was this question, that to have met it with a blunt plain-spoken dissent would have been to inflame his anger even farther. I merely shrugged my shoulders; and answered:

"What would you have me say? You yourself must admit that at this moment you are extremely excited."

"But how can I be calm?"

"No, there is that . . . "

"I am quite right, it seems to me!"

"Yes, yes, of course! But when one is in that state, my dear Ferro, it is also very easy to exaggerate things."

"Oh, so I am exaggerating, am I? Why, yes, . . . because people who are cool, people who reason, when they set to work quietly to commit a crime, *construct* it in such a way that inevitably, if discovered, it must appear exaggerated. Of course they do! They have constructed it in silence with such cunning, ever so quietly, with gloves on, oh yes, so as not to dirty their hands! In secret, yes, keeping it secret from themselves even! Oh, he has not the slightest idea that he is committing a crime! What! He would be horrified, if anyone were to call his attention to it. 'I, a crime? Go on! How you exaggerate!' But where is the exaggeration, by God? Reason

it out for yourself as I do! You take a man and
make him enter a cage, into which a tiger is to
be driven, and you say to him: 'Keep calm, now.
Take a careful aim, and fire. Oh, and remember
to bring it down with your first shot, see that
you hit it in the right spot; otherwise, even if you
wound it, it will spring upon you and tear you
in pieces!' All this, I know, if they choose a
calm, cool man, a skilled marksman, is nothing,
it is not a crime. But if they deliberately choose
a man like myself? Think of it, a man like myself! Go and tell him: he will be amazed:
'What? Ferro? Why, I chose him on purpose
because I know how brave he is!' There is the
treachery! There is where the crime lurks: in
that *knowing how brave I am!* In taking advantage of my courage, of my sense of honour,
you follow me? He knows quite well that courage is not what is required! He pretends to
think that it is! There is the crime! And go
and ask him why, at the same time, he is secretly
at work trying to pave the way for a friend of
his who would like to get back the woman, the
woman who is at present living with the very man
nominated by him to enter the cage. He will be
even more amazed! 'Why, what connexion is
there between the two things? Oh, but really,
he suspects this as well, does he? What an ex-
ag-ge-ra-tion!' Why, you yourself said that I
exaggerated. . . . But think it over carefully;

penetrate to the root of the matter; you will
discover what he himself refuses to see, hiding
beneath that artificial show of reason; tear off
his gloves, and you will find that the gentleman's
hands are red with blood!''

I myself too had often thought, that each of
us—however honest and upright he may esteem
himself, considering his own actions in the abstract, that is to say apart from the incidents
and coincidences that give them their weight and
value—may commit a crime *in secret even from
himself,* that I was stupefied to hear my own
thought expressed to me with such clearness,
such debating force, and, moreover, by a man
whom until then I had regarded as narrow-
minded and of a vulgar spirit.

I was, nevertheless, perfectly convinced that
Polacco was not acting *really* with any consciousness of committing a crime, nor was he favour-
ing Nuti for the purpose that Carlo Ferro suspected. But it might also, this purpose, be included *without his knowledge,* as well in the
selection of Ferro to kill the tiger as in the facilita-
tion of Nuti's coming: actions that only in appearance and in his eyes were unconnected. Certainly, since he could not *in any other way* rid
himself of the Nestoroff, the idea that she might
once more become the mistress of Nuti, his
friend, might be one of his secret aspirations, a
desire that was not however apparent. As the

mistress of one of his friends, the Nestoroff
would no longer be such an enemy; not only that,
but perhaps also Nuti, having secured what he
wanted, and being as rich as he was, would refuse to allow the Nestoroff to remain an actress,
and would take her away with him.

"But you," I said, "have still time, my dear
Ferro, if you think . . . "

"No, Sir!" he interrupted me sharply. "This
Signor Nuti, by Polacco's handiwork, has already bought the right to join the Kosmograph."

"No, excuse me; what I mean is, you have
still time to refuse the part that has been given
you. No one who knows you can think that you
are doing so from fear."

"They would all think it!" cried Carlo Ferro.
"And I should be the first! Yes, Sir . . . because
courage I can and do have, in front of a man,
but in front of a wild beast, if I have not calm
I cannot have courage; the man who does not
feel calm must feel afraid. And I should feel
afraid, yes Sir! Afraid not for myself, you
understand! Afraid for the people who care for
me. I have insisted that my mother should receive an insurance policy; but if to-morrow they
give her a wad of paper money stained with
blood, my mother will die! What do you expect
her to do with the money? You see the shame
that conjurer has brought on me! The shame
of saying these things, which appear to be dic-

tated by a tremendous, preposterously exaggerated fear! Yes, because everything that I do, and feel, and say is bound to strike everyone as exaggerated. Good God, they have shot ever so many wild beasts in every cinematograph company, and no actor has ever been killed, no actor has ever taken the thing so seriously. But I take it seriously, because here, at this moment, I see myself played with, I see myself trapped, deliberately selected with the sole object of making me lose my calm! I am certain that nothing is going to happen; that it will all be over in a moment and that I shall kill the tiger without the slightest danger to myself. But I am furious at the trap that has been set for me, in the hope that some accident will happen to me, for which Signor Nuti, there you have it, will be waiting ready to step in, with the way clear before him. That . . . that . . . is what I . . . I . . . "

He broke off abruptly; clenched his fists together and wrung his hands, grinding his teeth. In a flash of inspiration, I realised that the man was torn by all the furies of jealousy. So that was why he had shouted after me! That was why he had spoken at such length! That was why he was in such a state!

And so Carlo Ferro is not sure of the Nestoroff. I scanned him by the light of one of the infrequent street-lamps: his face was distorted, his eyes glared savagely.

"My dear Ferro," I assured him cordially, "if you think that I can be of use to you in any way, to the best of my ability . . . "

"Thanks!" he replied coldly. "No . . . it's not possible . . . *you* can't . . . "

Perhaps he meant to say at first: "You are of no use to me!" He managed to restrain himself, and went on:

"You can help me only in one way: by telling this Signor Polacco that I am not a man to be played with, because whether it is my life or the lady, I am not the sort of man to let myself be robbed of either of them as easily as he seems to think! That you can tell him! And that if anything should happen here—as it certainly will—it will be the worse for him: take the word of Carlo Ferro! Tell him this, and I am your grateful servant."

Barely indicating a contemptuous farewell with a wave of his hand, he lengthened his pace and left me.

And his offer of friendship?

How glad I was of this unexpected relapse into contempt! Carlo Ferro may think for a moment that he is my friend; he cannot feel any friendship for me. And certainly, to-morrow, he will hate me all the more, for having treated me this evening as a friend.

§ 5

I think that it would be a good thing for me if I had a different mind and a different heart.

Who will exchange with me?

Given my intention, which grows steadily more determined, to remain an impassive spectator, this mind, this heart are of little use to me. I have reason to believe (and more than once, before now, I have been glad of it) that the reality in which I invest other people corresponds exactly to the reality in which those people invest themselves, because I endeavour to feel them in myself as they feel themselves, to wish for them as they wish for themselves: a reality, therefore, that is entirely disinterested. But I see at the same time that, without meaning it, I am letting myself be caught by that reality which, being what it is, ought to remain outside me: matter, to which I give a form, not for my sake, but for its own; something to contemplate.

No doubt, there is an underlying deception, a mocking deception in all this. I see myself caught. So much so, that I am no longer able even to smile, if, beside or beneath a complication of circumstances or passions which grows steadily stronger and more unpleasant, I see escape some other circumstance or some other passion that might be expected to raise my

spirits. The case of Signorina Luisetta Cavalena, for instance.

The other day Polacco had the inspiration to
make that young lady come to the Bosco Sacro
and there take a small part in a film. I know
that, to engage her to take part in the remaining
scenes of the film, he has sent her father a five
hundred lire note and, as he promised, a
pretty sunshade for herself and a collar with
lots of little silver bells for the old dog, Piccinì.

He ought never to have done such a thing!

It appears that Cavalena had given his wife
to understand that, when he went with his
scenarios to the Kosmograph, each with its inevitable gallant suicide, and all of them, therefore, invariably rejected, he never saw anyone
there, except Cocò Polacco: Cocò Polacco and
then home again. And who knows how he had
described to her the interior of the Kosmograph:
perhaps as an austere hermitage, from which all
women were resolutely banished, like demons.
Only, alas, the other day, the fierce wife, becoming suspicious, decided to accompany her husband. I do not know what she saw, but I can
easily imagine it. The fact remains that this
morning, just as I was going into the Kosmograph, I saw all four Cavalena arrive in a carriage: husband, wife, daughter and little dog:
Signorina Luisetta, pale and trembling; Piccinì,
more surly than ever; Cavalena, looking as usual

like a mouldy lemon, among the curls of his wig
that protruded from under his broad-brimmed
hat; his wife, like a cyclone barely held in
check, her hat knocked askew as she dismounted
from the carriage.

Under his arm Cavalena had the long parcel
containing the sunshade presented by Polacco to
his daughter and in his hand the box containing
Piccinì's collar. He had come to return them.

Signorina Luisetta recognised me at once. I
hastened up to her to greet her; she wished to
introduce me to her mother and father, but could
not remember my name. I helped her out of her
difficulty, by introducing myself.

"The operator, the man who turns the handle,
you understand, Nene?" Cavalena at once explained, with timid haste, to his wife, smiling,
as though to implore a little condescension.

Heavens, what a face Signora Nene has! The
face of an old, colourless doll. A compact helmet of almost quite grey hair presses upon her
low, hard forehead, on which her eyebrows,
joined together, short, bushy, and straight, are
like a line boldly ruled to give a character of
stupid tenacity to the pale eyes that gleam with
a glassy stiffness. She seems apathetic; but, if
you study her closely, you observe on the surface of her skin certain strange nervous prick-
ings, certain sudden changes of colour, in
patches, which at once disappear. She also,

every now and then, makes rapid unexpected gestures, of the most curious nature. I caught her,
for instance, at one moment, in reply to a be-
seeching glance from her daughter, shaping her
mouth in a round O across which she laid her
finger. Evidently, this gesture was intended to
mean:

"Silly girl! Why do you look at me like
that?"

But they are always looking at her, surrepti-
tiously at least, her husband and daughter, perplexed and anxious in their fear lest at any
moment she may indulge in some flaming outburst of rage. And certainly, by looking at her
like that, they irritate her all the more. But
imagine the life they lead, poor creatures!

Polacco has already given me some account
of it. Perhaps she never thought of becoming
a mother, this woman! She found this poor man,
who, in her clutches, after all these years, has
been reduced to the most pitiable condition imaginable; no matter: she will fight for him; she
continues to fight for him savagely. Polacco tells
me that, when assailed by the furies of jealousy,
she loses all self-restraint; and in front of everyone, without a thought even of her daughter who
stands listening, looking on, she strips bare
(bare, as they flash before her eyes in those moments of fury) and lashes her husband's alleged
misdeeds: misdeeds that are highly improbable.

Certainly, in that hideous humiliation, Signorina
Luisetta cannot fail to see her father in a ridiculous light, albeit, as can be seen from the way
in which she looks at him, he must arouse so
much pity in her! Ridiculous, from the way
in which, stripped bare, lashed, the poor man
still seeks to gather up from all sides, to cover
himself in them hastily and as best he may, the
shreds and tatters of his dignity. Cocò Polacco
has repeated to me some of the phrases in which,
stunned by her savage, unexpected onslaughts,
he replies to his wife at such moments: sillier,
more ingenuous, more puerile things one could
not imagine! And for that reason alone I am
convinced that Cocò Polacco did not invent them
himself.

"Nene, for pity's sake, I am a man of five and
forty . . .

"Nene, I have held His Majesty's commission . . .

"Nene, good God, when a man has held a commission and gives you his word of honour . . . "

And yet, every now and then—oh, in the long
run even a worm will turn—wounded with a re-
finement of cruelty in his most sacred feelings,
barbarously chastised where the lash hurts most
—every now and then, he says, it appears that
Cavalena escapes from the house, bolts from his
prison. Like a madman, at any moment he may
be found wandering in the street, without a

penny in his pocket, determined to "take up the
threads of his life again" somewhere or other.
He goes here and there in search of friends; and
his friends, at first, welcome him joyously in
the *caffè*, in the newspaper offices, because they
like to see him enjoying himself; but the warmth
of their welcome begins at once to cool as soon
as he expresses his urgent need of finding employment once more among them, without a moment's delay, in order that he may be able to
provide for himself as quickly as possible. Yes
indeed! Because he has not even the price of a
cup of coffee, a mouthful of supper, a bed in an
inn for the night. Who will oblige him, for the
time being, with twenty lire or so? He makes
an appeal, among the journalists, to the spirit
of old comradeship. He will come round next
day with an article to his old paper. What?
Yes, something literary or light and scientific.
He has ever so much material stored up in his
head . . . new stuff, you know. . . . Such as?
Oh, Lord, such as, well, this . . . "

He has not finished speaking, before all these
good friends burst out laughing in his face. New
stuff? Why, Noah used to tell that to his sons,
in the ark, to beguile the tedium of their voyage
over the waters of the Deluge. . . .

Ah, I too know them well, those old friends of
the *caffè!* They all talk like that, in a forced
burlesque manner, and each of them becomes ex-

cited by the verbal exaggerations of the rest and
takes courage to utter an even grosser exaggeration, which does not however exceed the limit,
does not depart from the tone, so as not to be
received with a general outcry; they laugh at
one another in turn, making a sacrifice of all
their most cherished vanities, fling them in one
another's face with gay savagery, and apparently
no one takes offence; but the resentment within
grows, the bile ferments; the effort to keep the
conversation in that burlesque tone which pro-
vokes laughter, because amid general laughter
insults are tempered and lose their gall, becomes
gradually more laboured and difficult; then, the
prolonged, sustained effort leaves in each of them
a weariness of anger and disgust; each of them
is conscious with bitter regret of having done
violence to his own thoughts, to his own feelings;
more than remorse, an outraged sincerity; an inward uneasiness, as though the swelling, infuriated spirit no longer adhered to its own intimate
substance; and they all heave deep sighs to rid
themselves of the hot air of their own disgust;
but, the very next day, they all fall back into
that furnace, and scorch themselves, afresh,
miserable grasshoppers, doomed to saw frantically away at their own shell of boredom.

Woe to him who arrives a newcomer, or re-
turns after a certain interval to their midst!
But Cavalena perhaps does not take offence,

does not complain of the sacrifice that his good
friends make of him, tortured as he is in his
heart by the discovery that he has failed, in his
seclusion, to "keep in touch with life." Since
his last escape from the prison-house there have
passed, shall we say, eighteen months? Well;
it is as though there had passed eighteen cen-
turies! All of them, as they hear issuing from
his lips certain slang expressions, then the very
latest thing, which he has preserved like precious
jewels in the strong-box of his memory, screw
up their faces and gaze at him, as one gazes in
a chop-house at a warmed-up dish, which smells
of rancid fat a mile off! Oh, poor Cavalena,
just listen to him! Listen to him! He still ad-
mires the man who, eighteen months ago, was
the greatest man of the twentieth century. But
who was that? Ah, listen. . . . So and so of
Such and such. . . . That idiot! That bore!
That dummy! What, is he still alive? No, not
really alive? Yes, Cavalena swears he saw him,
actually alive, only a week ago; in fact, believing
that . . . (no, as far as being alive goes, he is
alive) still, if he is no longer a great man . . .
why, he proposed to write an article about him
. . . he won't write it now!

Utterly abased, his face livid with bile, but
with patches of red here and there, as though
his friends in their mortification of him had
amused themselves by pinching him on the brow,

the cheeks, the nose, Cavalena meanwhile is inwardly devouring his wife, like a cannibal after a three-days' fast: his wife, who has made him a public laughing-stock. He swears to himself that he will never again let himself fall into her clutches; but gradually, alas, his anxiety to resume "life" begins to transform itself into a mania which at first he is unable to define, but which becomes steadily more and more exasperating within him. For years past he has exercised all his mental faculties in defending his own dignity against the unjust suspicions of his wife. And now his faculties, suddenly diverted from this assiduous, desperate defence, are no longer adaptable, must make an effort to convert themselves and to devote themselves to other uses. But his dignity, so long and so strenuously defended, has now settled upon him, like the mould of a statue, immovable. Cavalena feels himself empty inside, but outwardly incrusted all over. He has become the walking mould of this statue. He cannot any longer scrape it off himself. Forever, henceforward, inexorably, he is the most dignified man in the world. And this dignity of his has so exquisite a sensibility that it takes umbrage, grows disturbed at the slightest indication that is vouchsafed to it of the most trifling transgression of his duties as a citizen, a husband, the father of a family. He has so often sworn to his wife that he has never proved false, even in thought, to these duties, that really now he cannot even think of transgressing them, and suffers, and turns all the colours of the rainbow when he sees other people so light-heartedly transgressing them. His friends laugh at him and call him a hypocrite. There, in their midst, incrusted all over, amid the noise and impetuous volubility of a life that knows no restraint either of faith or of affection, Cavalena feels himself outraged, begins to imagine that he is in serious peril; he has the impression that he is standing on feet of glass in the midst of a tumult of madmen who trample on him with iron shoes. The life imagined in his seclusion as full of attractions and indispensable to him reveals itself as being vacuous, stupid, insipid. How can he have suffered so keenly from being deprived of the company of these friends; of the spectacle of all their fatuity, all the wretched disorder of their life?

Poor Cavalena! The truth perhaps lies elsewhere! The truth is that in his harsh seclusion, without meaning it, he has become too much accustomed to converse with himself, that is to say with the worst enemy that any of us can have; and thus has acquired a clear perception of the futility of everything, and has seen himself thus lost, alone, surrounded by shadows and crushed by the mystery of himself and of everything. . . . Illusions? Hopes? Of what use are they?

Vanity. . . . And his own personality, prostrated,
annulled in itself, has gradually re-arisen as a
pitiful consciousness of other people, who are ignorant and deceive themselves, who are ignorant
and labour and love and suffer. What fault is it
of his wife, his poor Nene, if she is so jealous?
He is a doctor and knows that this fierce jealousy
is really and truly a mental disease, a form of
reasoning madness. Typical, a typical form of
paranoia, with persecution mania too. He goes
about telling everybody. Typical! Typical! She
has finally come to suspect, his poor Nene, that
he is seeking to kill her, in order to take possession, with the daughter, of her money! Ah,
what an ideal life they would lead then, without
her. . . . Liberty, liberty: one foot here, the
other there! She says this, poor Nene, because
she herself perceives that life, as she makes it
for herself and for the others, is not possible, it
is the destruction of life; she destroys herself,
poor Nene, with her ravings, and naturally supposes that the others wish to destroy her: with
a knife, no, because it would be discovered! By
concentrated spite! And she does not observe
that the spite originates with herself; originates
in all the phantoms of her madness to which she
gives substance. But is not he a doctor? And
if he, as a doctor, understands all this, does it
not follow that he ought to treat his poor Nene
as a sick patient, not responsible for the harm

she has done him and continues to do him? Why rebel? Against whom? He ought to feel for her and to shew pity, to stand by her lovingly, to endure with patience and resignation her inevitable cruelty. And then there is poor Luisetta, left alone in that hell, at the mercy of that mother who does not stop to think. . . . Ah, off with him, he must return home at once! At once. Perhaps, underlying his decision, masked by this pity for his wife and daughter, there is the need to escape from that precarious and uncertain life, which is no longer the life for him. Is he not, moreover, entitled to feel some pity for himself also? Who has brought him down to this state? Can he at his age take up life again, after having severed all the ties, after having closed all the doors, to please his wife? And, in the end, he goes back to shut himself up in his prison!

The poor man bears so clearly displayed in his whole appearance the great disaster that weighs upon him, he makes it so plainly visible in the embarrassment of his every step, his every glance, when he has his wife with him, by his constant terror lest she, in that step, in that glance, may find a pretext for a scene, that one cannot help laughing at him, sympathise with him as one may.

And perhaps I should have laughed at him too, this morning, had not Signorina Luisetta been

there. Who knows what she is made to suffer by
the inevitable absurdity of her father, poor girl.

A man of five and forty, reduced to that condition, whose wife is still so fiercely jealous of
him, cannot fail to be grotesquely absurd! All
the more so since, owing to another hidden tragedy, an indecent precocious baldness, the effect
of typhoid fever, which he managed by a miracle
to survive, the poor man is obliged to wear that
artistic wig under a hat large enough to cover
it. The effrontery of this hat and of all those
curled locks that protrude from it is in such
marked contrast to the frightened, shocked, cautious expression of his face, that it is nothing
short of ruination to his seriousness, and must
also, certainly, be a constant grief to his
daughter.

"No, one moment, my dear Sir . . . excuse me,
what did you say your name was?"

"Gubbio."

"Gubbio, thanks. Mine is Cavalena, at your
service."

"Cavalena, thanks, I know."

"Fabrizio Cavalena: in Rome I am better
known as . . . "

"I should say so, a buffoon!"

Cavalena turned round, pale as death, his
mouth agape, to gaze at his wife.

"Buffoon, buffoon, buffoon," she reiterated,
three times in succession.

"Nene, for heaven's sake, shew some respect.
. . . " Cavalena began threateningly; but all
of a sudden he broke off: shut his eyes, screwed
up his face, clenched his fists, as though seized
by a sudden, sharp internal spasm. . . . Not at
all! It was the tremendous effort which he has
to make every time to contain himself, to wring
from his infuriated animal nature the consciousness that he is a doctor and ought therefore to
treat and to pity his wife as a poor sick person.

"May I?"

And he took my arm in his, to draw me a little
way apart.

"Typical, you know? Poor thing. . . . Ah, it
requires true heroism, believe me, the greatest
heroism on my part to put up with her. I should
not be able, perhaps, if it were not for my poor
child here. But there! I was saying just now
. . . this Polacco, God in heaven . . . this
Polacco! But I ask you, is it a trick to play
upon a friend, knowing my misfortune? He
carries my daughter off to *pose* . . . with a light
woman . . . with an actor who, notoriously . . .
Can you imagine the scene that occurred at
home! And then he sends me these presents . . .
a collar too for the animal . . . and five hundred
lire!"

I tried to make it clear to him that, so far
at any rate as the presents and the five hundred
lire went, it did not appear to me that there was

any such harm in them as he chose to make out.
He? But he saw no harm in them whatsoever!
What harm should there be? He was delighted,
overjoyed at what had happened! Most grateful in his heart of hearts to Polacco for having
given that little part to his daughter! He had
to pretend to be so indignant to appease his
wife. I noticed this at once, as soon as I had
begun to speak. He was enraptured with the
argument that I set before him, proving that
after all no harm had been done. He gripped
me by the arm, led me impetuously back to his
wife.

"Do you hear? Do you hear? . . . I know
nothing about it. . . . This gentleman says . . .
Tell her, will you please, tell her what you said
to me. I don't wish to open my mouth. . . . I
came here with the presents and the five hundred
lire, you understand? To hand everything back.
But if that would be, as this gentleman says
I know nothing about it . . . a gratuitous insult
. . . replying with rudeness to a person who
never had the slightest intention to offend us,
to do us any harm, because he thinks that . . . I
know nothing, I know nothing . . . that there is
no occasion . . . I beg of you, in heaven's name,
my dear Sir, do you speak . . . repeat to my
wife what you have been so kind as to say to
me!"

But his wife did not give me time to speak:

she sprang upon me with the glassy, phosphorescent eyes of a maddened cat.

"Don't listen to this buffoon, hypocrite, clown! It is not his daughter he's thinking about, it is not the figure he would cut! He wants to hang about here all day, because here it would be like being in his own garden, with all the pretty ladies he's so fond of, artists like himself, mincing round him! And he's not ashamed, the scoundrel, to put his daughter forward as an excuse, to shelter behind his daughter, at the cost of compromising her and ruining her, the wretch! He would have the excuse of bringing his daughter here, you understand? He would come here for his daughter!"

"But you would come too," Fabrizio Cavalena shouted, losing all patience. "Aren't you here too? With me?"

"I?" roared his wife. "I, here?"

"Why not?" Cavalena went on unperturbed; and, turning again to myself: "Tell her, you tell her, does not Zeme come here as well?"

"Zeme?" inquired the wife in perplexity, knitting her brows. "Who is Zeme?"

"Zeme, the Senator!" exclaimed Cavalena. "A Senator of the Realm, a scientist of world-wide fame!"

"He must be as big a clown as yourself!"

"Zeme, who goes to the Quirinal? Invited to all the State Banquets? The venerable Senator

Zeme, the pride of Italy! The Keeper of the
Astronomical Observatory! Good Lord, you
ought to be ashamed of yourself! Shew some
respect, if not for me, for one of the glories of
the country! He has been here, hasn't he? But
speak, my dear Sir, tell her, for pity's sake, I
beg of you! Zeme has been here, he has helped
to arrange a film, hasn't he? He, Senator Zeme!
And if Zeme comes here, if Zeme offers his services, a world-famous scientist, then, I mean to
say . . . surely I can come here too, can offer
my services too. . . . But it doesn't matter to
me in the least! I shall not come again! I am
speaking now to make it clear to this woman
that this is not a place of ill-fame, to which I, for
immoral purposes, am seeking to lead my daughter to her ruin! You will understand, my dear
Sir, and forgive me: this is why I am speaking. It burns my ears to hear it said in front
of my daughter that I wish to compromise her,
to ruin her, by taking her to a place of ill-fame.
. . . Come, come, do me a favour: take me in at
once to Polacco, so that I may give him back
these presents and the money, and thank him for
them. When a man has the misfortune to possess a wife like mine, he ought to dig a grave
for himself, and finish things off once and for
all! Take me in to Polacco!''

What happened was not my fault on this occasion either, but, flinging open carelessly, without

knocking, the door of the Art Director's office, in which Polacco was to be found, I saw inside a spectacle which at once altered my state of mind completely, so that I was no longer able to give a thought to Cavalena, nor indeed to see anything clearly.

Huddled in the chair by Polacco's desk a man was sobbing, his face buried in his hands, desperately.

Immediately Polacco, seeing the door open, raised his head abruptly and made an angry sign to me to shut it.

I obeyed. The man who was sobbing inside the room was unquestionably Aldo Nuti. Cavalena, his wife, his daughter, looked at me in bewilderment.

"What is it?" Cavalena asked.

I could barely find the breath to answer:

"There's . . . there's some one there. . . . "

Shortly afterwards, there issued from the Art Director's office Cocò Polacco, in evident confusion. He saw Cavalena and made a sign to him to wait:

"You here? Excellent. I want to speak to you."

And without so much as a thought of greeting the ladies, he took me by the arm and drew me aside.

"He has come! He simply must not be left alone for a minute! I have mentioned you to him. He remembers you perfectly. Where are your lodgings? Wait a minute! Do you mind. . . . "

He turned and called to Cavalena.

"You let a couple of rooms, don't you? Are they vacant just now?"

"I should think so!" sighed Cavalena. "For the last three months and more. . . . "

"Gubbio," Polacco said to me, "I want you to give up your lodgings at once; pay whatever you have to pay, a month's rent, two months', three months'; take one of these two rooms at Cavalena's. The other will be for him."

"Delighted!" Cavalena exclaimed radiant, holding out both his hands to me.

"Hurry up," Polacco went on. "Off with you! You, go and get the rooms ready; you, pack up your traps and transport everything at once to Cavalena's. Then come back here! Is that all quite clear?"

I threw open my arms, resigned.

Polacco retired to his room. And I drove off with the Cavalena family, bewildered, and most anxious to have from me an explanation of all this mystery.

OF THE NOTES OF SERAFINO GUBBIO
CINEMATOGRAPH OPERATOR

BOOK V

§ 1

I HAVE just come from Aldo Nuti's room. It is nearly one o'clock. The house—in which I am spending my first night—is asleep. It has for me a strange atmosphere, which I cannot as yet breathe with comfort; the appearance of things, the savour of life, special arrangements, traces of unfamiliar habits.

In the passage, as soon as I shut the door of Nuti's room, holding a lighted match in my fingers, I saw close beside me, enormous on the opposite wall, my own shadow. Lost in the silence of the house, I felt my soul so small that my shadow there on the wall, grown so big, seemed to me the image of fear.

At the end of the passage, a door; outside this door, on the mat, a pair of shoes: Signorina Luisetta's. I stopped for a moment to look at my monstrous shadow, which stretched out in the direction of this door, and the fancy came to me that the shoes were there to keep my shadow away. Suddenly, from inside the door, the old dog Piccinì, who had already perhaps pricked

her ears, on the alert from the first sound of a
door being opened, uttered a couple of wheezy
barks. It was not at the sound that she barked;
but she had heard me stop in the passage for
a moment; had felt my thoughts make their way
into the bedroom of her young mistress, and so
she barked.

Here I am in my new room. But it should not
be this room. When I came here with my lug-
gage, Cavalena, who was genuinely delighted to
have me in the house, not only because of the
warm affection and strong confidence which I at
once inspired in him, but perhaps also because
he hopes that it may be easier for him, by my
influence, to find an opening in the Kosmograph,
had allotted to me the other room, larger, more
comfortable, better furnished.

Certainly neither he nor Signora Nene desired
or ordered the change. It must be the work of
Signorina Luisetta, who listened this morning in
the carriage so attentively and with such dismay, as we drove away from the Kosmograph,
to my summary account of Nuti's misadventures.
Yes, it must have been she, beyond question. My
suspicion was confirmed a moment ago by the
sight of her shoes outside the door, on the mat.

I am annoyed at the change for this reason
only, that I myself, if this morning they had let
me see both rooms, would have left the other to
Nuti and have chosen this one for myself. Sig-

norina Luisetta read my thoughts so clearly that
without saying a word to me she has removed
my things from the other room and arranged
them in this. Certainly, if she had not done so,
I should have been embarrassed at seeing Nuti
lodged in this smaller and less comfortable of
the rooms. But am I to suppose that she wished
to spare me this embarrassment? I cannot. Her
having done, without saying a word to me, what
I would have done myself, offends me, albeit I
realise that it is what had to be done, or rather
precisely because I realise that it is what had to
be done.

Ah, what a prodigious effect the sight of tears
in a man's eyes has on women, especially if they
be tears of love. But I must be fair: they have
had a similar effect on myself.

He has kept me in there for about four hours.
He wanted to go on talking and weeping: I
stopped him, out of compassion chiefly for his
eyes. I have never seen a pair of eyes brought
to such a state by excessive weeping.

I express myself badly. Not by excessive
weeping. Perhaps quite a few tears (he has shed
an endless quantity), perhaps only a few tears
would have been enough to bring his eyes to such
a state.

And yet, it is strange! It appears that it is
not he who is weeping. To judge by what he
says, by what he proposes to do, he has no

reason, nor, certainly, any desire to weep. The tears scald his eyes and cheeks, and therefore he knows that he is weeping; but he does not *feel* his own tears. His eyes are weeping almost for a grief that is not his, for a grief that is almost that of his tears themselves. His own grief is fierce, and refuses and scorns these tears.

But stranger still to my mind was this: that when at any point in his conversation his sentiments, so to speak, became lachrymose, his tears all at once began to slacken. While his voice grew tender and throbbed, his eyes, on the contrary, those eyes that a moment before were bloodshot and swollen with weeping, became dry and hard: fierce.

So that what he says and what his eyes say cannot correspond.

But it is there, in his eyes, and not in what he says that his heart lies. And therefore it was for his eyes chiefly that I felt compassion. Let him not talk and weep; let him weep and listen to his own weeping: it is the best thing that he can do.

There comes to me, through the wall, the sound of his step. I have advised him to go to bed, to try to sleep. He says that he cannot; that he has lost the power to sleep, for some time past. What has made him lose it? Not remorse, certainly, to judge by what he says.

Among all the phenomena of human nature one

of the commonest, and at the same time one of
the strangest when we study it closely, is this of
the desperate, frenzied struggle which every man,
however ruined by his own misdeeds, conquered
and crushed in his affliction, persists in keeping
up with his own conscience, in order not to acknowledge those misdeeds and not to make them
a matter for remorse. That others acknowledge
them and punish him for them, imprison him, inflict the cruellest tortures upon him and kill him,
matters not to him; so long as he himself does
not acknowledge them, but withstands his own
conscience which cries them aloud at him.

Who is he? Ah, if each one of us could for an
instant tear himself away from that metaphorical
ideal which our countless fictions, conscious and
unconscious, our fictitious interpretations of our
actions and feelings lead us inevitably to form
of ourselves; he would at once perceive that this
he is *another,* another who has nothing or but
very little in common with himself; and that the
true *he* is the one that is crying his misdeeds
aloud within him; the intimate being, often
doomed for the whole of our lives to remain unknown to us! We seek at all costs to preserve,
to maintain in position that metaphor of ourselves, our pride and our love. And for this
metaphor we undergo martyrdom and ruin ourselves, when it would be so pleasant to let ourselves succumb vanquished, to give ourselves up

to our own inmost being, which is a dread deity,
if we oppose ourselves to it; but becomes at once
compassionate towards our every fault, as soon
as we confess it, and prodigal of unexpected ten-
dernesses. But this seems a negation of self,
something unworthy of a man; and will ever
be so, so long as we believe that our humanity
consists in this metaphor of ourselves.

The version given by Aldo Nuti of the mishaps
that have brought him low—it seems impossible!
—aims above all at preserving this metaphor,
his masculine vanity, which, albeit reduced before
my eyes to this miserable plight, refuses nevertheless to humble itself to the confession that
it has been a silly toy in the hands of a woman:
a toy, a doll filled with sawdust, which the Nestoroff, after amusing herself for a while by making it open its arms and close them in an attitude
of prayer, pressing with her finger the too obvious spring in its chest, flings away into a corner,
breaking it in its fall.

It has risen to its feet again, this broken doll;
its porcelain face and hands in a pitiful state:
the hands without fingers, the face without a
nose, all cracked and chipped; the spring in its
chest has made a rent in the red woollen jacket
and dangles out, broken; and yet, no, what is
this: the doll cries out no, that it is not true
that that woman made it open its arms and
close them in an attitude of prayer to laugh at

it, nor that, after laughing at it, she has broken
it like this. It is not true!

By agreement with Duccella, by agreement
with Granny Rosa he followed the affianced lovers
from the villa by Sorrento to Naples, to save
poor Giorgio, too innocent, and blinded by the
fascination of that woman. It did not require
much to save him! Enough to prove to him, to
let him assure himself by experiment that the
woman whom he wished to make his by marrying
her, could be his, as she had been other men's,
as she would be any man's, without any necessity
of marrying her. And thereupon, challenged by
poor Giorgio, he set to work to make the experiment at once. Poor Giorgio believed it to be
impossible because, as might be expected, with
the tactics common among women of her sort,
the Nestoroff had always refused to grant him
even the slightest favour, and at Capri he had
seen her so contemptuous of everyone, so withdrawn and aloof! It was a horrible act of
treachery. Not his action, though, but Giorgio
Mirelli's! He had promised that on receiving
the proof he would at once leave the woman: instead, he killed himself.

This is the version that Aldo Nuti chooses
to give of the drama.

But how, then? Was it he, the doll, that was
playing the trick? And how comes he to be
broken like this? If it was so easy a trick?

Away with these questions, and away with all surprise. Here one must make a show of believing. Our pity must not diminish but rather increase at the overpowering necessity to lie in this poor doll, which is Aldo Nuti's vanity: the face without a nose, the hands without fingers, the spring in the chest broken, dangling out through the rent jacket, we must allow him to lie! Only, his lies give him an excuse for weeping all the more.

They are not good tears, because he does not wish to feel his own grief in them. He does not wish them, and he despises them. He wishes to do something other than weep, and we shall have to keep him under observation. Why has he come here? He has no need to be avenged on anyone, if the treachery lay in Giorgio Mirelli's action in killing himself and flinging his dead body between his sister and her lover. So much I said to him.

"I know," was his answer. "But there is still she, that woman, the cause of it all! If she had not come to disturb Giorgio's youth, to bait her hook, to spread her net for him with arts which really can be treacherous only to a novice, not because they are not treacherous in themselves, but because a man like myself, like you, recognises them at once for what they are: vipers, which we render harmless by extracting the teeth which we know to be venomous; now I should

not be caught like that: I should not be caught
like that! She at once saw in me an enemy, do
you understand? And she tried to sting me by
stealth. From the very beginning I, on purpose,
allowed her to think that it would be the easiest
thing in the world for her to sting me. I wished
her to shew her teeth, just so that I might draw
them. And I was successful. But Giorgio,
Giorgio, Giorgio had been poisoned for ever!
He should have let me know that it was useless
my attempting to draw the teeth of that
viper. . . . "

"Not a viper, surely!" I could not help ob-
serving. "Too much innocence for a viper,
surely! To offer you her teeth so quickly, so
easily. . . . Unless she did it to cause the death
of Giorgio Mirelli."

"Perhaps."

"And why? If she had already succeeded in
her plan of making him marry her? And did
she not yield at once to your trick? Did she not
let you draw her teeth before she had attained
her object?"

"But she had no suspicion!"

"In that case, how in the world is she a viper?
Would you have a viper not suspect? A viper
would have stung after, not before! If she stung
first, it means that . . . either she is not a viper,
or for Giorgio's sake she was willing to lose her
teeth. Excuse me . . . no, wait a minute . . .

please stop and listen to me . . . I tell you this
because . . . I am quite of your opinion, you
know . . . she did wish to be avenged, but at
first, only at the beginning, upon Giorgio. This
is my belief; I have always thought so."

"Be avenged for what?"

"Perhaps for an insult which no woman will
readily allow."

"Woman, you say! She!"

"Yes, indeed, a woman, Signor Nuti! You
who know her well, know that they are all the
same, especially on this point."

"What insult? I don't follow you."

"Listen: Giorgio was entirely taken up with
his art, wasn't he?"

"Yes."

"He found at Capri this woman, who offered
herself as an object of contemplation to him,
to his art."

"Precisely, yes."

"And he did not see, he did not wish to see in
her anything but her body, but only to caress
it upon a canvas with his brushes, with the play
of lights and colours. And then she, offended and
piqued, to avenge herself, seduced him (there I
agree with you!); and, having seduced him, to
avenge herself further, to avenge herself still
better, resisted him (am I right?) until Giorgio,
blinded, in order to secure her, proposed mar-

riage, took her to Sorrento to meet his grandmother, his sister."

"No! It was her wish! She insisted upon
it!"

"Very well, then; it was she; and I might say,
insult for insult; but no, I propose now to abide
by what you have said, Signor Nuti! And
what you have said makes me think, that she may
have insisted upon Giorgio's taking her there,
and introducing her to his grandmother and
sister, expecting that Giorgio would revolt
against this imposition, so that she might find an
excuse for releasing herself from the obligation
to marry him."

"Release herself? Why?"

"Why, because she had already attained her
object! Her vengeance was complete: Giorgio,
crushed, blinded, captivated by her, by her body,
to the extent of wishing to marry her! This was
enough for her, and she asked for nothing more!
All the rest, their wedding, life with him who
would be certain to repent immediately of their
marriage, would have meant unhappiness for her
and for him, a chain. And perhaps she was not
thinking only of herself; she may have felt some
pity also for him!"

"Then you believe?"

"But you make me believe it, you make me
think it, by maintaining that the woman is

treacherous! To go by what you say, Signor
Nuti, in a treacherous woman what she did is
not consistent. A treacherous woman who desires marriage, and before her marriage gives
herself to you so easily . . . "

"Gives herself to me?" came with a shout of
rage from Aldo Nuti, driven by my arguments
with his back to the wall. "Who told you that
she gave herself to me? I never had her, I never
had her. . . . Do you imagine that I can ever
have thought of having her? All I required was
the proof which she would not have failed to
provide . . . a proof to shew to Giorgio!"

I was left speechless for a moment, gazing at
him.

"And that viper let you have it at once? And
you were able to secure it without difficulty, this
proof? But then, but then, surely . . . "

I supposed that at last my logic had the victory
so firmly in its grasp that it would no longer be
possible to wrest it from me. I had yet to learn,
that at the very moment when logic, striving
against passion, thinks that it has secured the
victory, passion with a sudden lunge snatches
it back, and then with buffetings and kicks sends
logic flying with all its escort of linked con-
clusions.

If this unfortunate man, quite obviously the
dupe of this woman, for a purpose which I believe myself to have guessed, could not make

her his, and has been left accordingly with this
rage still in his body, after all that he has had
to suffer, because that silly doll of his vanity
believed honestly perhaps at first that it could
easily play with a woman like the Nestoroff;
what more can one say? Is it possible to induce
him to go away? To force him to see that he
can have no object in provoking another man,
in approaching a woman who does not wish to
have anything more to do with him?

Well, I have tried to induce him to go away,
and have asked him what, in short, he wanted, and
what he hoped from this woman.

"I don't know, I don't know," he cried. "She
ought to stay with me, to suffer with me. I can't
do without her any longer, I can't be left alone
any more like this. I have tried up to now, I
have done everything to win Duccella over; I
have made ever so many of my friends intercede
for me; but I realise that it is not possible. They
do not believe in my agony, in my desperation.
And now I feel a need, I must cling on to some
one, not be alone like this any more. You understand: I am going mad, I am going mad! I
know that the woman herself is utterly worthless; but she acquires a value now from everything that I have suffered and am suffering
through her. It is not love, it is hatred, it is
the blood that has been shed for her! And since
she has chosen to submerge my life for ever in

that blood, it is necessary now that we plunge
into it both together, clinging to one another, she
and I, not I alone, not I alone! I cannot be left
alone like this any more!"

I came away from his room without even the
satisfaction of having offered him an outlet which
might have relieved his heart a little. And now
I can open the window and lean out to gaze at
the sky, while he in the other room wrings his
hands and weeps, devoured by rage and grief.
If I went back now, into his room, and said to
him joyfully; "I say, Signor Nuti, there are
still the stars! You of course have forgotten
them, but they are still there!" what would happen? To how many men, caught in the throes of
a passion, or bowed down, crushed by sorrow,
by hardship, would it do good to think that there,
above the roof, is the sky, and that in the sky
there are the stars. Even if the fact of the
stars' being there did not inspire in them any
religious consolation. As we gaze at them, our
own feeble pettiness is engulfed, vanishes in the
emptiness of space, and every reason for our
torment must seem to us meagre and vain. But
we must have in ourselves, in the moment of
passion, the capacity to think of the stars. This
may be found in a man like myself, who for
some time past has looked at everything, himself
included, from a distance. If I were to go in there
and tell Signor Nuti that the stars were shining

in the sky, he would perhaps shout back at me
to give them his kind regards, and would turn
me out of the room like a dog.

But can I now, as Polacco would like, consti-
tute myself his guardian? I can imagine how
Carlo Ferro will glare at me presently, on seeing
me come to the Kosmograph with him by my
side. And God knows that I have no more reason
to be a friend of one than of the other.

All I ask is to continue, with my usual impassivity, my work as an operator. I shall not
look out of the window. Alas, since that cursed
Senator Zeme has been to the Kosmograph, I see
even in the sky a *marvel* of cinematography.

§ 2

"Then it is a serious matter?" Cavalena came
to my room, mysteriously, this morning to ask
me.

The poor man had three handkerchiefs in his
hand. At a certain point in the conversation,
after many expressions of pity for that "dear
Baron" (to wit, Nuti), and many observations
touching the innumerable misfortunes of the
human race, as though they were a proof of these
misfortunes he spread out before me the three
handkerchiefs, one after another, exclaiming:

"Look!"

They were all three in holes, as though they

had been gnawed by mice. I gazed at them with pity and wonder; after which I gazed at him, shewing plainly that I did not understand. Cavalena sneezed, or rather, I thought that he had sneezed. Not at all. He had said:

"Piccinì."

Seeing that I still gazed at him with that air of bewilderment, he shewed me the handkerchiefs once more and repeated:

"Piccinì."

"The little dog?"

He shut his eyes and nodded his head with a tragic solemnity.

"A hard worker, it seems," said I.

"And I must not say a word!" exclaimed Cavalena. "Because she is the one creature here, in my house, by whom my wife feels herself loved, and is not afraid of her playing her false. Ah, Signor Gubbio, nature is really wicked, believe me. No misfortune can be greater or worse than mine. To have a wife who feels that no one loves her but a dog! And it is not true, you know. That animal does not love anyone. My wife loves her, and do you know why? Because it is only with that animal that she can play at having a heart in her bosom that is overflowing with charity. And you should see how she consoles herself! A tyrant with all the rest of us, the woman becomes a slave to an old, ugly animal; ugly isn't the word—you've seen

it?—with claws like bill-hooks and bleared eyes.
. . . And she loves it all the more now that she
sees that an antipathy has been growing up for
some time between the dog and me, an antipathy,
Signor Gubbio, that is insuperable! Insuperable!
That nasty beast, being quite certain that I, who
know how she is protected by her mistress, will
never give her the kick that would turn her inside out, reduce her—I swear to you, Signor
Gubbio—to a jelly, shews me with the most
irritating calmness every possible and imaginable
sign of contempt, she positively insults me: she
is always dirtying the carpet in my study; she
lies on the armchairs, on the sofa in my study;
she refuses her food and gnaws all my dirty
linen: look at these, three handkerchiefs, yesterday, not to mention shirts, table-napkins, towels,
pillow-slips; and I have to admire her and thank
her, because do you know what this gnawing
means to my wife? Affection! I assure you. It
means that the dog smells her masters' scent.
'But how? When she eats it?' 'She doesn't
know what she is doing,' would be my wife's
answer. She has destroyed more than half our
linen-cupboard. I have to keep quiet, put a
stopper in, otherwise my wife would at once find
an excuse for reminding me once again, in so
many words, of my own brutality. That's just
how it is! A fortunate thing, Signor Gubbio,
a fortunate thing, as I always say, that I am a

Doctor! I am bound, as a Doctor, to realise that this passionate adoration for an animal is merely another symptom of the disease! Typical, don't you know?"

He stood gazing at me for a while, undecided, perplexed: then, pointing to a chair, asked:

"May I?"

"Why, of course!" I told him.

He sat down; studied one of the handkerchiefs, shaking his head, then, with a wan, almost imploring smile:

"I am not in your way, am I? I am not disturbing you?"

I assured him warmly that he was not disturbing me in the least.

"I know, I can see that you are a warm-hearted man . . . let me say it, a quiet man, but a man who can understand and feel for other people. And I . . . "

He broke off, with a worried expression, listened intently, then sprang to his feet:

"I think that was Luisetta calling me. . . . "

I too listened for a moment, then said:

"No, I don't think so."

Sorrowfully he raised his hands to his wig and straightened it on his head.

"Do you know what Luisetta said to me yesterday? 'Daddy, don't start again.' You see before you, Signor Gubbio, an exasperated man. Inevitably. Shut up here in the house from morning to night, without ever setting eyes on anyone, shut out from life, I can never find any outlet for my rage at the injustice of my fate! And Luisetta tells me that I drive all the lodgers away!"

"Oh, but I . . . " I began to protest.

"No, it is true, you know, it is true!" Cavalena interrupted me. "And, you, since you are so kind, must promise me that as soon as I begin to bore you, as soon as I am in your way, you will take me by the scruff of my neck and fling me out of the room! Promise me that, please. Right away; you must give me your hand and promise."

I gave him my hand, smiling:

"There . . . just as you please . . . to satisfy you."

"Thank you! Now I feel more at my ease. I am conscious, Signor Gubbio, you wouldn't believe! Conscious, do you know of what? Of being no longer myself! When a man reaches this depth, that is when he loses all sense of shame at his own disgrace, he is finished! But I should never have lost that sense of shame! I was too jealous of my dignity! It was that woman made me lose it, crying her madness aloud. My disgrace is known to everyone from now onwards? And it is obscene, obscene, obscene."

"But no . . . why?"

"Obscene!" shouted Cavalena. "Would you care to see it? Look! Here it is!"

And so speaking, he seized his wig between his fingers and plucked it from his head. I was left thunderstruck, gazing at that bare, pallid scalp, the scalp of a flayed goat, while Cavalena, the tears starting to his eyes, went on:

"Tell me, can it help being obscene, the disgrace of a man reduced to this state, whose wife is still jealous?"

"But you are a Doctor! You know that it is a disease!" I made haste to remind him, greatly distressed, raising my hands as though to help him to replace the wig on his head.

He settled it in its place, and said:

"But it is precisely because I am a Doctor and know that it is a disease, Signor Gubbio! That is the disgrace! That I am a Doctor! If I could only not know that she did it from madness, I should turn her out of the house, don't you see? Procure a separation from her, defend my own dignity at all costs. But I am a Doctor! I know that she is mad! And I know therefore that it is my duty to have sense for two, for myself and for her who has lost hers! But to have sense, for a madwoman, when her madness is so supremely ridiculous, Signor Gubbio, what does it mean? It means covering myself with ridicule, of course! It means resigning myself to endure the holocaust that madwoman makes of my dignity, before our daughter, before the servants, before everyone, in public; and so I lose all shame at my own disgrace!"

"Papa!"

Ah, this time, yes; it really was Signorina Luisetta calling.

Cavalena at once controlled himself, straightened his wig carefully, cleared his throat by way of changing his voice, and struck a sweet little playful, caressing note in which to answer:

"Here I am, Sesè."

And he hurried out, making a sign to me, with his finger, to be silent.

I too, shortly afterwards, left my room, to pay Nuti a visit. I listened for a moment outside the door of his room. Silence. Perhaps he was asleep. I stood there for a while in perplexity, then looked at my watch: it was already time for me to be going to the Kosmograph; only I did not wish to leave him, particularly as Polacco had expressly enjoined me to bring him with me. All of a sudden, I thought I heard what sounded like a deep sigh, a sigh of anguish. I knocked at the door. Nuti, from his bed, answered:

"Come in."

I went in. The room was in darkness. I went up to the bed. Nuti said:

"I think . . . I think I have a temperature. . . ."

I leaned over him; I felt one of his hands. It was trembling.

"Why, yes!" I exclaimed. "You have a temperature, and a high one. Wait a minute. I am going to call Signor Cavalena. Our landlord is a Doctor."

"No, don't bother . . . it will pass off!" he said. "I have been working too hard."

"Quite so," I replied. "But why won't you let me call in Cavalena? It will pass away all the sooner. Do you mind if I open the shutters a little?"

I looked at him by daylight; his appearance terrified me. His face was a brick red, hard, grim, rigid; the whites of his eyes, bloodshot overnight, were now almost black between their horribly swollen lids; his straggling moustache was glued to his parched, tumid, gaping lips.

"You must be feeling really bad."

"Yes, I do feel bad . . . " he said. "My head."

And he drew a hand from beneath the blankets to lay it with his fist clenched on his forehead.

I went to call Cavalena who was still talking to his daughter at the end of the passage. Signorina Luisetta, seeing me approach, stared at me with an icy frown.

She evidently supposed that her father had already found an outlet in me. Alas, I find myself unjustly condemned to atone thus for the excessive confidence which her father places in me.

Signorina Luisetta is my enemy already. But not only because of her father's excessive confidence in me, because also of the presence of another lodger in the house. The feeling aroused in her by this other lodger from the first moment rules out any friendliness towards me. I noticed this immediately. It is useless to argue about it. It is one of those secret, instinctive impulses by which our mental attitudes are determined and which at any moment, without any apparent reason, alter the relations between one person and another. Now, certainly, her ill-feeling will be increased by the tone of voice and the manner in which I—having noticed this—almost unconsciously, announced that Aldo Nuti was lying in bed, in his room, with a high temperature. She turned deathly pale, first of all; then blushed a deep crimson. Perhaps at that very moment she became aware of her still undefined feeling of aversion towards myself.

Cavalena at once hurried to Nuti's room; she stopped outside the door, as though she did not wish me to enter; so that I was obliged to say to her:

"May I pass, please?"

But a moment later, that is to say when her father told her to go and fetch the thermometer to take Nuti's temperature, she came into the

room also. I did not take my eyes from her face
for a moment, and saw that she, feeling that I
was looking at her, was making a violent effort
to conceal the mingled pity and dismay which
the sight of Nuti inspired in her.

The examination was prolonged. But, apart
from a high fever and headache, Cavalena was
unable to diagnose anything. When we had left
the room, however, after fastening the shutters
again, so that the patient should not be dazzled
by the light, Cavalena shewed signs of the utmost
consternation. He is afraid that it may be an
inflammation of the brain.

"We must send for another Doctor at once,
Signor Gubbio! I, especially as I am the owner
of the house, you understand, cannot assume
responsibility for an illness which I consider
serious."

He gave me a note for this other Doctor, his
friend, who receives calls at the neighbouring
chemist's, and I went off to leave the note and
then, being already behind my time, hastened
to the Kosmograph.

I found Polacco on tenterhooks, bitterly re-
penting his having let Nuti in for this mad enter-
prise. He says that he could never, never have
imagined that he would see him in the state in
which he suddenly appeared, unexpectedly, because from his letters written first from Russia,
then from Germany, afterwards from Switzer-

land, there was nothing to be made. He wished
to shew me these letters, in self-defence; but
then, all at once, seemed to have forgotten them.
The news of the illness has almost made him
cheerful, it has at any rate taken a great weight
off his mind for the moment.

"Inflammation of the brain? I say, Gubbio,
if he should die. . . . By Jove, when a man has
worked himself into that state, when he has become a danger to himself and to other people,
death . . . you might almost say . . . But let us
hope not; let us hope it is a good sign. It often
is, one never knows. I am sorry for you, poor
Gubbio, and also for that poor Cavalena. . . .
What a business. . . . I shall come and see you
this evening. But it's providential, you know.
So far, he has seen nobody here except yourself;
nobody knows that he is here. Mum's the word,
eh! You said to me that it would be advis-
able to relieve Ferro of his part in the tiger
film!

"But without letting him suppose . . . "

"Simpleton! You are talking to me. I have
thought of everything. Listen: yesterday afternoon, shortly after you people left, I had a visit
from the Nestoroff."

"Indeed? Here?"

"She must have felt in the air that Nuti had
come. My dear fellow, she's in a great fright!
Frightened of Ferro, not of Nuti. She came to

ask me . . . like that, just as if it was nothing
at all, whether it was really necessary that she
should continue to come to the Kosmograph, or
for that matter remain in Rome, as soon as, in a
few days from now, all four companies are employed on the tiger film, in which she is not to
take part. Do you follow? I caught the ball on
the rebound. I answered that Commendator
Borgalli's orders were that, before all four companies were amalgamated, we should finish the
three or four films that have been hung up for
various nature scenes, which will have to be taken
out of Rome. There's that one of the Otranto
sailors, the story Bertini gave us. 'But I have
no part in it,' said the Nestoroff. 'I know that,'
I told her, 'but Ferro has a part in it, the chief
part, and it might be better perhaps, more con-
venient for us, if we were to release him from
the part he is taking in the tiger film and send
him down South with Bertini. But perhaps he
won't agree. Now, if you were to persuade him,
Signora Nestoroff.' She looked me in the face
for a time . . . you know how she does . . . then
said: 'I might be able to. . . . ' And finally,
after thinking it over, 'In that case, he would
go down there by himself; I should remain here,
in his place, to take some part, even a minor part,
in the tiger film. . . . ' "

"Ah, no, in that case, no!" I could not help
interrupting Polacco. "Carlo Ferro will not go

down there by himself, you may be certain of
that!''

Polacco began to laugh.

"Simpleton! If she really wishes it, you may
be quite sure he will go! He would go to hell
for her!''

"I don't understand. Why does she wish to
remain here?''

"But it's not true. She says she does. . . .
Don't you understand that she's pretending, so
as not to let me see that she's afraid of Nuti?
She will go too, you'll see. Or perhaps . . . or
perhaps . . . who knows? She may really wish
to remain, to meet Nuti here by herself, without
interference, and make him give up the whole
idea. She is capable of that and of more; she
is capable of anything. Oh, what a business!
Come along; let us get to work. Tell me, though:
Signorina Luisetta? She simply must come here
for the rest of that film.''

I told him of Signora Nene's rage, and that
Cavalena, the day before, had come to return
(albeit unwillingly, so far as he was concerned)
the money and the presents. Polacco said once
more that he would come, this evening, to Cavalena's, to persuade him and Signora Nene to
send Signorina Luisetta back to the Kosmograph. We were by this time at the entrance to
the Positive Department: I ceased to be Gubbio
and became a hand.

§ 3

I have laid these notes aside for some days.
They have been days of sorrow and trepida-
tion. They are still not quite over; but now the
storm, which broke with terrific force in the soul
of this unhappy man whom all of us here have
vied with one another in helping compassionately
and with all the more devotion in that he was
virtually a stranger to us all and what little we
knew of him combined with his appearance and
the suggestion of fatality that he conveyed to
inspire in us pity and a keen interest in his most
wretched plight; this storm, I say, seems to be
shewing signs of gradually abating. Unless it is
only a brief lull. I fear it. Often, at the height
of a gale, a formidable peal of thunder succeeds
in clearing the sky for a little, but presently the
mass of clouds, rent asunder for a moment, return to accumulate slowly and ever more
menacingly, and the gale having increased its
strength breaks out afresh, more furious than
before. The calm, in fact, in which Nuti's spirit
seems gradually to be gathering strength after
his delirious ravings and the horrible frenzy of
all these days, is tremendously dark, just like
the calm of a sky in which a storm is gathering.

No one takes any notice, or seems to take any
notice of this, perhaps from the need which we

all feel to heave a momentary sigh of relief, saying that in any case the worst is over. We
ought, we intend to adjust first, to the best of our
ability, ourselves, and also everything round us,
swept by the whirlwind of his madness; because
there remains not only in all of us but even in
the room, in the very furniture of the room, a
sort of blind stupefaction, a strange uncertainty
in the appearance of everything, as it were an
air of hostility, suspended and diffused.

In vain do we detach ourselves from the outburst of a soul which from its profoundest depths
hurls forth, broken and disordered, the most
recondite thoughts, never yet confessed to itself
even, its most serious and awful feelings, the
strangest sensations which strip things of every
familiar meaning, to give them at once another,
unexpected meaning, with a truth that springs
forth and imposes itself, disconcerting and terri-
fying. The terror is due to our recognition, with
an appalling clarity, that madness dwells and
lurks within each of us and that a mere trifle
may let it loose: release it for a moment from
the elastic web of present consciousness, and lo,
all the imaginings accumulated in years past and
now wandering unconnected; the fragments of a
life that has remained hidden, because we could
not or would not let it be reflected in ourselves
by the light of reason; dubious actions, shameful
falsehoods, dark hatreds, crimes meditated in the

shadow of our inward selves and planned to the last detail, and forgotten memories and unconfessed desires burst in tumultuous, with diabolical fury, roaring like wild beasts. On more than one occasion, we all looked at one another with madness in our eyes, the terror of the spectacle of that madman being sufficient to release in us too for a moment the elastic net of consciousness. And even now we eye askance, and go up and touch with a sense of misgiving some object in the room which was for a moment illumined with the sinister light of a new and terrible meaning by the sick man's hallucinations; and, going to our own rooms, observe with stupefaction and repugnance that . . . yes, positively, we too have been overborne by that madness, even at a distance, even when alone: we find here and there clear signs of it, pieces of furniture, all sorts of things, strangely out of place.

We ought, we intend to adjust ourselves, we need to believe that the patient is now in this state, in this brooding calm, because he is still stunned by the violence of his final outbursts and is now exhausted, worn out.

There suffices to support this deception a slight smile of gratitude which he just perceptibly offers with his lips or eyes to Signorina Luisetta: a breath, an imperceptible glimmer which does not, in my opinion, emanate from the sick man, but is rather suffused over his face by his gentle

nurse, whenever she draws near and bends over
the bed.

Alas, how she too is worn out, his gentle nurse!
But no one gives her a thought; least of all herself. And yet the same storm has torn up and
swept away this innocent creature!

It has been an agony of which as yet perhaps
not even she can form any idea, because she
still perhaps has not with her, within her, her
own soul. She has given it to him, as a thing
not her own, as a thing which he in his delirium
might appropriate to derive from it refreshment
and comfort.

I have been present at this agony. I have done
nothing, nor could I perhaps have done anything
to prevent it. But I see and confess that I am
revolted by it. Which means that my feelings
are compromised. Indeed, I fear that presently
I may have to make another painful confession
to myself.

This is what has happened. Null, in his delirium, mistook Signorina Luisetta for Duccella
and, at first, inveighed furiously against her,
shouting in her face that her obduracy, her
cruelty to him were unjust, since he was in no
way to blame for the death of her brother, who,
of his own accord, like an idiot, like a madman,
had killed himself for that woman; then, as soon
as she, overcoming her first terror, grasping at
once the nature of his hallucination, went com-

passionately to his side, he refused to let her leave him for a moment, clasped her tightly to him, sobbing broken-heartedly or murmuring the most burning, the tenderest words of love to her, and caressing her or kissing her hands, her hair, her brow.

And she allowed him to do it. And all the rest of us allowed it. Because those words, those caresses, those embraces, those kisses were not intended for her: they were for a hallucination, in which his delirium found peace. And so we had to allow him. She, Signorina Luisetta, made her heart pitiful and loving for another girl's sake; and this heart, thus made pitiful and loving, she gave to him, as a thing not her own, but belonging to that other girl, to Duccella. And while he appropriated that heart, she could not, must not appropriate those words, those caresses, those kisses. . . . But she trembled at them in every fibre of her body, poor child, ready from the first moment to feel such pity for this man who was suffering so on account of the other woman. And not on her own behalf, who did really pity him, did it come to her to feel pitiful, but for that other, whom she naturally supposes to be harsh and cruel. Well, she has given her pity to the other, that the other might pass it on to him, and by him—through the medium of Luisetta's body—be loved and caressed in return. But love, love, who has given that? It was she

that had to give it, to give love, together with
her pity. And the poor child has given it. She
knows, she feels that she has given it, with all
her soul, with all her heart; and at the same
time she must suppose that she has given it for
the other.

The result has been as follows: that while
he, now, is gradually returning to himself
and collecting himself, and shutting himself
up again darkly in his trouble; she remains empty and lost, held in suspense, without a gleam in her eye, as though she had lost
her wits, a ghost, the ghost that entered into his
hallucination. For him, the ghost has vanished,
and with the ghost, love. But this poor child
who has emptied herself to fill that ghost with
herself, her love, her pity, is now herself left a
ghost; and he notices nothing. He barely smiles
at her in gratitude. The remedy has proved
effective: the hallucination has vanished; nothing more at present, is that it?

I should not be so distressed, had I not, for all
these days, seen myself obliged to bestow my
pity, also, to spend myself, to run in all directions, to sit up for several nights in succession,
not from a feeling that was genuinely my own,
that is to say one inspired in me by Nuti, as I
could have wished; but from a different feeling,
one of pity indeed, but of interested pity, so
interested that it made and still makes appear

false and odious to me the pity which I shewed
and am still shewing for Nuti.

I feel that, as a witness of the sacrifice (without doubt involuntary) which he has made of
Signorina Luisetta's heart, I, who seek to obey
my true feelings, ought to have withdrawn my
pity from him. I did indeed withdraw it inwardly, to pour it all upon that poor, tormented
little heart, but I continued to shew pity for him,
seeing that I could do no less, compelled by her
sacrifice, which was even greater. If she actually
subjected herself to that torture *out of pity* for
him, could I, could the rest of us shrink from
devotion, fatigue, proofs of Christian charity
that were far less? For me to draw back meant
my admitting and letting it be seen that she was
undergoing this torture not *out of pity only,* but
also *for love* of him, indeed principally *for love.*
And that could not, must not be. I have had to
pretend, because she has had to believe that she
was bestowing her love upon him for that other
woman. And I have pretended, albeit with self-
contempt, marvellously. Only in this way have
I been able to modify her attitude towards myself; to make her my friend again. And yet, by
shewing myself for her sake so compassionate towards Nuti, I have perhaps lost the one way that
remained to me of calling her back to herself;
that, namely, of proving to her that Duccella, on
whose behalf she imagines that she loves him,

has no reason whatever to feel any pity for him.
Were I to give Duccella her true shape, her
ghost, that loving and pitiful ghost, into which
she, Signorina Luisetta, has transformed herself,
would have to vanish, and leave her, Signorina
Luisetta, with her love *unjustified* and in no way
sought by him: because he has sought it from
the other, not from her, and she has given it
to him for the other, and not for herself, thus
publicly, before us all.

Very good, but if I know that she has really
given it to him, beneath this pious fiction of pity,
upon which I am now weaving sophistries?

As Aldo Nuti thinks Duccella hard and cruel,
so she would think me hard and cruel, were I
to tear from her the veil of this pious fiction.
She is a sham Duccella, simply because she is
in love; and she knows that the true Duccella
has not the slightest reason to be in love; she
knows it from the very fact that Aldo Nuti, now
that his hallucination has passed, no longer sees
any sign of love in her, and sadly just thanks
her for her pity.

Perhaps, at the cost of suffering a little more,
she might cover herself, but only on condition
that Duccella became really pitiful, upon learning the wretched plight to which her former
sweetheart had been brought, and appeared in
person here, by the bed upon which he lies, to
give him her love again and so to save him.

But Duccella will not come. And Signorina
Luisetta will continue to pretend to all of us and
also to herself, in good faith, that it is for her
sake that she is in love with Aldo Nuti.

§ 4

What fools all the people are who declare that
life is a mystery, wretches who seek to explain
by the use of reason what reason is powerless to
explain!

To set life before one as an object of study
is absurd, because life, when set before one like
that, inevitably loses all its real consistency and
becomes an abstraction, void of meaning and
value. And how after that is it possible to explain it to oneself? You have killed it. The
most you can do now is to dissect it.

Life is not explained; it is lived.

Reason exists in life; it cannot exist apart
from it. And life is not to be set before one,
but felt within one and lived. How many of us,
emerging from a passion as we emerge from a
dream, ask ourselves:

"I? How can I have been like that? How
could I do such a thing?"

We are no longer able to account for it; just
as we are powerless to explain how other people
can give a meaning and a value to certain things
which for us have ceased or have not yet begun

to have either. The reason, which lies in these things, we seek outside them. Can we find it? Outside life there is nullity. To observe this nullity, with the reason which abstracts itself from life, is still to live, is still a *nullity* in our life: a sense of mystery: religion. It may be desperate, if it has no illusions; it may appease itself by plunging back into life, no longer as of old but there, into that *nullity,* which at once becomes *all.*

How clearly I have learned all this in a few days, since I began really to feel! I mean, since I began to feel *myself also,* for other people I have always felt within me, and have found it easy therefore to explain them to myself and to sympathise with them.

But the feeling that I have of myself, at this moment, is most bitter.

On your account, Signorina Luisetta, for all that you are so compassionate! Indeed, just because you are so compassionate. I cannot say it to you, I cannot make you understand. I would rather not say it to myself, I would rather not understand it myself either. But no, I am no longer *a thing,* and this silence of mine is no longer an *inanimate* silence. I wished to draw other people's attention to this silence, but now I *suffer* from it myself, so keenly.

I go on, nevertheless, welcoming everyone into it. I feel, however, that everyone hurts me now

who comes into it, as into a place of certain
hospitality. My silence would like to draw ever
more closely round about me.

Here, in the meantime, is Cavalena, who has
settled himself in it, poor man, as in his own
home. He comes, whenever he can, to talk over
with me, always with fresh arguments, or on
the most futile pretexts, his own misfortunes.
He tells me that it is impossible, on account of
his wife, to keep Nuti in the house any longer,
and that I shall have to find him a lodging elsewhere, as soon as he has recovered. Two dramas,
side by side, cannot be kept going. Especially
since Nuti's drama is one of passion, of women.
. . . Cavalena requires lodgers with judgment
and self-control. He would gladly pay out of
his own pocket to have all men serious, dignified, pure and enjoying a spotless reputation for
chastity, with which to crush his wife's furious
hatred for the whole of the male sex. It falls to
him every evening to pay the penalty—the fine,
he calls it—for all the misdeeds of men, recorded
in the columns of the newspapers, as though he
were the author or the necessary accomplice of
every seduction, of every adultery.

"You see?" his wife screams at him, her finger
pointing to the paragraph in the paper: "You
see what *you men* are capable of?"

And in vain does the poor wretch try to make
her see that in each case of adultery, for every

erring man who betrays his wife, there must be also an erring woman, his accomplice in the betrayal. Cavalena thinks that he has found a triumphant argument, instead of which he sees Signora Nene's mouth form that round O with her finger across it, the familiar expression which means:

"Fool!"

Excellent logic! That we know! And does not Signora Nene hate the whole of the female sex as well?

Drawn on by the unreal, pressing arguments of that terrible reasoning insanity which never comes to a halt at any conclusion, he always finds himself, in the end, lost or bewildered, in a false situation, from which he has no idea how to escape. Why, inevitably! If he is compelled to alter, to complicate the most obvious and natural things, to conceal the simplest and commonest actions; an acquaintance, an introduction, a chance meeting, a look, a smile, a word, in which his wife might suspect who knows what secret understandings and plots; then inevitably, even when he is engaged upon an abstract discussion with her, there must emerge incidents, contradictions which all of a sudden, unexpectedly, reveal him and represent him, with every appearance of truth, a liar and impostor. Revealed, caught out in his own innocent deception, which however he himself now sees cannot any longer appear innocent in his wife's eyes; exasperated, with his back to the wall, in the face of the evidence, he still persists in denying it, and so, over and over again, for no reason, they come to quarrels, scenes, and Cavalena escapes from the house and stays away for a fortnight or three weeks, until he is once more conscious of being a doctor and the thought recurs to him of his abandoned daughter, "poor, dear, sweet little soul," as he calls her.

It is a great pleasure to me when he begins to talk to me of her; but for that very reason I never do anything to incite him to speak of her: I should feel that I was taking a base advantage of her father's weakness to penetrate, by way of his confidences, into the private life of that poor, dear, sweet little soul. No, no! Often I have even been on the point of forbidding him to continue.

Ages ago, it seems to Cavalena, his Sesè ought to have married, to have had a life of her own away from the hell of this house! Her mother, on the other hand, does nothing but shout at her, day after day:

"Never marry, mind! Don't marry, you fool! Don't do anything so mad!"

"And Sesè? Sesè?" I feel tempted to ask him; but, as usual, I remain silent.

Poor Sesè, perhaps, does not know herself what she would like to do. Perhaps, on some days, like her father, she would wish it to be to-morrow; on other days she will feel the bitterest disgust when she sees some hint of it pass between her parents. For undoubtedly they, with their degrading scenes, must have rent asunder all her illusions, all of them, one after another, shewing her through the rents the most sickening crudities of married life.

They have prevented her, meanwhile, from securing her freedom in any other way, the means of providing henceforward for herself, of being able to leave this house and live on her own. They will have told her that, thank heaven, there is no need for her to do so: an only child, she will some day have the whole of her mother's fortune for herself. Why degrade herself by becoming a teacher or looking out for some other employment? She can read, study what she pleases, play the piano, do embroidery, a free woman in her own home.

A fine freedom!

The other evening, fairly late, when we had all left the room in which Nuti had already fallen asleep, I saw her sitting on the balcony. We live in the last house in Via Veneto, and have in front of us the open space of the Villa Borghese. Four little balconies on the top floor, on the cornice of the building. Cavalena was sitting on another balcony, and appeared to be lost in contemplation of the stars.

Suddenly, in a voice that seemed to come from

a distance, almost from the sky, suffused with infinite pain, I heard him say:

"Sesè, do you see the Pleiads?"

She pretended to look: perhaps her eyes were filled with tears.

And her father:

"There they are . . . above your head . . . that little cluster of stars . . . do you see them?"

She nodded her head; yes, she saw them.

"Fine, aren't they, Sesè? And do you see how bright Capella is?"

The stars . . . Poor Papa! A fine distraction. . . . And with one hand he straightened, stroked on his temples the curling locks of his artistic wig, while with the other . . . what? Why, yes . . . he was holding on his knee Piccinì, his enemy, and was stroking her head. . . . Poor Papa! This must be one of his most tragic and pathetic moments!

There came from the Villa a long, slow slight rustle of leaves; from the deserted street an occasional sound of footsteps and the rapid clattering sound of a carriage driven in haste. The clang of the bell and the long-drawn whine of the trolley running along the electric wire of the tramway seemed to tear the street apart and fling it violently in its wake, with the houses and trees. Then all was silent, and in the weary calm returned the distant sound of a piano from one of the houses. It was a gentle, almost veiled, melancholy sound, which drew the spirit, fixed it at a definite point, as though to enable it to perceive how heavy was the cloak of sadness suspended over everything.

Ah, yes—Signorina Luisetta was perhaps thinking—marriage. . . . She was imagining, perhaps, that it was she who was playing, in a strange house, far away, that piano, to lull to sleep the pain of the sad, early memories which have poisoned her life for all time.

Will it be possible for her to illude herself? Will she be able to prevent from falling, withered, like the petals of flowers, on the silent air, chill with a want of confidence that is now perhaps insuperable, all the innocent graces that from time to time spring up in her soul?

I observe that she is spoiling herself, deliberately; she makes herself, every now and then, hard, bristling, so as not to appear tender and credulous. Perhaps she would like to be gay, frolicsome, as in more than one light moment of oblivion, when she has just risen from her bed, her eyes have suggested to her, from her mirror: those eyes of hers, which would so gladly laugh, keen and brilliant, and which she instead condemns to appear absent, or shy and sullen. Poor, lovely eyes! How often under her knitted brows does she not fix them on the empty air, while through her nostrils she breathes a long sigh in silence, as though she did not wish it to reach

even her own ears! And how they cloud over
and change colour, whenever she breathes one of
those silent sighs.

Certainly she must have learned long ago to
distrust her own impressions, perhaps in the
fear lest she be gradually seized by the same
malady as her mother. This is clearly shewn by
her abrupt changes of expression, a sudden pallor following a sudden crimson flushing of her
whole face, a smiling return to serenity after
a fleeting cloud. Who knows how often, as she
walks the streets with her father and mother, she
must feel herself stabbed by every sound of
laughter, and how often she must have the
strange feeling that even that little blue frock,
of Swiss silk, light as a feather, is weighing upon
her like the habit of a cloistered nun and that
the straw hat is crushing her head; and be
tempted to tear off the blue silk, to wrench the
straw from her head and tear it in pieces furiously with both hands and fling it . . . in her
mother's face? No . . . in her father's, then?
No . . . on the ground, on the ground, trampling
it underfoot. Because it must seem to her a
masquerade, an idiotic farce, to go about dressed
like that, like a respectable person, like a young
lady who is under the illusion that she is cutting
a figure, or rather who lets it be seen that she
has some beautiful dream in her mind, when
presently at home, and even now in the street,

everything that is most ugly, most brutal, most
savage in life must be disclosed, must spring to
light in those almost daily scenes between her
parents, to smother her in misery and shame
and disgrace.

And this reflexion more than any other seems
to me to have profoundly penetrated her soul:
that in the world, as her parents create it for
themselves and round about her with their comic
appearance, with the grotesque absurdity of that
furious jealousy, with the disorder of their existence, there can be no room, air nor light for her
charm. How can charm shew itself, breathe, refresh itself in a delicate, light and airy hue, in
the midst of that ridicule which holds it down
and stifles and obscures it?

She is like a butterfly cruelly fastened down
with a pin, while still alive. She dares not beat
her wings, not only because she has no hope of
freeing herself, but also and even more because
she might attract attention.

§ 5

I have landed in a regular volcanic region.
Eruptions and earthquakes without end. A big
volcano, apparently snow-clad but inwardly in
perpetual ebullition, Signora Nene. That one
knew. But now there has come to light, unexpectedly, and has given its first eruption a little
volcano, in whose bowels the fire has been lurk-

ing, hidden and threatening, albeit kindled but a few days ago.

The cataclysm was brought about by a visit from Polacco, this morning. Having come to persist in his task of persuading Nuti that he ought to leave Rome and return to Naples, to complete his convalescence, and after that should resume his travels, to distract his mind and be cured altogether, he had the painful surprise of finding Nuti up, as pale as death, with his moustache shaved clean to shew his firm intention of beginning at once, this very day, his career as an actor with the Kosmograph.

He shaved his moustache himself, as soon as he left his bed. It came as a surprise to all of us as well, because only last night the Doctor ordered him to keep absolutely quiet, to rest and not to leave his bed, except for an hour or so before noon; and last night he promised to obey these instructions.

We stood open-mouthed when we saw him appear shaved like that, completely altered, with that face of death, still not very steady on his legs, exquisitely attired.

He had cut himself slightly in shaving, at the left corner of his mouth; and the dried blood, blackening the cut, stood out against the chalky pallor of his face. His eyes, which now seemed enormous, with their lower lids stretched, as it were, by his loss of flesh, so as to shew the white of the eyeball beneath the line of the cornea, wore in confronting our pained stupefaction a terrible, almost a wicked expression of dark contempt and hatred.

"What in the world . . . " exclaimed Polacco.

He screwed up his face, almost baring his teeth, and raised his hands, with a nervous tremor in all his fingers; then, in the lowest of tones, indeed almost without speaking, he said:

"Leave me, leave me alone!"

"But you aren't fit to stand!" Polacco shouted at him.

He turned and looked at him suspiciously:

"I can stand. Don't worry me. I have . . . I have to go out . . . for a breath of air."

"Perhaps it is a little soon, you know," Cavalena tried to intervene, "if you will allow me. . . . "

"But I tell you, I want to go out!" Nuti cut him short, barely tempering with a wry smile the irritation that was apparent in his voice.

This irritation springs from his desire to tear himself away from the attentions which we have been paying him recently, and which may have given us (though not me, I assure you) the illusion that he in a sense belongs to us from now onwards, is one of ourselves. He feels that this desire is held in check by his respect for the debt of gratitude which he owes to us, and sees no other way of breaking that bond of respect than by shewing indifference and contempt for his own health and welfare, so that we may begin to feel a resentment for the attentions we have paid him, and this resentment, at once creating a breach between him and ourselves, may absolve him from that debt of gratitude. A man in that state of mind dares not look people in the face. And for that matter he, this morning, was not able to look any of us straight in the face.

Polacco, confronted by so definite a resolution, could see no other way out of the difficulty than to post round about him to watch, and, if need be, to defend him, as many of us as possible, and principally one who more than any of us has shewn pity for him and to whom he therefore owes a greater consideration; and, before going off with him, begged Cavalena emphatically to follow them at once to the Kosmograph, with Signorina Luisetta and myself. He said that Signorina Luisetta could not leave the film half-finished in which by accident she had been called upon to play a part, and that such a desertion would moreover be a real pity, because everyone was agreed that, in that short but by no means easy part, she had shewn a marvellous aptitude, which might lead, by his intervention, to a contract with the Kosmograph, an easy, safe and thoroughly respectable source of income, under her father's protection.

Seeing Cavalena agree enthusiastically to this

proposal, I was more than once on the point of going up to him to pluck him gently by the sleeve.

What I feared did, as a matter of fact, occur.

Signora Nene assumed that it was all a plot engineered by her husband—Polacco's morning call, Nuti's sudden decision, the offer of a contract to her daughter—to enable him to go and flirt with the young actresses at the Kosmograph. And no sooner had Polacco left the house with Nuti than the volcano broke out in a tremendous eruption.

Cavalena at first tried to stand up to her, putting forward the anxiety for Nuti which obviously—as how in the world could anyone fail to see—had suggested this idea of a contract to Polacco. What? She didn't care two pins about Nuti? Well, neither did he! Let Nuti go and hang himself a hundred times over, if once wasn't enough! It was a question of seizing this golden opportunity of a contract for Luisetta! It would compromise her? How in the world could she be compromised, under the eyes of her father?

But presently, on Signora Nene's part, argument ended, giving way to insults, vituperation, with such violence that finally Cavalena, indignant, exasperated, furious, rushed out of the house.

I ran after him down the stairs, along the

street, doing everything in my power to stop him, repeating I don't know how many times:

"But you are a Doctor! You are a Doctor!"

A Doctor, indeed! For the moment he was a wild beast in furious flight. And I had to let him escape, so that he should not go on shouting in the street.

He will come back when he is tired of running about, when once again the phantom of his tragi-comic destiny, or rather of his conscience, appears before him, unrolling the dusty parchment certificate of his medical degree.

In the meantime, he will find a little breathing-space outside.

Returning to the house, I found, to my great and painful surprise, an eruption of the little volcano; an eruption so violent that the big volcano was almost overwhelmed by it.

She no longer seemed herself, Signorina Luisetta! All the disgust accumulated in all these years, from a childhood that had passed without ever a smile amid quarrels and scandal; all the disgraceful scenes which they had made her witness, she hurled in her mother's face and at the back of her retreating father. Ah, so her mother was thinking now of her being compromised? When for all these years, with her idiotic, shameful insanity, she had destroyed her daughter's existence, irreparably! Submerged in the sickening shame of a family which no one

could approach without a feeling of revulsion!
It was not compromising her, then, to keep her
tied to that shame? Did her mother not hear
how everyone laughed at her and at such a
father? She had had enough, enough, enough!
She had no wish to be tormented any longer by
that laughter; she wished to free herself from
the disgrace, and to make her escape by the way
that was opening now before her, unsought, along
which nothing worse could conceivably befall
her! Away! Away! Away!

She turned to me, heated and trembling.

"You come with me, Signor Gubbio! I am
going to my room to put on my hat, and then let
us start at once!"

She ran off to her room. I turned to look at
her mother.

Left speechless before her daughter who had
at last risen to crush her with a condemnation
which she at once felt to be all the more deserved
inasmuch as she knew that the thought of her
daughter's being compromised was nothing more,
really, than an excuse brought forward to prevent
her husband from accompanying the girl to the
Kosmograph; now, left face to face with me, with
drooping head, her hands pressed to her bosom,
she was endeavouring in a hoarse groan to
liberate the cry of grief from her wrung, contracted bowels.

It pained me to see her.

All of a sudden, before her daughter returned, she raised her hands from her bosom and joined them in supplication, still powerless to speak, her whole face contracted in expectation of the tears which she had not yet succeeded in drawing up from their fount. In this attitude, she said to me with her hands what certainly she would never have said to me with her lips. Then she buried her face in them and turned away, as her daughter entered the room.

I drew the latter's attention, pityingly, to her mother as she went off sobbing to her own room.

"Would you like me to go by myself?" Signorina Luisetta said menacingly.

"I should like you," I answered sadly, "at least to calm yourself a little first."

"I shall calm myself on the way," she said, "Come along, let us be off."

And a little later, when we had got into a carriage at the end of Via Veneto, she added:

"Anyhow, you'll see, we are certain to find Papa at the Kosmograph."

What made her add this reflexion? Was it to free me from the thought of the responsibility she was making me assume, in obliging me to accompany her? Then she is not really sure of her freedom to act as she chooses. In fact, she at once went on:

"Does it seem to you a possible life?"

"But if it is madness!" I reminded her. "If,

as your father says, it is a typical form of paranoia?"

"Quite so, but for that very reason! Is it possible to go on living like that? When people have trouble of that sort, they can't have a home any more; nor a family; nor anything. It is an endless struggle, and a desperate one, believe me! It can't go on! What is to be done? What is to stop it? One flies off one way, another another. Everyone sees us, everyone knows. Our house stands open to the world. There is nothing left to keep secret! We might be living in the street. It is a disgrace! A disgrace! Besides, you never know, perhaps this meeting violence with violence will make her shake off this madness which is driving us all mad! At least, I shall be doing something . . . I shall see things, I shall move about . . . I shall shake off this degradation, this desperation!"

"But if for all these years you have put up with this desperation, how in the world can you now, all of a sudden," I found myself asking her, "rebel so fiercely?"

If, immediately after that little part which she had played in the Bosco Sacro, Polacco had suggested engaging her at the Kosmograph, would she not have recoiled from the suggestion, almost with horror? Why, of course! And yet the conditions at home were just the same then.

Whereas now here she is racing off with me

to the Kosmograph! In desperation? Yes, but not on account of that mother of hers who gives her no peace.

How pale she turned, how ready she seemed to faint, as soon as her father, poor Cavalena, appeared with a face of terror in the doorway of the Kosmograph to inform us that "he," Aldo Nuti, was not there, and that Polacco had telephoned to the management to say that he would not be coming there that day, so that there was nothing for it but to turn back.

"I can't myself," I said to Cavalena. "I have to remain here. I am very late as it is. You must take the Signorina home."

"No, no, no, no!" shouted Cavalena. "I shall keep her with me all day; but afterwards I shall bring her back here, and you will oblige me, Signor Gubbio, by seeing her home, or she shall go alone. I, no; I decline to set foot in the house again! That will do, now! That will do!"

And off he went, accompanying his protests with an expressive gesture of his head and hands. Signorina Luisetta followed her father, shewing clearly in her eyes that she no longer saw any reason for what she had done. How cold the little hand was that she held out to me, and how absent her glance and hollow her voice, when she turned to take leave of me and to say to me:

"Till this evening."

Book VI

OF THE NOTEBOOKS OF SERAFINO GUBBIO CINEMATOGRAPH OPERATOR

BOOK VI

§ 1

SWEET and cool is the pulp of winter pears,
but often, here and there, it hardens in a
bitter knot. Your teeth, in the act of biting, come
upon the hard piece and are set on edge. So
is it with our position, which might be sweet and
cool, for two of us at any rate, were we not conscious of the intrusion of something bitter and
hard.

We have been going together, for the last three
days, every morning, Signorina Luisetta, Aldo
Nuti and I, to the Kosmograph.

Of the two of us, Signora Nene trusts me, certainly not Nuti, with her daughter. But the said
daughter, of the two of us, certainly seems rather
to be going with Nuti than to be coming with me.

Meanwhile:

I see Signorina Luisetta, and do not see
Nuti;

Signorina Luisetta sees Nuti and does not
see me;

Nuti sees neither me nor Signorina Luisetta.

So we proceed, all three of us, side by side,

but without seeing ourselves in one another's company.

Signorina Nene's confidence ought to irritate me, ought to . . . what else? Nothing. It ought to irritate me, it ought to degrade me: instead of which, it does not irritate me, it does not degrade me. It moves me, if anything. So as to make me feel more contemptuous than ever.

And so I consider the nature of this confidence, in an attempt to overcome my contemptuous emotion.

It is certainly an extraordinary tribute to my incapacity, on one hand; to my capacity, on the other. The latter—I mean the tribute to my capacity—might in one respect flatter me; but it is quite certain that this tribute has not been paid me by Signora Nene without a slight trace of derisive pity.

A man who is incapable of doing evil cannot, in her eyes, be a man at all. So that this other capacity of mine cannot be a manly quality.

It appears that we cannot help doing evil, if we are to be regarded as men. For my own part, I know quite well, perfectly well, that I am a man: evil I have done, and in abundance! But it appears that other people do not choose to notice it. And that makes me furious. It makes me furious because, obliged to assume that certificate of incapacity—which both is and is not mine—I often find my shoulders bowed, by the

arrogance of other people, under a fine cloak of
hypocrisy. And how often have I groaned beneath the weight of that cloak! At no time, I
am certain, so often as during the last few days.
I feel almost inclined to go and look Signora
Nene in the face in a certain fashion, so that.
. . . But, no, no, what an idea, poor woman! She
has grown so meek, all of a sudden, so helpless
rather, after that furious outbreak by her daughter and this sudden determination to become a
cinematograph actress! You ought to see her
when, shortly before we leave the house, every
morning, she comes up to me and, behind her
daughter's back, raises her hands ever so
slightly, with a furtive movement, and with a
piteous look in her eyes:

"Take care of her," she stammers.

The situation, as soon as we arrive at the
Kosmograph, changes and becomes highly serious, notwithstanding the fact that at the entrance,
every morning, we find—punctual to a second and
trembling all over with anxiety—Cavalena. I
have already told him, the day before yesterday and again yesterday, of the change in his
wife; but Cavalena shews no sign as yet of becoming a Doctor again. Far from it! The day
before yesterday and again yesterday, he seemed
to be carried away before my eyes in a fit of
distraction, as though trying not to let himself
be affected by what I was saying to him:

"Oh, indeed? Good, good . . . " was his answer. "But I, for the present. . . . What is that you say? No, excuse me, I thought. . . . I am glad, don't you know? But if I go back, it will all come to an end. Heaven help us! What I have to do at present is to stay here and consolidate Luisetta's position and my own."

Ah yes, consolidate: father and daughter might be treading on air. I reflect that their life might be easy and comfortable, their story unfold in a sweet, serene peace. There is the mother's fortune; Cavalena, honest man, could attend quietly to his profession; there would be no need to take strangers into their home, and Signorina Luisetta, on the window sill of a peaceful little house in the sun, might gracefully cultivate, like flowers, the fairest dreams of girlhood. But no! This fiction which ought to be the reality, as everyone sees, for everyone admits that Signora Nene has absolutely no reason to torment her husband, this thing which ought to be the reality, I say, is a dream. The reality, on the other hand, must be something different, utterly remote from this dream. The reality is Signora Nene's madness. And in the reality of this madness—which is of necessity an agonised, exasperated disorder—here they are flung out of doors, straying, helpless, this poor man and this poor girl. They wish to consolidate their position, both of them, in this reality of madness, and so they have been wandering about here for the last two days, side by side, sad and speechless, through the studios and grounds.

Cocò Polacco, to whom with Nuti they report on their arrival, tells them that there is nothing for them to do at present. But the engagement is in force; the salary is mounting up. It is unnecessary, therefore, for Signorina Luisetta to take the trouble to come; if she is not to *pose*, she does not lose anything.

But this morning, at last, they have made her *pose*. Polacco lent her to his fellow producer Bongarzoni for a small part in a coloured film, in eighteenth century costume.

I have been working for the last few days with Bongarzoni. On reaching the Kosmograph I hand over Signorina Luisetta to her father, go to the Positive Department to fetch my camera, and often it happens that for hours on end I see nothing more of Signorina Luisetta, nor of Nuti, nor of Polacco, nor of Cavalena. So that I was not aware that Polacco had given Bongarzoni Signorina Luisetta for this small part. I was thunderstruck when I saw her appear before me as if she had stepped out of a picture by Watteau.

She was with the Sgrelli, who had just completed a careful and loving supervision of her toilet in the "costume" wardrobe, and with one finger was pressing to her cheek a silken patch

that refused to stick. Bongarzoni was lavish
with his compliments, and the poor child made
an effort to smile without moving her head, for
fear of overbalancing the enormous pile of hair
above it. She did not know how to move her
limbs in that billowing silken skirt.

And now the little scene is arranged. An outside staircase, leading down to a stretch of park.
The little lady appears from a glazed balcony;
trips down a couple of steps; leans over the
pillared balustrade to gaze out across the park,
timid, perplexed, in a state of anxious alarm:
then runs quickly down the remaining steps and
hides a note, which is in her hand, under the
laurel that is growing in a bowl on the pillar at
the foot of the balustrade.

"Are you ready? Shoot!"

Never before have I turned the handle of my
machine with such delicacy. This great black
spider on its tripod has had her twice, now, for
its dinner. But the first time, out in the Bosco
Sacro, my hand, in turning the handle to give
her to the machine to eat, did not yet *feel*.
Whereas, on this occasion . . .

Ah, I am ruined, if ever my hand begins to
feel! No; Signorina Luisetta, no: it is evident
that you must not continue in this vile trade.
Quite so, I know why you are doing it! They
all tell you, Bongarzoni himself told you this
morning that you have a quite exceptional nat-

ural gift for the scenic art; and I tell you so too; not because of this morning's rehearsal, though. Oh, you went through your part as well as anyone could wish; but I know very well, I know very well how you were able to give such a marvellous rendering of anxious alarm, when, after coming down the first two steps, you leaned over the balustrade to gaze into the distance. I know so well that almost, now and then, I turned my head too to gaze where you were gazing, to see whether at that moment the Nestoroff might not have arrived.

For the last three days, here, you have been living in this state of anxiety and alarm. Not you only; although more, perhaps, than anyone else. At any moment, indeed, the Nestoroff may arrive. She has not been seen for more than a week. But she is in Rome; she has not left. Only Carlo Ferro has left, with five or six other actors and Bertini, for Taranto.

On the day of Carlo Ferro's departure (about a fortnight ago), Polacco came to me radiant, as though a stone had been lifted from his chest.

"What did I tell you, simpleton? He would go to hell if she told him to!"

"I only hope," I answered, "that we shan't see him burst in here suddenly like a bomb."

But it is already a great thing, certainly, and one that to me remains inexplicable, that he should have gone.　His words still echo in my ears:

"I may be a wild beast when I'm face to face with a man, but as a man face to face with a wild beast I'm worth nothing!"

And yet, with the consciousness of being worth nothing, on a point of honour, he did not draw back, he did not refuse to face the beast; now, having a man to face, he has fled.　Because it is indisputable that his departure, the day after Nuti's arrival, has every appearance of flight.

I do not deny that the Nestoroff has such power over him that she can compel him to do what she wishes.　But I have heard roaring in him, simply because of Nuti's coming, all the fury of jealousy.　His rage at Polacco's having put him down to kill the tiger was not due only to the suspicion that Polacco was hoping in this way to get rid of him, but also and even more to the suspicion that he has made Nuti come here at the same time in order that Nuti may be free to recapture the Nestoroff.　And it seems obvious to me that he is not sure of her.　Why then has he gone?

No, no: there is most certainly something behind this, a secret agreement; this departure must be concealing a trap.　The Nestoroff could never have induced him to go by shewing him that she was afraid of losing him, in any event, by allowing him to remain here to await the com-

ing of a man who was certainly coming with the
deliberate intention of provoking him. A fear
of that sort would never have made him go. Or,
at least, she would have gone with him. If she
has remained here and he has gone, leaving the
field clear for Nuti, it means that an agreement
must have been reached between them, a net
woven so strongly and securely that he himself
has been able to pack up his jealousy in it and so
keep it in check. No sign of fear can she have
shewn him; rather, the agreement having been
reached, she must have demanded this proof of
his faith in her, that he should leave her here alone
to face Nuti. In fact, for several days after
Carlo Ferro's departure, she continued to come
to the Kosmograph, evidently prepared for an
encounter with Nuti. She cannot have come for
any other reason, free as she now is from any
professional engagement. She ceased to come,
when she learned that Nuti was seriously ill.

But now, at any moment, she may return.

What is going to happen?

Polacco is once again on tenterhooks. He
never lets Nuti out of his sight; if he is obliged
to leave him for a moment, he first of all makes
a covert signal to Cavalena. But Nuti, for all
that, now and again, some slight obstacle makes
him break out in a way that points to an exasperation forcibly held in check, is relatively calm;
he seems also to have shaken off the sombre

mood of the early days of his convalescence; he allows himself to be led about everywhere by Polacco and Cavalena; he shews a certain curiosity to make a closer acquaintance with this world of the cinematograph and has carefully visited, with the air of a stern inspector, both the departments.

Polacco, hoping to distract him, has twice suggested that he should try some part or other. He has declined, saying that he wishes to gain a little experience first by watching the others act.

"It is a labour," he observed yesterday in my hearing, after he had watched the production of a scene, "and it must also be an effort that destroys, alters and exaggerates people's expressions, this acting without words. In speaking, the action comes automatically; but without speaking. . . . "

"You speak to yourself," came with a marvellous seriousness from the little Sgrelli (La Sgrellina, as they all call her here). "You speak to yourself, so as not to force the action. . . . "

"Exactly," Nuti went on, as though she had taken the words out of his mouth.

The Sgrellina then laid her forefinger on her brow and looked all round her with an assumption of silliness which asked, with the most delicate irony:

"Who said I wasn't intelligent?"

We all laughed, including Nuti. Polacco could

hardly refrain from kissing her. Perhaps he hopes that she, Nuti having taken the place here of Gigetto Fleccia, may decide that he ought also to take Fleccia's place in her affections, and may succeed in performing the miracle of detaching him from the Nestoroff. To enhance and give ample food to this hope, he has introduced him also to all the young actresses of the four companies; but it seems that Nuti, although exquisitely polite to all of them, does not shew the slightest sign of wishing to be detached. Besides, all the rest, even if they were not already, more or less, bespoke, would take great care not to stand in the Sgrellina's way. And as for the Sgrellina, I am prepared to bet that she has already observed that she would be doing an injury, herself, to a certain young lady, who has been coming for the last three days to the Kosmograph with Nuti and with *Shoot*.

Who has not observed it? Only Nuti himself! And yet I have a suspicion that he too has observed it. And the strange thing is this, and I should like to find a way of pointing it out to Signorina Luisetta: that his perception of her feeling for him creates an effect in him the opposite of that for which she longs: it turns him away from her and makes him strain all the more ardently after the Nestoroff. Because it is obvious now that Nuti remembers having identified her, in his delirium, with Duccella; and since

he knows that she cannot and does not wish to
love him any longer, the love that he perceives
in Signorina Luisetta must of necessity appear
to him a sham, no longer pitiful, now that his
delirium has passed; but rather pitiless: a burning memory, which makes the old wound ache
again.

It is impossible to make Signorina Luisetta
understand this.

Glued by the clinging blood of a victim to his
love for two different women, each of whom re-
jects him, Nuti can have no eyes for her; he may
see in her the deception, that false Duccella, who
for a moment appeared to him in his delirium;
but now the delirium has passed, what was a pitiful deception has become for him a cruel memory,
all the more so the more he sees the phantom
of that deception persist in it.

And so, instead of retaining him, Signorina
Luisetta with this phantom of Duccella drives
him away, thrusts him more blindly than ever
into the arms of the Nestoroff.

For her, first of all; then for him, and lastly
—why not?—for myself, I see no other remedy
than an extreme, almost a desperate attempt:
that I should go to Sorrento, reappear after all
these years in the old home of the grandparents,
to revive in Duccella the earliest memory of her
love and, if possible, take her away and make
her come here to give substance to this phantom,

which another girl, here, for her sake, is desperately sustaining with her pity and love.

§ 2

A note from the Nestoroff, this morning at eight o'clock (a sudden and mysterious invitation to call upon her with Signorina Luisetta on our way to the Kosmograph), has made me postpone my departure.

I remained standing for a while with the note in my hand, not knowing what to make of it. Signorina Luisetta, already dressed to go out, came down the corridor past the door of my room; I called to her.

"Look at this. Read it."

Her eyes ran down to the signature; as usual, she turned a deep red, then deadly pale; when she had finished reading it, she fixed her eyes on me with a hostile expression, her brow contracted in doubt and alarm, and asked in a faint voice:

"What does she want?"

I waved my hands in the air, not so much because I did not know what answer to make as in order to find out first what she thought about it.

"I am not going," she said, with some confusion. "What can she want with me?"

"She must have heard," I explained, "that he . . . that Signor Nuti is staying here, and . . . "

"And?"

"She may perhaps have some message to give, I don't know . . . for him."

"To me?"

"Why, I imagine, to you too, since she asks you to come with me. . . . "

She controlled the trembling of her body; she did not succeed in controlling that of her voice:

"And where do I come in?"

"I don't know; I don't come in either," I pointed out to her. "She wants us both. . . . "

"And what message can she have to give me . . . for Signor Nuti?"

I shrugged my shoulders and looked at her with a cold firmness to call her back to herself and to indicate to her that she, in so far as her own person was concerned—she, as Signorina Luisetta, could have no reason to feel this aversion, this disgust for a lady for whose kindness she had originally been so grateful.

She understood, and grew even more disturbed.

"I suppose," I went on, "that if she wishes to speak to you also, it will be for some good purpose; in fact, it is certain to be. You take offence. . . . "

"Because . . . because I cannot . . . possibly . . . imagine . . . " she broke out, hesitating at first, then with headlong speed, her face catching fire as she spoke, "what in the world she can have to say to me, even if, as you suppose, it is for a good purpose. I . . . ''

"Stand apart, like myself, from the whole affair, you mean?" I at once took her up, with increasing coldness. "Well, possibly she thinks that you may be able to help in some way. . . . ''

"No, no, I stand apart; you are quite right," she hastened to reply, stung by my words. "I intend to remain apart, and not to have anything to do, so far as Signor Nuti is concerned, with this lady."

"Do as you please," I said. "I shall go alone. I need not remind you that it would be as well not to say anything to Nuti about this invitation."

"Why, of course not!"

And she withdrew.

I remained for a long time considering, with the note in my hand, the attitude which, quite unintentionally, I had taken up in this short conversation with Signorina Luisetta.

The kindly intentions with which I had credited the Nestoroff had no other foundation than Signorina Luisetta's curt refusal to accompany me in a secret manoeuvre which she instinctively felt to be directed against Nuti. I stood up for the Nestoroff simply because she, in inviting Signorina Luisetta to her house in my company, seems to me to have been intending to detach her from Nuti and to make her my companion, supposing her to be my friend.

Now, however, instead of letting herself be detached from Nuti, Signorina Luisetta has detached herself from me and has made me go alone to the Nestoroff. Not for a moment did she stop to consider the fact that she had been invited to come with me; the idea of keeping me company had never even 'occurred to her; she had eyes for none but Nuti, could think only of him; and my words had certainly produced no other effect on her than that of ranging me on the side of the Nestoroff against Nuti, and consequently against herself as well.

Except that, having now failed in the purpose for which I had credited the other with kindly intentions, I fell back into my original perplexity and in addition became a prey to a dull irritation and began to feel in myself also the most intense distrust of the Nestoroff. My irritation was with Signorina Luisetta, because, having failed in my purpose, I found myself obliged to admit that she had after all every reason to be distrustful. In fact, it suddenly became evident to me that I only needed Signorina Luisetta's company to overcome all my distrust. In her absence, a feeling of distrust was beginning to take possession of me also, the distrust of a man who knows that at any moment he may be caught in a snare which has been spread for him with the subtlest cunning.

In this state of mind I went to call upon the

Nestoroff, unaccompanied. At the same time
I was urged by an anxious curiosity as to what
she would have to say to me, and by the desire
to see her at close quarters, in her own house,
albeit I did not expect either from her or from
the house any intimate revelation.

I have been inside many houses, since I lost
my own, and in almost all of them, while waiting
for the master or mistress of the house to
appear, I have felt a strange sense of mingled
annoyance and distress, at the sight of the more
or less handsome furniture, arranged with taste,
as though in readiness for a stage performance.
This distress, this annoyance I feel more
strongly than other people, perhaps, because in
my heart of hearts there lingers inconsolable the
regret for my own old-fashioned little house,
where everything breathed an air of intimacy,
where the old sticks of furniture, lovingly cared
for, invited us to a frank, familiar confidence and
seemed glad to retain the marks of the use we
had made of them, because in those marks, even
if the furniture was slightly damaged by them,
lingered our memories of the life we had lived
with it, in which it had had a share. But really
I can never understand how certain pieces of
furniture can fail to cause if not actually distress at least annoyance, furniture with which
we dare not venture upon any confidence, because
it seems to have been placed there to warn us

with its rigid, elegant grace, that our anger, our
grief, our joy must not break bounds, nor rage
and struggle, nor exult, but must be controlled
by the rules of good breeding. Houses made for
the rest of the world, with a view to the part
that we intend to play in society; houses of outward appearance, where even the furniture round
us can make us blush if we happen for a moment
to find ourselves behaving in some fashion that
is not in keeping with that appearance nor consistent with the part that we have to play.

I knew that the Nestoroff lived in an expen-
sive furnished flat in Via Mecenate. I was shewn
by the maid (who had evidently been warned of
my coming) into the drawing-room; but the maid
was a trifle disconcerted owing to this previous
warning, since she expected to see me arrive
with a young lady. You, to the people who do
not know you, and they are so many, have no
other reality than that of your light trousers or
your brown greatcoat or your "English" moustache. I to this maid was a person who was to
come with a young lady. Without the young
lady, I might be some one else. Which explains
why, at first, I was left standing outside the
door.

"Alone? And your little friend?" the Nestoroff was asking me a moment later in the drawing-room. But the question, when half uttered,
between the words "your" and "little," sank,

or rather died away in a sudden change of feeling. The word "friend" was barely audible.

This sudden change of feeling was caused by the pallor of my bewildered face, by the look in my eyes, opened wide in an almost savage stupefaction.

Looking at me, she at once guessed the reason of my pallor and bewilderment, and at once she too turned pale as death; her eyes became strangely clouded, her voice failed, and her whole body trembled before me as though I were a ghost.

The assumption of that body of hers into a prodigious life, in a light by which she could never, even in her dreams, have imagined herself as being bathed and warmed, in a transparent, triumphant harmony with a nature round about her, of which her eyes had certainly never beheld the jubilance of colours, was repeated six times over, by a miracle of art and love, in that drawing-room, upon six canvases by Giorgio Mirelli.

Fixed there for all time, in that divine reality which he had conferred on her, in that divine light, in that divine fusion of colours, the woman who stood before me was now what? Into what hideous bleakness, into what wretchedness of reality had she now fallen? And how could she have had the audacity to dye with that strange coppery colour the hair which there, on those six

canvases, gave with its natural colour such frank-
ness of expression to her earnest face, with its
ambiguous smile, with its gaze plunged in the
melancholy of a sad and distant dream?

She humbled herself, shrank back as though
ashamed into herself, beneath my gaze which
must certainly have expressed a pained contempt.
From the way in which she looked at me, from
the sorrowful contraction of her eyebrows and
lips, from her whole attitude I gathered that not
only did she feel that she deserved my contempt,
but she accepted it and was grateful to me for
it, since in that contempt, which she shared, she
tasted the punishment of her crime and of her
fall. She had spoiled herself, she had dyed her
hair, she had brought herself to this wretched
reality, she was living with a coarse and violent
man, to make a sacrifice of herself: so much
was evident; and she was determined that henceforward no one should approach her to deliver
her from that self-contempt to which she had
condemned herself, in which she reposed her
pride, because only in that firm and fierce determination to despise herself did she still feel
herself worthy of the luminous dream, in which
for a moment she had drawn breath and to which
a living and perennial testimony remained to her
in the prodigy of those six canvases.

Not the rest of the world, not Nuti, but she,
she alone, of her own accord, doing inhuman

violence to herself, had torn herself from that
dream, had dashed headlong from it. Why? Ah,
the reason, perhaps, was to be sought elsewhere,
far away. Who knows the secret ways of the
soul? The torments, the darkenings, the sudden,
fatal determinations? The reason, perhaps, must
be sought in the harm that men had done to her
from her childhood, in the vices by which she
had been ruined in her early, vagrant life, and
which in her own conception of them had so outraged her heart that she no longer felt it to
deserve that a young man should with his love
rescue and ennoble it.

As I stood face to face with this woman so
fallen, evidently most unhappy and by her unhappiness made the enemy of all mankind and
most of all of herself, what a sense of degradation, of disgust assailed me suddenly at the
thought of the vulgar pettiness of the relations
in which I found myself involved, of the people
with whom I had undertaken to deal, of the importance which I had bestowed and was bestowing upon them, their actions, their feelings! How
idiotic that fellow Nuti appeared to me, and how
grotesque in his tragic fatuity as a fashionable
dandy, all crumpled and soiled in his starched
finery clotted with blood! Idiotic and grotesque
the Cavalena couple, husband and wife! Idiotic
Polacco, with his air of an invincible leader of
men! And idiotic above all my own part, the

part which I had allotted to myself of a comforter on the one hand, on the other of the guardian, and, in my heart of hearts, the saviour of a poor little girl, whom the sad, absurd confusion of her family life had led also to assume a part almost identical with my own; namely that of the phantom saviour of a young man who did not wish to be saved!

I felt myself, all of a sudden, alienated by this disgust from everyone and everything, including myself, liberated and so to speak emptied of all interest in anything or anyone, restored to my function as the impassive manipulator of a photographic machine, recaptured only by my original feeling, namely that all this clamorous and dizzy mechanism of life can produce nothing now but stupidities. Breathless and grotesque stupidities! What men, what intrigues, what life, at a time like this? Madness, crime or stupidity. A cinematographic life? Here, for instance: this woman who stood before me, with her coppery hair. There, on the six canvases, the art, the luminous dream of a young man who was unable to live at a time like this. And here, the woman, fallen from that dream, fallen from art to the cinematograph. Up, then, with a camera and turn the handle! Is there a drama here? Behold the principal character.

"Are you ready? Shoot!"

§ 3

The woman, as from the expression on my face she had at once realised my contempt for her, realised also the sense of degradation, the disgust that filled me, and the impulse that followed them.

The first, my contempt, had pleased her, possibly because she intended to make use of it for her own secret ends, submitting to it before my eyes with an air of pained humility. My sense of degradation, my disgust had not displeased her, perhaps because she herself felt them also and even more than I. What she resented was my sudden coldness, was seeing me all at once resume the cloak of my professional impassivity. And she too stiffened; looked at me coldly, and said:

"I expected to see you with Signorina Cavalena."

"I gave her your note to read," I replied. "She was just starting for the Kosmograph. I asked her to come."

"She would not?"

"She did not like to. Perhaps in her capacity as a hostess ... "

"Ah!" she threw back her head. "Why," she went on, "that was precisely why I asked her to come, because she was acting as a hostess."

"I pointed that out to her," I said.

"And she did not think that she ought to come?"

I raised my hands.

She remained for a moment in thought; then, almost with a sigh, said:

"I have made a mistake. That day (do you remember?) when we all went together to the Bosco Sacro, she struck me as so charming, and pleased, too, at having my company, I realise that she was not a hostess then. But, surely, you are her guest also?"

She smiled, hoping to hurt me, as she aimed this question at me like a treacherous blow. And indeed, notwithstanding my determination to remain aloof from everything and everyone, I did feel hurt. So much so that I replied:

"But with two guests, as you must know, one may seem more important than the other."

"I thought it was just the opposite," she replied. "You don't like her?"

"I neither like her nor dislike her, Signora."

"Is that really so? Forgive me, I have no right to expect you to be frank with me. But I decided that I would be frank with you to-day."

"And I have come . . . "

"Because Signorina Cavalena, as you tell me, wished to let it be seen that she attaches more importance to her other guest?"

"No, Signora. Signorina Cavalena said that she wished to remain apart."

"And you too?"

"I have come."

"And I thank you, most cordially. But you have come alone! And that—perhaps I am again mistaken—does not encourage me, not that I suppose for a moment, mind, that you, like Signorina Cavalena, attach more importance to the other guest; on the contrary. : . . "

"You mean?"

"That this other guest is of no importance to you whatever; not only that, but that you would actually be glad if he were to meet with some accident, if only because Signorina Cavalena, by refusing to come with you, has shewn that she placed his interests above yours. Do I make myself clear?"

"Ah, no, Signora, you are mistaken!" I exclaimed sharply.

"It does not annoy you?"

"Not in the least. That is to say . . . well, to be honest, . . . it does annoy me, but it no longer affects me personally. I do really feel that I stand apart."

"There, you see?" she interrupted me. "I feared as much, when I saw you come in by yourself. Confess that you would not feel yourself so much apart at this moment if the Signorina had come with you. . . . "

"But if I have come myself!"

"To remain apart."

"No, Signora. Listen, I have done more than you think. I have discussed the whole matter fully with that poor fellow and have tried in every possible way to make it clear to him that he has no right to expect anything after all that has happened, according to his own account at least."

"What has he told you?" asked the Nestoroff, in a tone of determination, her face darkening.

"All sorts of silly things, Signora," I replied. "He is raving. And his state is all the more alarming, believe me, since he is incapable, to my mind, of any really serious and deep feeling. As is already shewn by the fact of his coming here with a certain plan. . . . "

"Of revenge?"

"Not exactly of revenge. He doesn't know himself, even, what he feels. It is partly remorse . . . a remorse which he does not wish to feel; the irritating sting of which he feels only upon the surface, because, I repeat, he is equally incapable of a true, a sincere repentance which might mature him, make him recover his senses. And so it is partly the irritation of this remorse, which is maddening; partly rage, or rather (rage is too strong a word to apply to him) let us say vexation, a bitter vexation, which he does not admit, at having been tricked."

"By me?"

"No. He will not admit it!"

"But you think so?"

"I think, Signora, that you never took him seriously, that you made use of him to break away from. . . . "

I refused to utter the name: I pointed towards the six canvases. The Nestoroff knitted her brows, lowered her head. I stood gazing at her for a moment and, deciding to go on to the bitter end, pressed the point:

"He speaks of a betrayal. Of his betrayal by Mirelli, who killed himself because of the proof that he wished to give him that it was easy to obtain from you (if you will pardon my saying so) what Mirelli himself had failed to obtain."

"Ah, he says that, does he?" broke from the Nestoroff.

"He says it, but he admits that he never obtained anything from you. He is raving. He wishes to attach himself to you, because if he goes on like this (he says) he will go mad "

The Nestoroff looked at me almost with terror.

"You despise him?" she asked me.

I replied:

"I certainly do not admire him. Sometimes he makes me feel contempt for him, at other times pity."

She sprang to her feet as though urged by an irrepressible impulse:

"I despise," she said, "people who feel pity."

I replied calmly:

"I can quite understand your feeling like that."

"And you despise me?"

"No, Signora, far from it!"

She gazed at me for a while; smiled with a bitter disdain:

"You admire me, then?"

"I admire in you," was my answer, "what may perhaps arouse contempt in other people; the contempt, for that matter, which you yourself wish to arouse in other people, so as not to provoke their pity."

She gazed at me more fixedly; came forward until we stood face to face, and asked me:

"And don't you mean by that, in a sense, that you also feel pity for me?"

"No, Signora. Admiration. Because you know how to punish yourself."

"Indeed? so you understand that?" she said, with a change of colour, and a shudder, as though she had felt a sudden chill.

"For some time past, Signora."

"In spite of everyone's despising me?"

"Perhaps it was just because everyone despised you."

"I too have been aware of it for some time," she said, holding out her hand and clasping mine tightly. "Thank you! But I can punish other people too, you know!" she at once added, in a threatening tone, withdrawing her hand and rais-

ing it in the air with outstretched forefinger. "I
can punish other people too, without pity, because I have never sought any pity for myself
and seek none now!"

She began to pace up and down the room, repeating:

"Without pity . . . without pity. . . . "

Then, coming to a halt:

"You see?" she said, with an evil gleam in her
eyes. "I do not admire you, for instance, who
can overcome contempt with pity."

"In that case, you ought not to admire yourself either," I said with a smile. "Think for a
moment, and then tell me why you invited me
to call upon you this morning."

"You think it was out of pity for that . . .
poor fellow, as you call him?"

"For him, or for some one else, or for yourself."

"Nothing of the sort!" her denial was em
phatic. "No! No! You are mistaken! Not a
scrap of pity for anyone! I wish to be what I
am; I intend to remain myself. I asked you to
come in order that you might make him understand that I do not feel any pity for him and
never shall!"

"Still, you do not wish to do him any injury."

"I do indeed wish to do him an injury, by leaving him where he is and as he is."

"But since you are so pitiless, would you not

be doing him a greater injury if you were to call
him back to you? Instead of driving him
away. . . . ''

"That is because I wish, I myself, to remain
as I am! I should be doing a greater injury to
him, yes; but I should be conferring a benefit on
myself, since I should take my revenge upon
him instead of taking it upon myself. And what
harm do you suppose could come to me from a
man like him? I do not wish him any, you understand. Not because I feel any pity for him, but
because I prefer not to feel any for myself. I
am not interested in his sufferings, nor would it
interest me to make him suffer more. He has
had enough trouble. Let him go and weep somewhere else! I have no intention of weeping."

"I am afraid," I said, "that he has no longer
any intention of weeping either."

"Then what does he intend to do?"

"Well! Being, as I have already told you, incapable of doing anything, in the state of mind
in which he is at present, he might unfortunately
become capable of anything."

"I am not afraid of him! The point is this,
you see. I asked you to come and see me in
order to tell you this, to make you understand
this, so that you in turn may make him understand. I am not afraid that any harm can come
to me from him, not even if he were to kill me,
not even if, on his account, I had to go and end

my days in prison! I am running that risk as
well, you know! Deliberately, I have exposed
myself to that risk as well. Because I know the
man I have to deal with. And I am not afraid.
I have let myself imagine that I was feeling a little afraid; imagining that, I have
made an effort to send away from here a
man who was threatening me, and everyone, with
violence. It is not true. I have acted in cold
blood, not out of fear! Any evil, even that,
would count for less with me. Another crime,
imprisonment, death itself, would be lesser evils
to me than what I am now suffering and wish
to keep on suffering. So take care not to try
and arouse any pity in me for myself or for him.
I have none! If you have any for him, you who
have so much pity for everyone, make him, make
him go away! That is what I want from you,
simply because I am not afraid of anything!"

As she made this speech, she shewed in her
whole person a desperate rage at not really feeling what she would have liked to feel.

I remained for some time in a state of perplexity in which dismay, anguish and also admiration were mingled; then I threw up my hands,
and, so as not to make a vain promise, told her
of my plan of going down to the villa by
Sorrento.

She stood and listened to me, recoiling upon
herself, perhaps to deaden the smart that the

memory of that villa and of the two disconsolate women caused her; shut her eyes sorrowfully; shook her head; said:

"You will gain nothing."

"Who knows?" I sighed. "One can at least try."

She pressed my hand:

"Perhaps," she said, "I too shall do something for you."

I gazed at her face, with more consternation than curiosity:

"For me? What can that be?"

She shrugged her shoulders; made an effort to smile:

"I said, *perhaps*. . . . Something. You will see."

"I thank you," I added. "But really I do not see what you can possibly do for me. I have always asked so little of life, and I mean now to ask less than ever. Indeed, I ask it for nothing more, Signora."

I said good-bye to her and left the house, my thoughts filled with this mysterious promise.

What does she propose to do? In cold blood, as I supposed at the time, she has sent away Carlo Ferro, with the knowledge, which does not cause her the slightest alarm, either for herself or for him or for the rest of us, that at any moment he may come rushing upon the scene here and commit a crime on his own account. How

can she, knowing this, think of doing anything for
me? What can she do? Where do I come in,
in all this wretched entanglement? Does she intend to involve me in it in some way? With
what object? She failed to get anything out of
me, beyond an admission of my friendship long
ago with Giorgio Mirelli and of a vague sentiment now for Signorina Luisetta. She cannot
seize hold of me either by that friendship with a
man who is now dead or by this sentiment which
is already dying in me.

And yet, one never knows. I cannot set my
mind at rest.

§ 4

The villa.

Was this it? Is it possible that this was it?

And yet, there was nothing altered about it, or
very little. Only that gate, a little higher, that
pair of pillars, a little higher, replacing the little
pillars of the old days, from one of which Grandfather Carlo had had the marble tablet with his
name on it torn down.

But could this new gate have changed so completely the whole appearance of the old villa.

I saw that it was the same house, and it seemed
to me impossible that it could be; I saw that it
had remained much the same; why then did it
appear a different house?

What a tragedy! The memory that seeks to

live again, and cannot find its way among places that seem changed, that seem different, because our sentiments have changed, our sentiments are different. And yet I imagined that I had come hurrying to the villa with the sentiments of those days, the heart of long ago!

There it is. Knowing quite well that places have no other life, no other reality than that which we bestow on them, I saw myself obliged to admit with dismay, with infinite regret: "How I have changed!" The reality now is this. Something different.

I rang the bell. A different sound. But now I no longer knew whether this were due to some change in myself or to there being a different bell. How depressing!

There appeared an old gardener, without a coat, his shirt sleeves rolled up to the elbows, with a watering-can in his hand and a brimless hat perched on the crown of his head like a priest's biretta.

"Donna Rosa Mirelli?"

"Who?"

"Is she dead?"

"Who' do you mean?"

"Donna Rosa. . . . "

"Ah, you want to know if she's dead? How should I know?"

"She doesn't live here any longer?"

"I don't know what Donna Rosa you're talking about. She doesn't live here. It's Pèrsico lives here, Don Filippo, the Cavaliere."

"Has he a wife? Donna Duccella?"

"No, Sir. He's a widower. He lives in town."

"Then there's no one living here?"

"There's myself here, Nicola Tavuso, the gardener."

The flowers in the borders on either side of the path from the gate to the house, red, yellow, white, hung motionless like discs of enamel in the limpid, silent air, dripping still from their recent bath. Flowers born yesterday, but upon those old borders. I looked at them: they disconcerted me; they said that it really was Tavuso who was living there now, as far as they were concerned, that he watered them well every morning, and that they were grateful to him for it: fresh, scentless, smiling with all those drops of water.

Fortunately, there appeared on the scene an old peasant woman, all breast and belly and hips, enormous under a big basket of greenstuff, with one eye shut, imprisoned beneath its swollen red lid, and the other keenly alert, clear, sky-blue, glazed with tears.

"Donna Rosa? Eh, the old mistress. . . . Many's the long year since she left here. . . . Alive, yes, Sir, why not, poor soul? An old woman now . . . with the grandchild, yes, Sir, . . . Donna Duccella, yes, Sir. . . . Good folk!

All for God. . . . No use for this world, or anything. . . . The house here they sold, yes, Sir, years ago, to Don Filippo the *'surer.* . . . "

"Pèrsico, the Cavaliere."

"Go on, Don Nicò, everyone knows Don Filippo! Now, Sir, you come along with me, and I'll take you to Donna Rosa's, next door to the New Church."

Before leaving it, I took a final look at the villa. There was nothing left of it now; all of a sudden, nothing left; as though in a moment a cloud had passed from before my eyes. There it was: poverty-stricken, old, empty . . . nothing left! And in that case, perhaps, . . . Granny Rosa, Duccella. . . . Nothing left, of them either? Phantoms of a dream, my sweet phantoms, my dear phantoms, and nothing more?

I felt chilled. A bare, dull, icy hardness. That stout peasant's words: "Good folk! All for God. . . . No use for this world. . . . " I could feel the Church in them: hard, bare, icy. Across those green fields that smiled no longer. . . . But then?

I allowed myself to be led away. I cannot say what long account followed of that Don Filippo, who was aptly named *'surer,* because . . . a never-ending because . . . the old Government . . . not him, no, his father . . . a man of God too, he was, but . . . his father, or so the story went, at least. And with my weariness, in my

weariness, as I went, all those impressions of a
sordid reality, hard, bare, icy, . . . a donkey
covered in flies, that refused to move, the squalid
road, a crumbling wall, the fetid odour of the
stout woman. . . . Oh, what a temptation to dash
to the station and take the train home again!
Twice, three times, I was on the point of doing
it; I checked myself; said to myself: "Let us
see!"

A narrow stair, filthy, damp, almost in pitch
darkness; and the old woman shouting to me
from below:

"Straight on, keep straight on. . . . The second floor. . . . The bell is broken, Sir. . . . Knock
loud; she doesn't hear; knock loud."

As though I were deaf too. . . . "Here?" I
said to myself as I climbed the stair. "How have
they come down to this? Lost all their money?
Perhaps, two women by themselves. . . . That
Don Filippo . . . "

On the landing of the second floor, two old
doors, low in the lintel, freshly painted. By one
hung the broken cord of its bell. The other had
none. This one or that? I knocked first at this
one, loud, with my fist, once, twice, thrice. I
tried to pull the bell of the other: it did not ring.
Was it this one, then? I knocked at it, loud,
three times, four times. . . . No answer! But
how in the world? Was Duccella deaf too? Or
was she not living with her grandmother? I

knocked again, more loudly. I was turning to go, when I heard on the stair the heavy step and breathing of somebody coming up. A short, thickset woman, in one of those garments that signify devotion, with the penitential cord round her waist: a coffee-coloured garment, of devotion to Our Lady of Mount Carmel. Over her head and shoulders a *spagnoletta* of black lace; in her hand, a fat prayer-book and the key of the house.

She stopped on the landing and looked at me with pale, lifeless eyes from a fat white face ending in a flaccid chin: on her upper lip, here and there, at the corners of her mouth, a few hairs sprouted. Duccella.

I had had enough; I wished only to make my escape! Ah, if only she had remained with that apathetic, stupid air with which she stopped short in front of me, still a little breathless, on the landing! But no: she wanted to entertain me, she wanted to be polite—she, now, like that —with those eyes that were no longer hers, with that fat, colourless nun's face, with that short, stout body, and a voice, a voice and a kind of smile which I did not recognise: entertainment, compliments, ceremonies, as though I were shewing her a great condescension; and she was absolutely determined that I should come in and see her grandmother, who would be so delighted at the honour . . . why, yes, why, yes. . . .

"Step inside, please, step inside. . . . "

To remove her from my path I would have given her a shove, even at the risk of sending her flying downstairs! What a flabby horror! What an object! That deaf old woman, doddering with age, without a tooth in her head, with her pointed chin that protruded horribly towards the tip of her nose, chewing and mumbling, and her pallid tongue shewing between her flaccid, wrinkled lips, and those huge spectacles, monstrously enlarging her sightless eyes, scarred by an operation for cataract, between their sparse lashes, long as the feelers of an insect!

"You have made a position for yourself." (With the soft Neapolitan z—*posi-zzi-o-ne.*)

She could think of nothing else to say to me.

I made my escape without its ever having occurred to me for a moment to suggest the plan for which I had come. What was I to say? What was there to do? Why ask them to tell me their story? If they had really fallen into poverty, as might be supposed from the appearance of the house? Perfectly content with everything, stolid and happy with God! Oh, what a horrible thing faith is! Duccella, the blushing flower . . . Granny Rosa, the garden of the villa with its jasmines. . . .

In the train, I felt as though I were rushing towards madness, through the night. In what world was I? My travelling companion, a man

of middle age, dark, with oval eyes, like discs of
enamel, and hair that gleamed with oil, he be-
longed certainly to this world; firm and well
established in the consciousness of his own calm
and well cared for beastliness, he understood it
all to perfection, without worrying about anything; he knew quite well all that it concerned
him to know, where he was going, why he was
travelling, the house at which he would arrive,
the supper that was being prepared for him.
But I? Was I of the same world? His journey
and mine . . . his night and mine. . . . No, I
had no time, no world, no anything. The train
was his; he was travelling in it. How on earth
did I come to be travelling in it also? What was
I doing in the world in which he lived? How, in
what respect was this night mine, when I had
no means of living it, nothing to do with it? He
had his night and all the time he wanted, that
middle-aged man who was now twisting his neck
about with signs of discomfort in his immaculate
starched collar. No, no world, no time, nothing:
I stood apart from everything, absent from myself and from life; and no longer knew where I
was nor why I was there. Images I carried in me,
not my own, of things and people; images,
aspects, faces, memories of people and things
which had never existed in reality, outside me,
in the world which that gentleman saw round him

and could touch. I had thought that I saw them,
and could touch them also, but no, they were all
imagination! I had never found them again, because they had never existed: phantoms, a
dream. . . . But how could they have entered my
mind? From where? Why? Was I there too,
perhaps, then? Was there an I there then that
now no longer existed? No; the middle-aged
gentleman opposite to me told me, no: that other
people existed, each in his own way and with his
own space and time: I, no, I was not there;
albeit, not being there, I should have found it
hard to say where I really was and what I was,
being thus without time or space.

I no longer understood anything. And I
understood nothing when, arriving in Rome and
coming to the house, about ten o'clock at night,
I found in the dining-room, as gay as though
nothing had happened, as though a new life had
begun during my absence, Fabrizio Cavalena, a
Doctor once more and restored to the bosom of
his family, Aldo Nuti, Signorina Luisetta and
Signora Nene, sitting round the table.

How? Why? What had happened?

I could not get rid of the impression that they
were sitting there, gay and reconciled to one another, to make a fool of me, to reward me with
the sight of their gaiety for the trouble that I
had taken on their behalf; not only this, but that,

knowing the state of mind in which I should return from the expedition, they had clubbed together to confound me utterly, making me find here also a reality such as I should never have expected.

More than any of the rest she, Signorina Luisetta, filled me with scorn, Signorina Luisetta who was impersonating Duccella in love, that Duccella, the blushing flower, of whom I had so often spoken to her! I would have liked to shout in her face how I had found her that afternoon, down at Sorrento, that Duccella, and to bid her give up this play-acting, which was an unworthy and grotesque contamination! And he too, the young man, who seemed by a miracle to be the same young man of years ago, I would have liked to shout in his face how and where I had found Duccella and Granny Rosa.

But good souls all of you! Down there, those two poor women, happy in God, and you happy here in the devil! Dear Cavalena, why yes, changed back not merely into a Doctor, but into a boy, a bridegroom, sitting by his bride! No, thank you: there is no place for me among you: don't get up; don't disturb yourselves: I am neither hungry nor thirsty! I can do without everything, I can. I have wasted upon you a little of what is of no use to me; you know it; a little of that heart which is of no use to me;

because to me only my hand is of use: there is
no need, therefore, to thank me! Indeed, you
must excuse me if I have disturbed you. The
fault is mine, for trying to interfere. Keep
your seats, don't get up, good night.

OF THE NOTES OF SERAFINO GUBBIO
CINEMATOGRAPH OPERATOR

BOOK VII

§ 1

I UNDERSTAND, at last.

Upset? No, why should I be? So much water has passed under the bridges; the past is dead and distant. Life is here now, this life: a different life. Lawns, round about, and stages, the buildings miles away, almost in the country, between green grass and blue sky, of a cinematograph company. And she is here, an actress now. . . . He an actor too? Just fancy! Why, then, they must be colleagues? Splendid; I am so glad. . . .

Everything perfect, everything smooth as oil. Life. That rustle of her blue silk skirt, now, with that curious white lace jacket, and that little winged hat like the helmet of the god of commerce, on her copper-coloured hair . . . yes. Life. A little heap of gravel turned up by the point of her sunshade; and an interval of silence, with her eyes wandering, fixed on the point of her sunshade that is turning up that little heap of gravel.

"What? Yes, of course, dear: a great bore."

This is undoubtedly what must have happened

yesterday, during my absence. The Nestoroff, with those wandering eyes of hers, strangely wide open, must have gone to the Kosmograph on purpose, in the hope of meeting him; she must have strolled up to him with an indifferent air, as one goes up to a friend, an acquaintance whom one happens to meet again after many years, and the butterfly, without the least suspicion of the spider, must have begun to flap his wings, quite exultant.

But how in the world did not Signorina Luisetta notice anything?

Well, that is a satisfaction which Signora Nestoroff must have had to forego. Yesterday, Signorina Luisetta, to celebrate her father's return home, did not go with Signor Nuti to the Kosmograph. And so Signora Nestoroff cannot have had the pleasure of shewing this proud young lady who, the day before, had declined her invitation, how she, at any moment, whenever the fancy took her, could tear from the side of any proud young lady and recapture for herself all the mad young gentlemen who threatened tragedies, *pst!,* like that, by holding up a finger, and at once tame them, intoxicate them with the rustle of a silk skirt and a little heap of gravel turned up with the point of a sunshade. A bore, yes, a great bore unquestionably, because to this pleasure which she has had to forego Signora Nestoroff attached great importance.

That evening, knowing nothing of what had happened, Signorina Luisetta saw the young gentleman return home completely transformed, radiant with happiness. How was she to suppose that this transformation, this radiance could be due to a meeting with the Nestoroff, if, whenever she thinks with terror of that meeting, she sees red, black, confusion, madness, tragedy? And so this change, this radiance, was the effect of Papa's return home on him also? Well, that it is of any great importance to him, her father's return home, Signorina Luisetta cannot suppose, no; but that he should take pleasure in it, and seek to attune himself to other people's rejoicing, why in the world not? How else is his jubilation to be explained? And it is something to be thankful for; it is a thing to rejoice in, because this jubilation shews that his heart has become lighter, more open, so that he can readily assimilate the joy of other people.

These must certainly have been the thoughts of Signorina Luisetta. Yesterday; not to-day.

To-day she came to the Kosmograph with me, her face clouded. She had found, greatly to her surprise, that Signor Nuti had already left the house at an early hour, while it was still dark. She did not wish to display, as we went along, resentment and alarm, after the spectacle offered me last night of her gaiety; and so asked me where I had been yesterday and what I had done.

"I? Oh, only a little pleasure jaunt. . . . " And had I enjoyed myself? "Oh, immensely, to begin with at least. Afterwards. . . . " The way things happen. We make all the arrangements for a pleasure party; we imagine that we have thought of everything, have taken every precaution so that the excursion may be a success, with no unfortunate incident to mar it; and yet there is always something, one of the many things, of which we have not thought; one thing escapes us . . . well, for instance, suppose there is a family with a number of children, who propose to go and spend a fine summer day picnicking in the country, there are the second child's shoes, in one of which there is a nail, a mere nothing, a tiny nail, inside, sticking up in the heel, which needs hammering down. The mother remembered it, as soon as she got out of bed; but afterwards, you know what happens—with everything to get ready for the excursion, she forgot all about it. And that pair of shoes, with their little tongues sticking up like the pricked ears of a wily rabbit, standing in the row among all the other pairs, cleaned and polished and all ready for the children to put on, wait there and seem to be gloating in silence over the trick they are going to play on the mother who has forgotten all about them and who now, at the last moment, is in a greater bustle than ever, in wild confusion, because the father is down below at

the foot of the stair shouting to her to make
haste and all the children round her shout to her
to make haste, they are so impatient. That pair
of shoes, as the mother takes them to thrust
them hurriedly on the child's feet, say to her
with a mocking laugh:

"Ah yes, mother dear; but us, you know?
You have forgotten about us; and you'll see that
we shall spoil the whole day for you: when you
are half way there that little nail will begin to
hurt your child's foot and make it cry and limp."

Well, something of that sort happened to me
too. No, not a nail to be hammered down in my
boot. Another little detail had escaped my
memory. . . . "What?" Nothing: another little
detail. I did not wish to tell her. Another thing,
Signorina Luisetta, which perhaps had long ago
broken down in me.

To say that Signorina Luisetta paid me any
close attention would not be true. And, as we
went on our way, while I allowed my lips to go
on speaking, I was thinking:

"Ah, you are not interested, my dear child, in
what I am telling you? My misadventure leaves
you indifferent, does it? Well, you shall see
with what an air of indifference I, in my turn,
to pay you back in your own coin, am going to
receive the unpleasant surprise that is in store
for you, as soon as you enter the Kosmograph
with me: you shall see!"

In fact, before we had advanced five yards across the tree-shaded lawn in front of the first building of the Kosmograph, there we saw, strolling side by side, like the dearest of friends, Signor Nuti and Signora Nestoroff: she, with her sunshade open, resting upon her shoulder, and twirling the handle.

What a look Signorina Luisetta gave me! And I:

"You see? They are taking a quiet stroll. She is twirling her sunshade."

So pale, however, so pale had the poor child turned, that I was afraid of her falling to the ground, in a faint: instinctively I put out my hand to support her arm; she withdrew her arm angrily, and looked me straight in the face. Evidently the suspicion flashed across her mind that it was my doing, a plot on my part (by arrangement, very possibly, with Polacco), that quiet and friendly reconciliation of Nuti and Signora Nestoroff, the first-fruits of the visit paid by me to that lady two days ago, and perhaps also of my mysterious absence yesterday. It must have seemed to her a vile mockery, all this secret machination, as it entered her mind in a flash. To make her dread the imminence, day after day, of a tragedy, should those two meet; to make her conceive such a terror of their meeting; to make her suffer such agony in order to pacify his ravings with a piteous deception, which had

cost her so dear, and to what purpose? To offer
her as a final reward the delicious picture of
those two taking their quiet morning stroll under
the trees on the lawn? Oh, villainy! Was it for
this? For the amusement of laughing at a poor
child who had taken it all seriously, plunged into
the midst of this sordid, vulgar intrigue? She
looked for nothing pleasant, in the absurd,
miserable conditions of her life; but why this as
well? Why mockery also? It was vile!

All this I read in the poor child's eyes. Could
I prove to her, there and then, that her suspicion
was unjust, that life is like that—to-day more
than ever it was before—made to offer such
spectacles; and that I myself was in no way to
blame?

I had hardened my heart; I was glad that she
should pay for the injustice of her suspicion by
her suffering at that spectacle, at the sight of
those people, to whom I as well as she, unasked,
had given something of ourselves, something that
was now smarting, bruised and wounded, inside
us. But we deserved it! And now, it pleased
me to have her at this moment as my companion,
while those two strolled up and down there without so much as seeing us. Indifference, indifference, Signorina Luisetta, there you are!
"If you will excuse me," it occurred to me to
say to her, "I shall go and get my camera, and
take my place here, as is my duty, impassive."

And I felt a strange smile on my lips, which was almost the grin of a dog when he bares his teeth at some secret thought. I was looking meanwhile towards the door of the building beyond, from which emerged, coming towards us, Polacco, Bertini and Fantappiè. Suddenly there occurred a thing which I ought really to have expected, which justified Signorina Luisetta in trembling so violently and rebuked me for having chosen to remain indifferent. My mask of indifference I was obliged to throw aside in a moment, at the threat of a danger which did really seem to all of us imminent and terrible. I caught the first glimpse of it in the appearance of Polacco, who had come close up to us with Bertini and Fantappiè. They were talking among themselves, evidently of that couple who were still strolling beneath the trees, and all three were laughing at some witticism that had fallen from Fantappiè, when all of a sudden they stopped short in front of us with faces of chalk, staring eyes, all three of them. But most of all in the face of Polacco I read terror. I turned to look over my shoulder: Carlo Ferro!

He was coming up behind us, still with his travelling cap on his head, as he had left the train a few minutes earlier. And those two, meanwhile, continued to stroll up and down, together, without the least suspicion, under the trees. Did

he see them? I cannot say. Fantappiè had the
presence of mind to shout:

"Hallo, Carlo Ferro!"

The Nestoroff turned round, left her companion standing, and then one saw—free of charge—
the moving spectacle of a lion-tamer who amid
the terror of the spectators advances to meet an
infuriated animal. Calmly she advanced, without haste, still balancing her open sunshade on
her shoulder. And she had a smile on her lips,
which said to us, without her deigning to look at
us: "What are you afraid of, you idiots! I
am here, a'nt I?" And a look in her eyes which
I shall never forget, the look of one who knows
that everyone must see that no fear can find a
place in a person who looks straight ahead and
advances so. The effect of that look on the
savage face, the disordered person, the excited
gait of Carlo Ferro was remarkable. We did not
see his face, we saw his body grow limp and his
pace slacken steadily as the fascination drew
nearer to him. And the one sign that she too
must be feeling somewhat agitated was this: she
began to address him in French.

None of us cast a glance beyond her, where
Aldo Nuti remained by himself, planted among
the trees, but suddenly I became aware that one
of us, she, Signorina Luisetta, was looking in
that direction, was looking at him, and had per-

haps looked at nothing else, as though for her
the terror lay there and not in the two at whom
the rest of us were gazing, in dismayed suspense.

But nothing occurred for the moment. To
break the storm, making a great din, there
dashed upon the lawn, in the nick of time, Commendator Borgalli accompanied by various mem-
bers of the firm and employees from the
manager's office. Bertini and Polacco, who were
with us, were swept away; but the managing
director's fierce reproaches were aimed also at
the other two producers who were absent. The
work was going to pieces! No control of production; the wildest confusion; a perfect Tower of
Babel! Fifteen, twenty subjects left in the air;
the companies scattered here, there and everywhere, when it had been announced, weeks ago,
that they must be assembled and ready to get to
work on the tiger film, on which thousands and
thousands of lire had been spent! Some were off
to the hills, some to the sea; eating their heads
off! What was the use of keeping the tiger there?
There was still the whole part of the actor who
was to kill it wanting? And where was the actor?
Oh, he had just arrived, had he? How was that?
Where had he been?

Actors, supers, scene-painters had come pouring in a crowd from every direction at the shouts
of Commendator Borgalli, who had the satisfac-

tion of measuring thus the extent of his own
authority, and the fear and respect in which he
was held, by the silence in which all these people
stood round and then dispersed, when he con-
cluded his harangue with the words:

"To your work! Get along back to work!"

There vanished from the lawn, as though it
had been first of all submerged by this tide of
people, then carried away by their ebb, every
trace of the—shall we say—dramatic situation
of a moment earlier; there, in the foreground, the
Nestoroff and Carlo Ferro; beyond them, Nuti,
solitary, apart, under the trees. The ground lay
empty before us. I heard Signorina Luisetta
sobbing by my side:

"Oh, heavens, oh, heavens," and she wrung
her hands. "Oh, heavens, what next? What will
happen next?"

I looked at her with irritation, but tried, nevertheless, to comfort her:

"Why, what do you want to happen? Keep
calm! Didn't you see? All arranged beforehand. . . . At least, that is my impression. Yes,
of course, keep calm! This surprise visit from
Ferro. . . . I bet she knew all about it; I
shouldn't be surprised if she telegraphed to him
yesterday to come; why yes, of course, to let him
find her here engaged in a friendly conversation
with Signor Nuti. You may be sure that is what
it is."

"But he? He?"

"Who is *he?* Nuti?"

"If it is all a trick played by those two. . . . ''

"You are afraid he may notice it?"

"Yes! Yes!"

And the poor child began again to wring her hands.

"Well? And what if he does notice it?" said I. "You needn't worry yourself; he won't do anything. Depend upon it, this was arranged beforehand too."

"By whom? By her? By that woman?"

"By that woman. She must first have made quite certain, before talking to him, that the other man would be able to turn up in time, without any danger to anyone; keep calm! Otherwise, Ferro would not have come upon the scene."

We were quits. My statement embodied a profound contempt for Nuti; if Signorina Luisetta desired peace of mind, she was bound to accept it. She did so long to secure peace of mind, Signorina Luisetta; but on these terms, no; she would not. She shook her head violently: no, no.

There was nothing then to be done! But as a matter of fact, notwithstanding my faith in the Nestoroff's cold perspicacity, in her power, when I reminded myself of Nuti's desperate ravings, I did not feel any too certain myself that

it was with him that we should concern ourselves.
But this thought increased my irritation, already
moved by the spectacle of that poor, terrified
child. Despite my resolution to place and keep
all these people in front of my machine as food
for its hunger while I stood impassively turning
the handle, I saw myself too obliged to continue
to take an interest in them, to occupy myself with
their affairs. There came back to me also the
threats, the fierce protestations of the Nestoroff,
that she feared nothing from any man, because
any other evil—a fresh crime, imprisonment,
death itself—she would reckon as less than the
evil which she was suffering in secret and pre-
ferred to endure. Had she perhaps suddenly
grown tired of enduring it? Could this be the
reason of her deciding yesterday, during my
absence, to take the first step towards Nuti,
in contradiction of what she had said to me the
day before?

"No pity," she had said to me, "neither for
myself nor for him!"

Had she suddenly felt pity for herself? Not
for him, certainly! But pity for herself means
to her extricating herself by any means in her
power, even at the cost of a crime, from the punishment she has inflicted on herself by living
with Carlo Ferro. Suddenly making up her
mind, she has gone to meet Nuti and has made
Carlo Ferro return.

What does she want? What is going to happen
next?

This is what happened, in the meantime, at
midday beneath the pergola of the tavern, where
—dressed some of them as Indians and others
as English tourists—a crowd of actors and
actresses from the four companies had assembled. All of them were or pretended to be infuriated and upset by Commendator Borgalli's
outburst that morning, and had for some time
been taunting Carlo Ferro, letting him clearly
understand that they were indebted to him for
that outburst, he having first of all advanced all
those silly claims and then tried to back out of
the part allotted to him in the tiger film, and
having left Rome, as though there were really
a great risk attached to the killing of an animal
cowed by all those months of captivity: an insurance for one hundred thousand lire, agree-
ments, conditions, etc. Carlo Ferro was seated
at a table, a little way off, with the Nestoroff.
His face was yellow; it was quite evident that
he was making an enormous effort to control
himself; we all expected him at any moment to
break out, to turn upon us. We were, therefore,
left speechless at first when, instead of him, another man, to whom no one had given a thought,
broke out all of a sudden and turned upon him,
going up to the table at which Ferro and the
Nestoroff were sitting. It was he, Nuti, as pale

as death. In a silence that throbbed with a violent
tension, a faint cry of terror was heard, to which
Varia Nestoroff promptly replied by laying her
hand, imperiously, upon Carlo Ferro's arm.

Nuti said, looking Ferro straight in the face:
"Are you prepared to give up your place and
your part to me? I promise before everyone
here to take it on unconditionally."

Carlo Ferro did not spring to his feet nor did
he fly at the tempter. To the general amazement
he sank down, sprawled awkwardly in his chair;
leaned his head to one side, as though to look up
at the speaker, and before replying raised the arm
upon which the Nestoroff's hand was resting, saying to her:

"Please. . . . "

Then, turning to Nuti:

"You? My part? Why, I shall be delighted,
my dear Sir. Because I am a fearful coward
. . . you wouldn't believe how frightened I am
Delighted, my dear Sir, delighted!"

And he laughed, as I never saw a man laugh
before!

His laughter made us all shudder, and, what
with this general shudder and the whiplash of
his laughter, Nuti was left quite helpless, his mind
certainly vacillating from the impulse which had
driven him to face his rival and had now col-
lapsed, in the face of this awkward and teasingly
submissive reception. He looked round him, and

then, all of a sudden, at the sight of that pale, puzzled face, everyone began to laugh at him, broke into peals of loud, irrepressible laughter. The painful tension was broken in this way, in this enormous laugh of relief, at the challenger's expense. Exclamations of derision sounded here and there, like jets of water amid the clamour of the laughter: "He's cut a pretty figure!" "Caught in the trap!" "Like a mouse!"

Nuti would have done better to join in the laughter as well; but, most unfortunately, he chose to persist in the ridiculous part he had adopted, looking round for some one to whom he might cling, to keep himself afloat in this cyclone of hilarity, and stammered:

"Then . . . then, you agree? . . . I am to play the part . . . you agree!"

But even I myself, however reluctantly, at once took my eyes from him to look at the Nestoroff, whose dilated pupils gleamed with an evil light.

§ 2

Trapped. That is all. This and this only is what Nestoroff wished—that it should be he who entered the cage.

With what object? That seems to me easily understood, after the way in which she has arranged things: that is to say that everyone, first of all, heaping contempt upon Carlo Ferro whom she had persuaded or forced to go away, should insist that there was no danger involved in entering the cage, so that afterwards the challenge of Nuti's offer to enter it should seem all the more ridiculous, and, by the laughter with which that challenge was greeted, the other's self-esteem might emerge if not unscathed still with the least possible damage; with no damage at all, indeed, since, with the malign satisfaction which people feel on seeing a poor bird caught in a snare, that the snare in question was not a pleasant thing everyone is now prepared to admit; all the more credit, therefore, to Ferro who has managed to free himself from it at this sparrow's expense. In short, this to my mind is clearly what she wished: to take in Nuti, by shewing him her heartfelt determination to spare Ferro even a trifling inconvenience and the mere shadow of a remote danger, such as that of entering a cage and firing at an animal which everyone says is cowed by all these months of captivity. There: she has taken him neatly by the nose and amid universal laughter has led him into the cage.

Even the most moral of moralists, unintentionally, between the lines of their fables, allow us to observe their keen delight in the cunning of the fox, at the expense of the wolf or the rabbit or the hen: and heaven only knows what the fox

represents in those fables! The moral to be
drawn from them is always this: that the loss
and the ridicule are borne by the foolish, the
timid, the simple, and that the thing to be valued
above all is therefore cunning, even when the fox
fails to reach the grapes and says that they are
sour. A fine moral! But this is a trick that the
fox is always playing on the moralists, who, do
what they may, can never succeed in making him
cut a sorry figure. Have you laughed at the
fable of the fox and the grapes? I never did.
Because no wisdom has ever seemed to me wiser
than this, which teaches us to cure ourselves of
every desire by despising its object.

This, you understand, I am now saying of myself, who would like to be a fox and am not. I
cannot find it in me to say sour grapes to Signorina Luisetta. And that poor child, whose heart
I have not been able to reach, here she is doing
everything in her power to make me, in her company, lose my reason, my calm impassivity,
abandon the fine wise course which I have repeatedly declared my intention of following, in
short all my boasted *inanimate silence*. I should
like to despise her, Signorina Luisetta, when I
see her throwing herself away like this upon that
fool; I cannot. The poor child can no longer
sleep, and comes to tell me so every morning in
my room, with eyes that change in colour, now
a deep blue, now a pale green, with pupils that

now dilate with terror, now contract to a pair
of pin-points which seem stabbed by the most
acute anguish.

I say to her: "You don't sleep? Why not?"
prompted by a malicious desire, which I would
like to repress but cannot, to annoy her. Her
youth, the calm weather ought surely to coax
her to sleep. No? Why not? I feel a strong
inclination to force her to tell me that she lies
awake because she is afraid that he . . . Indeed?
And then: "No, no, sleep sound, everything is
going well, going perfectly. You should see the
energy with which he has set to work to inter-
pret his part in the tiger film! And he does it
really well, because as a boy he used to say that
if his grandfather had allowed it, he would have
gone upon the stage; and he would not have been
wrong! A marvellous natural aptitude; a true
thoroughbred distinction; the perfect composure
of an English gentleman following the perfidious
Miss on her travels in the East! And you ought
to see the courteous submission with which he
accepts advice from the professional actors, from
the producers Bertini and Polacco, and how delighted he is with their praise! So there is nothing to be afraid of, Signorina. He is perfectly
calm. . . . " "How do you account for that?"
"Why, in this way, perhaps, that having never
done anything, lucky fellow, in his life, now that,
by force of circumstances, he has set himself to

do something, and the very thing that at one
time he would have liked to do, he has taken a
fancy to it, finds distraction in it, flatters his
vanity with it."

No? Signorina Luisetta says no, persists in
repeating no, no, no; that it does not seem to
her possible; that she cannot believe it; that
he must be brooding over some act of violence,
which he is keeping dark.

Nothing could be easier, when a suspicion of
this sort has taken root, than to find a corrobo-
rating significance in every trifling action. And
Signorina Luisetta finds so many! And she
comes and tells me about them every morning in
my room: "He is writing," "He is frowning,"
"He never looked up," "He forgot to say good
morning. . . . "

"Yes, Signorina, and what about this; he blew
his nose with his left hand this morning, instead
of using his right!"

Signorina Luisetta does not laugh: she looks
at me, frowning, to see whether I am serious:
then goes away in a dudgeon and sends to my
room Cavalena, her father, who (I can see) is
doing everything in his power, poor man, to overcome in my presence the consternation which his
daughter has succeeded in conveying to him in
its strongest form, trying to rise to abstract considerations.

"Women!" he begins, throwing out his hands.

"You, fortunately for yourself (and may it always remain so, I wish with all my heart, Signor Gubbio!) have never encountered the Enemy upon your path. But look at me! What fools the men are who, when they hear woman called 'the enemy,' at once retort: 'But what about your mother? Your sisters? Your daughters?' as though to a man, who in that case is a son, a brother, a father, those were women! Women, indeed! One's mother? You have to consider your mother in relation to your father, and your sisters or daughters in relation to their husbands; then the true woman, the enemy will emerge! Is there anything dearer to me than my poor darling child? Yet I have not the slightest hesitation in admitting, Signor Gubbio, that even she, undoubtedly, even my Sesè is capable of becoming, like all other women when face to face with man, the enemy. And there is no goodness of heart, there is no submissiveness that can restrain them, believe me! When, at a turn in the road, you meet her, the particular woman, to whom I refer, the enemy: then one of two things must happen: either you kill her, or you have to submit, as I have done. But how many men are capable of submitting as I have done? Grant me at least the meagre satisfaction of saying very few, Signor Gubbio, very few!"

I reply that I entirely agree with him.

Whereupon: "You agree?" asks Cavalena, with

a surprise which he makes haste to conceal, fear‚ ing lest from his surprise I may divine his pur- pose. "You agree?"

And he looks me timidly in the face, as though seeking the right moment to descend, without marring our agreement, from the abstract con- sideration to the concrete instance. But here I quickly stop him.

"Good Lord, but why," I ask him, "must you believe in such a desperate resolution on Signora Nestoroff's part to be Signor Nuti's enemy?"

"What's that? But surely? Don't you think so? But she is! She is the enemy!" exclaims Cavalena. "That seems to me to be unquestion- able!"

"And why?" I persisted. "What seems to me unquestionable is that she has no desire to be his friend or his enemy or anything at all."

"But that is just the point!" Cavalena inter- rupts me. "Surely; or do you mean that we ought to consider woman in and by herself? Always in relation to a man, Signor Gubbio! The greater enemy, in certain cases, the more indifferent she is! And in this case, indifference, really, at this stage? After all the harm that she has done him? And she doesn't stop at that; she must make a mock of him, too. Really!"

I gaze at him for a while in silence, then with a sigh return to my original question:

"Very good. But why must you now believe
that the indifference and mockery of Signora
Nestoroff have provoked Signor Nuti to (what
shall I say?) anger, scorn, violent plans of revenge? On what do you base your argument?
He certainly shews no sign of it! He keeps
perfectly calm, he is looking forward with evident pleasure to his part as an English
gentleman. . . . "

"It is not natural! It is not natural!" Cavalena protests, shrugging his shoulders. "Believe
me, Signor Gubbio, it is not natural! My daughter is right. If I saw him cry with rage or grief,
rave, writhe, waste away, I should say *amen*.
You see, he is tending towards one or other alter-
native."

"You mean?"

"The alternatives between which a man can
choose when he is face to face with the enemy.
Do you follow me? But this calm, no, it is not
natural! We have seen him go mad here, for
this woman, raving mad; and now. . . . Why, it
is not natural! It is not natural!"

At this point I make a sign with my finger,
which poor Cavalena does not at first understand.

"What do you mean?" he asks me.

I repeat the sign; then, in the most placid of
tones:

"Go up higher, my friend, go up higher. . . . "

"Higher . . . what do you mean?"

"A step higher, Signor Fabrizio; rise a step above these abstract considerations, of which you began by giving me a specimen. Believe me, if you are in search of comfort, it is the only way. And it is the fashionable way, too, to-day."

"And what is that?" asks Cavalena, bewildered.

To which I:

"Escape, Signor Fabrizio, escape; fly from the drama! It is a fine thing, and it is the fashion, too, I tell you. Let yourself e-va-po-rate in (shall we say?) lyrical expansion, above the brutal necessities of life, so ill-timed and out of place and illogical; up, a step above every reality that threatens to plant itself, in its petty crudity, before our eyes. Imitate, in short, the songbirds in cages, Signor Fabrizio, which do indeed, as they hop from perch to perch, cast their droppings here and there, but afterwards spread their wings and fly: there, you see, prose and poetry; it is the fashion. Whenever things go amiss, whenever two people, let us say, come to blows or draw their knives, up, look above you, study the weather, watch the swallows dart by, or the bats if you like, count the passing clouds; note in what phase the moon is, and if the stars are of gold or silver. You will be considered original, and will appear to enjoy a vaster understanding of life."

Cavalena stares at me open-eyed: perhaps he thinks me mad.

Then: "Ah," he says, "to be able to do that!"

"The easiest thing in the world, Signor Fabrizio! What does it require? As soon as a drama begins to take shape before you, as soon as things promise to assume a little consistency and are about to spring up before you solid, concrete, menacing, just liberate from within you the madman, the frenzied poet, armed with a suction pump; begin to pump out of the prose of that mean and sordid reality a little bitter poetry, and there you are!"

"But the heart?" asks Cavalena.

"What heart?"

"Good God, the heart! One would need to be without one!"

"The heart, Signor Fabrizio! Nothing of the sort. Foolishness. What do you suppose it matters to my heart if Tizio weeps or Cajo weds, if Sompronio slays Filano, and so on? I escape, I avoid the drama, I expand, look, I expand!"

What do expand more and more are the eyes of poor Cavalena. I rise to my feet and say to him in conclusion:

"In a word, to your consternation and that of your daughter, Signor Fabrizio, my answer is this: that I do not wish to hear any more; I am weary of the whole business, and should like to send you all to blazes. Signor Fabrizio, tell your daughter this: my job is to be an operator, there!"

And off I go to the Kosmograph.

§ 3

And now, God willing, we have reached the end. Nothing remains now save the final picture of the killing of the tiger.

The tiger: yes, I prefer, if I must be distressed, to be distressed over her; and I go to pay her a visit, standing for the last time in front of her cage.

She has grown used to seeing me, the beautiful creature, and does not stir. Only she wrinkles her brows a little, annoyed; but she endures the sight of me as she endures the burden of this sunlit silence, lying heavy round about her, which here in the cage is impregnated with a strong bestial odour. The sunlight enters the cage and she shuts her eyes, perhaps to dream, perhaps so as not to see descending upon her the stripes of shadow cast by the iron bars. Ah, she must be tremendously bored with life also; bored, too, with my pity for her; and I believe that to make it cease, with a fit reward, she would gladly devour me. This desire, which she realises that the bars prevent her from satisfying, makes her heave a deep sigh; and since she is lying outstretched, her languid head drooping on one paw, I see, when she sighs, a cloud of dust rise from

the floor of the cage. Her sigh really distresses
me, albeit I understand why she has emitted it;
it is her sorrowful recognition of the depriva-
tion to which she has been condemned of her
natural right to devour man, whom she has every
reason to regard as her enemy.

"To-morrow," I tell her. "To-morrow, my
dear, this torment will be at an end. It is true
that this torment still means something to you,
and that, when it is over, nothing will matter to
you any more. But if you have to choose between this torment and nothing, perhaps nothing
is preferable! A captive like this, far from your
savage haunts, powerless to tear anyone to
pieces, or even to frighten him, what sort of
tiger are you? Hark! They are making ready
the big cage out there. . . . You are accustomed
already to hearing these hammer-blows, and pay
no attention to them. In this respect, you see,
you are more fortunate than man: man may
think, when he hears the hammer-blows: 'There,
those are for me; that is the undertaker, getting
my coffin ready.' You are already there, in
your coffin, and do not know it: it will be a far
larger cage than this; and you will have the comfort of a touch of local colour there too: it will
represent a glade in a forest. The cage in which
you now are will be carried out there and placed
so that it opens into the other. A stage hand
will climb on the roof of this cage, and pull

up the door, while another man opens the door
of the other cage; and you will then steal in between the tree trunks, cautious and wondering.
But immediately you will notice a curious ticking
noise. Nothing! It will be I, winding my machine on its tripod; yes, I shall be in the cage
too, beside you; but don't pay any attention to
me! Do you see? Standing a little way in front
of me is another man, another man who takes
aim at you and fires, ah! there you are on the
ground, a dead weight, brought down in your
spring. . . . I shall come up to you; with no risk
to the machine, I shall register your last con-
vulsions, and so good-bye!"

If it ends like that . . .

This evening, on coming out of the Positive
Department, where, in view of Borgalli's
urgency, I have been lending a hand myself in
the developing and joining of the sections of this
monstrous film, I saw Aldo Nuti advancing upon
me with the unusual intention of accompanying
me home. I at once observed that he was trying,
or rather forcing himself not to let me see that
he had something to say to me.

"Are you going home?"

"Yes."

"So am I."

When we had gone some distance he asked:

"Have you been in the rehearsal theatre
to-day?"

"No. I've been working downstairs, in the dark room."

Silence for a while. Then he made a painful effort to smile, with what he intended for a smile of satisfaction.

"They were trying my scenes. Everyone was pleased with them. I should never have imagined that they would come out so well. One especially. I wish you could have seen it."

"Which one?"

"The one that shews me by myself for a minute, close up, with a finger on my lips, like this, engaged in thinking. It lasts a little too long, perhaps . . . my face is a little too prominent . . . and my eyes. . . . You can count my eyelashes. I thought I should never disappear from the screen."

I turned to look at him; but he at once took refuge in an obvious reflexion:

"Yes!" he said. "Curious the effect our own appearance has on us in a photograph, even on a plain card, when we look at it for the first time. Why is it?"

"Perhaps," I answered, "because we feel that we are fixed there in a moment of time which no longer exists in ourselves; which will remain, and become steadily more remote."

"Perhaps!" he sighed. "Always more remote for us. . . . "

"No," I went on, "for the picture as well.

The picture ages too, just as we gradually age. It ages, although it is fixed there for ever in that moment; it ages young, if we are young, because that young man in the picture becomes older year by year with us, in us."

"I don't follow you."

"It is quite easy to understand, if you will think a little. Just listen: the time, there, of the picture, does not advance, does not keep moving on, hour by hour, with us, into the future; you expect it to remain fixed at that point, but it is moving too, in the opposite direction; it recedes farther and farther into the past, that time. Consequently the picture itself is a dead thing which as time goes on recedes gradually farther into the past: and the younger it is the older and more remote it becomes."

"Ah, yes, I see what you mean. . . . Yes, yes," he said. "But there is something sadder still. A picture that has grown old young and empty."

"How do you mean, empty?"

"The picture of somebody who has died young."

I again turned to look at him; but he at once added:

"I have a portrait of my father, who died quite young, at about my age; so long ago that I don't remember him. I have kept it reverently, this picture of him, although it means nothing to me.

It has grown old too, yes, receding, as you say, into the past. But time, in ageing the picture, has not aged my father; my father has not lived through this period of time. And he presents himself before me empty, devoid of all the life that for him has not existed; he presents himself before me with his old picture of himself as a young man, which says nothing to me, which cannot say anything to me, because he does not even know that I exist. It is, in fact, a portrait he had made of himself before he married; a portrait, therefore, of a time when he was not my father. I do not exist in him, there, just as all my life has been lived without him."

"It is sad. . . . "

"Sad, yes. But in every family, in the old photograph albums, on the little table by the sofa in every provincial drawing-room, think of all the faded portraits of people who no longer mean anything to us, of whom we no longer know who they were, what they did, how they died. . . . "

All of a sudden he changed the subject to ask me, with a frown:

"How long can a film be made to last?"

He no longer turned to me as to a person with whom he took pleasure in conversing; but in my capacity as an operator. And the tone of his voice was so different, the expression of his face had so changed that I suddenly felt rise up in

me once again that contempt which for some
time past I have been cherishing for everything
and everybody. Why did he wish to know how
long a film could last? Had he attached himself
to me to find out this? Or from a desire to make
my flesh creep, leaving me to guess that he intended to do something rash that very day, so
that our walk together should leave me with a
tragic memory or a sense of remorse?

I felt tempted to stop short in front of him
and to shout in his face:

"I say, my dear fellow, you can drop all that
with me, because I don't take the slightest interest in you! You can do all the mad things
you please, this evening, to-morrow: I shan't
stir! You may perhaps have asked me how long
a film can last to make me think that you are
leaving behind you that picture of yourself with
your finger on your lips? And you think perhaps
that you are going to fill the whole world with
pity and terror with that enlarged picture, in
which *they can count your eyelashes?* How long
do you expect a film to last?"

I shrugged my shoulders and answered:

"It all depends upon how often it is used."

He too from the change in my tone must have
realised that my attitude towards him had
changed also, and he began to look at me in a
way that troubled me.

The position was this: he was still here on

earth a petty creature. Useless, almost a non-entity; but he existed, and was walking beside me, and was suffering. It was true that he was suffering, like all the rest of us, from life which is the true malady of us all. He was suffering for no worthy reason; but whose fault was it if he had been born so petty? Petty as he was, he was suffering, and his suffering was great for him, however unworthy. . . . It was from life that he suffered, from one of the innumerable accidents of life, which had fallen upon him to take from him the little that he had in him and rend and destroy him! At the moment he was here, still walking by my side, on a June evening, the sweetness of which he could not taste; to-morrow perhaps, since life had so turned against him, he would no longer exist: those legs of his would never be set in motion again to walk; he would never see again this avenue along which we were going, and he would never again clothe his feet in those fine patent leather shoes and those silk socks, would never again take pleasure, even in the height of his desperation, as he stood before the glass of his wardrobe every morning, in the elegance of the faultless coat upon his handsome slim body which I could put out my hand now and touch, still living, conscious, by my side.

"Brother. . . . "

No, I did not utter that word. There are cer-

tain words that we hear, in a fleeting moment;
we do not say them. Christ could say them, who
was not dressed like me and was not, like me, an
operator. Amid a human society which delights
in a cinematographic show and tolerates a profession like mine, certain words, certain emotions
become ridiculous.

"If I were to call this Signor Nuti *brother*,"
I thought, "he would take offence; because . . .
I may have taught him a little philosophy as
to pictures that grow old, but what am I
to him? An operator: a hand that turns a
handle."

He is a "gentleman," with madness already
latent perhaps in the ivory box of his skull, with
despair in his heart, but a rich "titled gentleman" who can well remember having known me
as a poor student, a humble tutor to Giorgio
Mirelli in the villa by Sorrento. He intends to
keep the distance between me and himself, and
obliges me to keep it too, now, between him and
myself: the distance that time and my profession have created. Between him and me, the
machine.

"Excuse me," he asked, just as we were reaching the house, "how will you manage to-morrow
about taking the scene of the shooting of the
tiger?"

"It is quite easy," I answered. "I shall be
standing behind you."

"But won't there be the bars of the cage, all the plants in between?"

"They won't be in my way. I shall be inside the cage with you."

He stood and stared at me in surprise:

"You will be inside the cage too?"

"Certainly," I answered calmly.

"And if . . . if I were to miss?"

"I know that you are a crack shot. Not that it will make any difference. To-morrow all the actors will be standing round the cage, looking on. Several of them will be armed and ready to fire if you miss."

He stood for a while lost in thought, as though this information had annoyed him.

Then: "They won't fire before I do?" he said.

"No, of course not. They will fire if it is necessary."

"But in that case," he asked, "why did that fellow . . . that Signor Ferro insist upon all those conditions, if there is really no danger?"

"Because in Ferro's case there might perhaps not have been all those others, outside the cage, armed."

"Ah! Then they are for me? They have taken these precautions for me? How ridiculous! Whose doing is it? Yours, perhaps?"

"Mine, no. What have I got to do with it?"

"How do you know about it, then?"

"Polacco said so."

"Said so to you? Then it was Polacco? Ah, I shall have something to say to him to-morrow morning! I won't have it, do you understand? I won't have it!"

"Are you addressing me?"

"You too!"

"Dear Sir, let me assure you that what you say leaves me perfectly indifferent: hit or miss your tiger; do all the mad things you like inside the cage: I shall not stir a finger, you may be sure of that. Whatever happens, I shall remain quite impassive and go on turning my handle. Bear that in mind, if you please!"

§ 4

Turn the handle; I have turned it. I have kept my word: to the end. But the vengeance that I sought to accomplish upon the obligation imposed on me, as the slave of a machine, to serve up life to my machine as food, life has chosen to turn back upon me. Very good. No one henceforward can deny that I have now arrived at perfection.

As an operator I am now, truly, perfect.

About a month after the appalling disaster which is still being discussed everywhere, I bring these notes to an end.

A pen and a sheet of paper: there is no other way left to me now in which I can communicate

with my fellow-men. I have lost my voice; I am
dumb now for ever. Elsewhere in these notes I
have written: "I suffer from this silence of
mine, into which everyone comes, as into a place
of certain hospitality. *I should like now my
silence to close round me altogether.*" Well, it
has closed round me. I could not be better qualified to act as the servant of a machine.

But I must tell you the whole story, as it
happened.

The wretched fellow went, next morning, to
Borgalli to complain forcibly of the ridiculous
figure which, as he was informed, Polacco intended to make him cut with these precautions.
He insisted at all costs that the orders should be
cancelled, offering to give them all a specimen,
if they needed it, of his well-known skill as a
marksman. Polacco excused himself to Borgalli,
saying that he had taken these measures not
from any want of confidence in Nuti's courage
or sureness of eye, but from prudence, knowing
Nuti to be extremely nervous, as for that matter
he was shewing himself to be at that moment by
uttering this excited protest, instead of the grateful, friendly thanks which Polacco had a right to
expect from him.

"Besides," he unfortunately added, pointing
to me, "you see, Commendatore, there's Gubbio
here too, who has to go into the cage. . . ."

The poor wretch looked at me with such contempt that I immediately turned upon Polacco, exclaiming:

"No, no, my dear fellow! Don't bother about me, please! You know very well that I shall go on quietly turning my handle, even if I see this gentleman in the jaws and claws of the beast!"

There was a laugh from the actors who had gathered round to listen; whereupon Polacco shrugged his shoulders and gave way, or pretended to give way. Fortunately for me, as I learned afterwards, he gave secret instructions to Fantappiè and one of the others to conceal their weapons and to stand ready for any emergency. Nuti went off to his dressing-room to put on his sporting clothes; I went to the Negative Department to prepare my machine for its meal. Fortunately for the company, I drew a much larger supply of film than would be required, to judge approximately by the length of the scene. When I returned to the crowded lawn, by the side of the enormous cage, set with a forest scene, the other cage, with the tiger inside it, had already been carried out and placed so that the two cages opened into one another. It only remained to pull up the door of the smaller cage.

Any number of actors from the four companies had assembled on either side, close to the cage, so that they could see between the tree trunks and branches that concealed its bars. I hoped

for a moment that the Nestoroff, having secured
her object, would at least have had the prudence
not to come. But there she was, alas!

She stood apart from the crowd, a little way
off, with Carlo Ferro, dressed in bright green,
and was smiling as she repeatedly nodded her
head in agreement with what Ferro was saying
to her, albeit from the grim attitude in which
he stood by her side it seemed evident that
such a smile was not the appropriate answer to his
words. But it was meant for the others, that
smile, for all of us who stood watching her, and
was also for me, a brighter smile, when I fixed
my gaze on her; and it said to me once again
that she was not afraid of anything, because the
greatest possible evil for her I already knew:
she had it by her side—there it was—Ferro;
he was her punishment, and to the very end she
was determined, with that smile, to taste its
full flavour in the coarse words which he was
probably addressing to her at that moment.

Taking my eyes from her, I sought those of
Nuti. They were clouded. Evidently he too had
caught sight of the Nestoroff there in the distance; but he chose to pretend that he had not.
His face had grown stiff. He made an effort
to smile, but smiled with his lips alone, a faint,
nervous smile, at what some one was saying to
him. With his black velvet cap on his head, with
its long peak, his red coat, a huntsman's brass

horn slung over his shoulder, his white buckskin breeches fitting close to his thighs; booted and spurred, rifle in hand: he was ready.

The door of the big cage, through which he and I were to enter, was opened from outside; to help us to climb in, two stage hands placed a pair of steps beneath it. He entered the cage first, then I. While I was setting up my machine on its tripod, which had been handed to me through the door of the cage, I noticed that Nuti first of all knelt down on the spot marked out for him, then rose and went across to thrust apart the boughs at one side of the cage, as though he were making a loophole there. I alone was in a position to ask him:

"Why?"

But the state of feeling that had grown up between us did not allow of our exchanging a single word at this stage. His action might therefore have been interpreted by me in several ways, which would have left me uncertain at a moment when the most absolute and precise certainty was essential. And then it was just as though Nuti had not moved at all; not only did I not think any more about his action, it was exactly as though I had not even noticed it.

He took his stand on the spot marked out for him, raising his rifle; I gave the signal:

"Ready."

We heard from the other cage the sound of the

door being pulled up. Polacco, perhaps seeing
the animal begin to move towards the open door,
shouted amid the silence:

"Are you ready? Shoot!"

And I began to turn the handle, with my eyes
on the tree trunks in the background, through
which the animal's head was now protruding,
lowered, as though peering out to explore the
country; I saw that head slowly drawn back, the
two forepaws remain firm, close together, and
the hindlegs gradually, silently gather strength
and the back rise in an arch in readiness for the
spring. My hand was impassively keeping the time
that I had set for its movement, faster, slower,
dead slow, as though my will had flowed down—
firm, lucid, inflexible—into my wrist, and from
there had assumed entire control, leaving my
brain free to think, my heart to feel; so that my
hand continued to obey even when with a pang
of terror I saw Nutl take his aim from the beast
and slowly turn the muzzle of his rifle towards
the spot where a moment earlier he had opened
a loophole among the boughs, and fire, and the
tiger immediately spring upon him and become
merged with him, before my eyes, in a horrible
writhing mass. Drowning the most deafening
shouts that came from all the actors outside the
cage as they ran instinctively towards the Nestoroff who had fallen at the shot, drowning the
cries of Carlo Ferro, I heard there in the cage

the deep growl of the beast and the horrible gasp
of the man as he lay helpless in its fangs, in its
claws, which were tearing his throat and chest;
I heard, I heard, I kept on hearing above that
growl, above that gasp, the continuous ticking of
the machine, the handle of which my hand, alone,
of its own accord, still kept on turning; and I
waited for the beast to spring next upon me,
having brought him down; and the moments of
waiting seemed to me an eternity, and it seemed
to me that throughout eternity I had been count-
ing them as I turned, still turned the handle,
powerless to stop, when finally an arm was thrust
in between the bars, carrying a revolver, and
fired a shot point blank into the tiger's ear over
the mangled corpse of Nuti; and I was pulled
back and dragged from the cage with the handle
of the machine so tightly clasped in my fist that
it was impossible at first to wrest it from me. I
uttered no groan, no cry: my voice, from terror,
had perished in my throat for ever.

Well, I have rendered the firm a service from
which they will reap a fortune. As soon as I
was able, I explained to the people who gathered
round me terror-struck, first of all by signs, then
in writing, that they were to take good care of
the machine, which had been wrenched from my
hand: that machine had in its maw the life of a
man; I had given it that life to eat to the very
last, until the moment when that arm had been

thrust in to kill the tiger. There was a fortune to be extracted from this film, what with the enormous publicity and the morbid curiosity which the sordid atrocity of the drama of that slaughtered couple would everywhere arouse.

Ah, that it would fall to my lot to feed literally on the life of a man one of the many machines invented by man for his pastime, I could never have guessed. The life which this machine has devoured was naturally no more than it could be in a time like the present, in an age of machines; a production stupid in one aspect, mad in another, inevitably, and in the former more, in the latter rather less stamped with a brand of vulgarity.

I have found salvation, I alone, in my silence, with my silence, which has made me thus— according to the standard of the times—perfect. My friend Simone Pau will not understand this, more and more determined to drown himself in *superfluity,* the perpetual inmate of a Casual Shelter. I have already secured a life of ease with the compensation which the firm has given me for the service I have rendered it, and I shall soon be rich with the royalties which have been assigned to me from the hire of the monstrous film. It is true that I shall not know what to do with these riches; but I shall not reveal my embarrassment to anyone; least of all to Simone Pau, who comes every day to shake me, to abuse

me, in the hope of forcing me out of this inanimate silence, which makes him furious. He
would like to see me weep, would like me at least
with my eyes to shew distress or anger; to make
him understand by signs that I agree with him,
that I too believe that life is there, in that
superfluity of his. I do not move an eyelid; I
sit gazing at him, rigid, motionless, until he flies
from the house in a rage. Poor Cavalena, from
another angle, is studying on my behalf text-
books of nervous pathology, suggests injections
and electric batteries, hovers round me to persuade me to agree to a surgical operation on my
vocal chords; and Signorina Luisetta, penitent,
heartbroken at my calamity, in which she chooses
to detect an element of heroism, timidly lets me
see now that she would like to hear issue, if not
from my lips, at any rate from my heart a "yes"
for herself.

No, thank you. Thanks to everybody. I have
had enough. I prefer to remain like this. The
times are what they are; life is what it is; and
in the sense that I give to my profession, I
intend to go on as I am—alone, mute and impassive—being the operator.

Is the stage set?

"Are you ready? Shoot. . . . "

THE END

Dedalus's 1990 publishing programme consists of the following 14 titles:

A Dedalus Nobel Prize Winner

The Notebooks of Serafino Gubbio - Pirandello £7.99
Dreams of Roses and Fire - Johnson £7.99

Decadence from Dedalus

Torture Garden - Octave Mirbeau £6.99
Triumph of Death - Gabriele D'Annunzio £6.99
The Dedalus Book of Decadence: Moral Ruins -
ed Brian Stableford £7.99

Dedalus European Classics

Undine - Fouqué de la Motte £5.99
The Wandering Jew - Eugene Sue £9.99
Tales from the Saragossa Manuscript - Jan Potocki £5.99
The Phantom of the Opera - Gaston Leroux £0.99
The Lost Musicians - William Heinesen £6.99
The Quest of the Absolute - Balzac £4.95
The Devil in Love - Cazotte £5.99

Original Fiction / Fantasy

The Acts of the Apostates - G. Farrington £6.99

A Dedalus Anthology

Tales of the Wandering Jew - ed Brian Stableford £8.99